Advance Praise

"Arora's writing is highly descriptive and evocative, with rich details about Indian culture and way of life. From a Sikh religious wedding to college romance, Arora has written a coming of age story, the difficult intersection of arriving and learning American ways, and the many complications of family secrets. I highly recommend this debut novel."

— Cari Scribner, author of *A Girl Like You* and *A Place Like This*

From Ash to Ashes

From Ash to Ashes

Krishma Tuli Arora

First Edition

Library of Congress Control Number: 2022950112

Hardcover ISBN: 978-1-62720-425-5
Paperback ISBN: 978-1-62720-426-2
Ebook ISBN: 978-1-62720-427-9

Design by Claire Marino
Editorial Development by Sienna Whalen
Promotional Development by Corrine Moulds

Published by Apprentice House Press

Loyola University Maryland
4501 N. Charles Street, Baltimore, MD 21210
410.617.5265
www.ApprenticeHouse.com

info@ApprenticeHouse.com

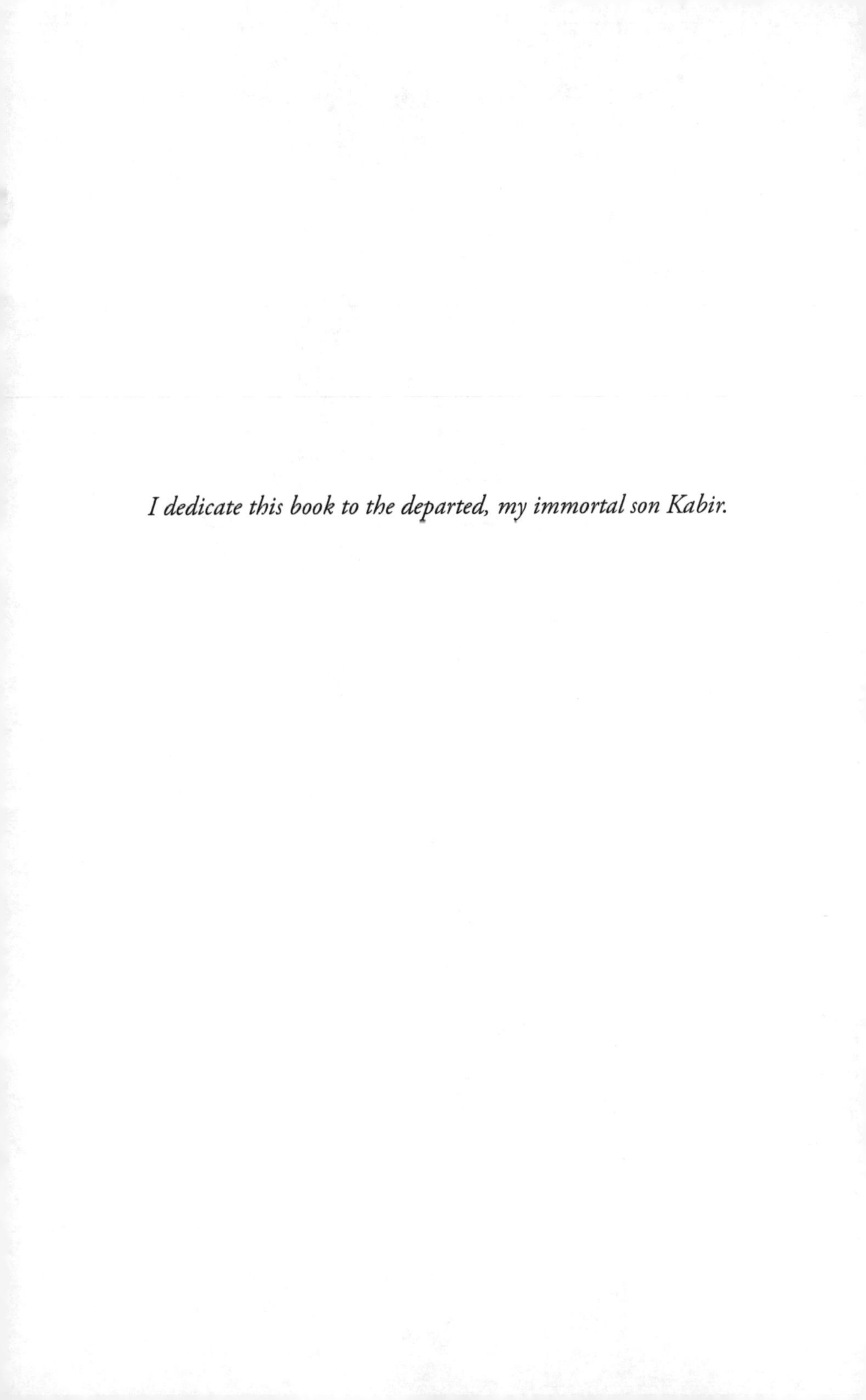

I dedicate this book to the departed, my immortal son Kabir.

Preface

I see my shadow in the rise and fall of others. Their stories, their lives, their moments of perfection are what I want from my story. Our lives, yours and mine, the mundane and routine actions, may feel like they will wither with time and the memories created might disappear. But the true moments of our stories will be remembered. This story isn't mine alone—it lives on in the stories to come. Different names, different lives, but the same story.

Chapter 1

1998

Insecure and cold like a newborn unaccustomed to air and light, I was alone on the crowded train. Knowing I'd left the womb of home for good, the once-familiar train felt strange. Gone were the tattered red-and-blue leather seats; shiny, green-striped leather seats with a new-car smell had taken their place. The train, like time, kept moving forward. Time's unrelenting flow and merciless pursuit of the future nudged me to drift with its current. Yet, frozen and still, wanting to remain bound to the past, I resisted moving on. Though experience told me he was approaching, I didn't hear the distant clicking of the train conductor punching holes through tickets bound for New York's Pennsylvania Station. My mind was set on hiding my jumbled thoughts from the middle-aged man sporting a charcoal woolen overcoat sitting opposite me. He stole a peek at my face from the corners of his icy-blue eyes. Shuddering, I turned my face toward the window, hoping he would disappear, and I could be hidden again.

I had been hiding at home for the last few months, praying that I could stay hibernating like a bear, warm and safe, where my wounds could heal into scabs. Shielded from the cruel winter of the world, I wanted to stay there in that place of false safety without being reminded of the memories that would rip open again the place where I bled. But there was no use trying to escape it now; I was already exposed, out of my cave and on my way, with no choice but to bear the bone-chilling winds of fate.

The cloudy images of trees and water appeared for a moment in the foggy window, and in a flash, their reflections were gone. Blurry memories of my happy childhood had similarly vanished in an instant, as distant as the houses in the window left behind miles ago, as if they had happened in another lifetime. Years had passed almost as quickly as the images of the world in my view. Even I could not recall every moment from those years, and those that I cherished seemed unreal now, just another story from a book I may have read. I was not that little girl from my childhood, naive and gullible, open to the world. A wiser darkness, an unearthing of truth, coldness of life had settled within me.

"Miss, your ticket?"

I was abruptly brought back into the here and now. "Oh, sorry." I half-smiled as I handed my ticket to the conductor and stole a quick glance at Overcoat stuffing his monthly card back into his inner coat pocket. The conductor, unmoved by my apology, punched my ticket and went on his way, repeating his mantra, "Tickets please."

I looked down to study my pale, cold hands. Caressing the raggedy edge of the holes in my ticket with the velvety pads of my fingertips brought me back to the here and now, a time I seldom lived in. The ticket stub read, *Off-Peak, One Way, Penn, LIRR, March 1998*, and a computer-generated female voice on the speaker caught my attention. "This is the train to Penn Station. The next stop is Douglaston." I used to take the train from Manhasset every weekend, but it had been months since my last trip, and since I missed the express, the local train would take a painstaking forty-two minutes to reach Penn Station.

The cold wind swooped my long, dark hair forward as the doors opened at the Douglaston station, and a new set of people boarded the train. An older woman with silver hair squeezed next to Overcoat, who shifted his knees toward mine. Avoiding his gaze, I couldn't help but smile back at the wrinkled face and faded eyes whose smile was as endearing and comforting as if she were my own kin. A kind of smile whose warmth I could feel through the air. Her old eyes saw beyond the delicate profile of my face, knowing all too well the kind of struggle hidden under my passive gaze. Her reassuring smile spoke words of hope and perseverance and a history of life experiences. Her bright aura illuminated the train but felt unfamiliar within the lifelessness I had grown accustomed to. I turned away from the golden warmth and once again stared blankly into the gray, frozen landscape outside the window. I was frozen, unwilling, and unable to embrace the warmth being offered. I still heard their voices, "You're young, and you will move on from this...," but I didn't believe them.

The sudden jolt of the train stopping in the darkness alongside the underground platform at Penn Station cut my thoughts in half, and my body shifted gear, into autopilot. After disembarking the train, I ran up the flight of stairs to the main hall, a sudden energy vibrating me to the core. The pace of people around me was fast; the aroma of fresh bread from Hot and Crusty filled my lungs; the array of brightly colored fruit lined up outside Smoothie King caught my eyes. Yet none of these enticed my numbed senses to embrace my old home, New York City. The A, C, E train had taken me downtown to my destination, Eighth Street, and I walked up aboveground to Fifth Avenue. Crossing over two blocks to Tenth Street, I reached my dorm, Rubin Hall, at New York University. I paused outside in front of the revolving doors of the brick building with a large purple flag embossed with the letters *NYU* swaying in the wind. Despite the cold air and the puff of breath exhaling from my lungs, I didn't want to go in yet to the loud chatter of students and to the stink of youth that permeated the lobby.

Instead, I stared at the Empire State Building jutting into the heavens ahead of me and its tricolored band lighting the sky. In the exact opposite direction, over the arch in Washington Square Park, my gaze took in the two soaring pillars of the World Trade Center, and my heart swelled. It was my daily habit as a child to look longingly at the stars in the deep-black sky before going to bed. Since I moved into Rubin Hall, my daily ritual had been to seek out the towers through the black-iron-fitted window of my dorm room every night before sleeping. The concrete jungle I lived in could not take away from the overwhelming presence of nature, but it never ceased to pull me in with its magnetic prowess. Loss and nothingness had brought me to see the largeness of life outside the artificial creation of humankind. I remained in awe of what we could create, how much we could endure, and how far we had come.

I took a deep breath to swallow the immensity of the grand skyscrapers that surrounded me. Vulnerable, small, and insignificant before these daunting structures, I feebly resorted to entering the dorm. After what felt like years away, I took the old elevator to the eighth floor and finally arrived at my room, 8C. I didn't want to return to school—hiding was all I wanted from life—but I had missed almost a semester, so my parents forced me to come back. I dropped my luggage on the floor and flung myself onto the bed. A ghost trapped inside the young body of a first-year college student reluctantly dragging myself through the motions of life, breath after breath.

"Mira! I haven't seen you for so long!" I heard Katy's voice before I saw her. Before I could open my eyes, Katy gave me a long hug, holding me tightly. "Are you OK? You didn't tell me you were coming back today, but I'm so glad to see you!" Katy, my roommate and my best friend, coaxed me gently to look at her.

Looking up at her face from my tear-stained pillow, I saw her concern and sympathy. "I'll be OK," I lied. Overwhelmed by the questions racing in my mind, I finally broke. "Why is this all happening to me, to my family, and all at once? There's an old Indian saying, 'When God gives, he tears the ceiling apart and pours it in!' Except in our case, it's not blessings; it's misery," I said between choking sobs. I couldn't hold the weight of the pain inside any longer, so I let it flood Katy and the rest of the room.

"I'm so sorry for everything that's happened," Katy said, rubbing my back. "And I know you're really hurt and upset right now, but I know you, and I know how strong you are. You have strong faith, you've always had it, and I promise you it will pull you through this, just like it used to pull you through other problems. Have you and your family thought about seeing a therapist for family counseling?"

"Oh, Katy," I almost laughed as I said her name. "In my culture, having to see a therapist to discuss our family's innermost secrets and problems would be volunteering to bring shame to our own family. It is like admitting that we all have a mental disease. My parents would never agree. Although I bet, we could all benefit from it! Unfortunately, Indian people like my family refuse to let outsiders into their private family issues and live in denial of the fact that mental health is a real thing."

Katy sighed with a soft breath. "That's a shame because depression is such an awful thing to battle alone."

Her gentle face reminded me of him. Maybe that was why I took to her so quickly when we first met. She had the same soft skin, calm expression, and like him, a gentle voice. We understood each other. Katy knew me better than I knew myself; it was only Waheguru, God, who could carry me through this. My faith was the only thing that lasted, the only thing that remained when all hope in people and the world was lost. I had to force myself to pray. I was angry and wanted answers, but there was no use fighting and resisting when you were up against a force like destiny, so I meekly resigned myself to my daily ritual. Rehras, the evening prayers, flowed through my lips like silky milk, sweet and melodious. Katy patiently waited for me to finish, and we went down to the dining hall later than usual to avoid other friends and eat quietly together. I had not eaten properly for months, but with the comfort of Katy by my side, and the aroma of hot food, I finally gave in to the temptation of my most primal need. A small bud of hope to live again was beginning to bloom in me, even if its origin was only one small meal and an overstimulated journey into New York City.

Back in my room, I stared at my large green computer hogging all the space on my desk but didn't email Dev, my boyfriend, to let him know I was back. I didn't know what to say to him. I didn't want to crush him with my misery. I didn't want him to run away from me because of my problems. And worst of all, I didn't know if I should see him anymore. Releasing my thoughts of Dev, I climbed into my four-wooden post bed pushed against the bare wall of the square room, delving into deeper thoughts about Waheguru and why life was tied with the knot of death, each holding the other. Exhaustion wrapped around my bones as I floated in oversized flannel pajamas, but I was too tired to sleep.

"Goodnight, Mira." Katy slipped under her covers after

switching off the light.

"Goodnight," I whispered, staring into the darkness.

Wails and cries of mourners filled my ears. "Why did this have to happen?" They asked me as if I knew the answers to the universe. Haunted by that day and reminiscing of a bygone life, I sensed that sleep was almost in reach. I began drifting into a life I used to know. My dreams were taking me back to my life in the past, to my foolish youth in our house on Ash Lane, to the trials and tribulations of those days. I dreamed of the years, of the days gone by in what I was now sure could have been a different lifetime.

Chapter 2

1993

I remembered the story so well like I still breathed it, still lived it. My dreams took me back to the old room with its white-washed walls, the glossy wooden floors that creaked in soft spots, the mini attic door that kept childhood fears lurking behind its dark corners, and a jute rug brightening the floor with its vivid colors. The view of the setting sun from the bedroom window was breathtaking—its rays painted the sky with new fiery colors unprecedented in the day—and I gazed at it till it made my eyes water.

Mom always warned me not to play in the hot sun too long for fear that I may become tan and somehow ugly, so the sunset became my favorite time of the day. When I told my American friends why I couldn't go to the beach with them, they laughed and said I was already tan. But in this moment, the sun made my long, thick, black hair shine a brownish tint, and I was delighted in its transformation. Its rays seeped into my brown eyes, which became dewy and hazel, and my wheat-colored skin basked as a golden hue. While the sunset lasted, I pranced by the window, gazing at myself in the mirror, imagining all the while that I was a white American girl with short, brown hair.

"What are you doing, Mira? You're so weird!" My sister, Ritu, caught me fantasizing in front of the mirror. I felt my thirteen-year-old cheeks sting with embarrassment. I jumped on the bed and pretended that I had just been reading a novel. Ritu, uninterested in my denial of teenage silliness, dived to the real point of her visit: "Isn't it interesting, Mira, that this morning I was searching for my blue daisy necklace, and I couldn't find it anywhere, but when I got back this evening, it was right there in my jewelry box on the dresser?"

I avoided Ritu's sharp-edged stare and simply shrugged in response. My nonchalant attitude angered Ritu, whose voice rose to a shrill shout. "Mira, I know you wore it without asking me and sneaked it out this morning in your backpack and put it back after school!"

"What is the matter?!" Our mother wearily came up the creaking wooden stairs of our small house.

"Mom, Mira wears my things without my permission, and when I need them, I can't find them. She is not allowed to touch my things!" Ritu's voice towered above the room, and her small nostrils flared hot with anger.

"Ritu, stop it!" Shouted Mom. "Don't cause unpleasantness in the house, and I don't want you screaming at your baby sister."

"You always take her side. Why don't you tell her that she shouldn't steal my things, that she should ask me first?!" Ritu shouted back.

Somehow the argument had shifted from Ritu and me to her and Mom. Ritu had raised her twenty-year-old voice against an elder, and regardless of whether her complaint was right or wrong, Ritu's disrespect would have to be punished.

"Shut up! Don't raise your voice at me, and I told you, don't cause unpleasantness!" Ritu's cause was cut down by Mom, and Ritu saying anything more to defend herself would have instigated further argument. Mom and Ritu had their differences,

Mom always won, and Ritu had learned to bitterly step down.

Today, Mom had more serious worries to deal with, since Dad was away again to India for work. Mom had to manage their handicrafts wholesale business in his absence; back home with her mom hat on, she ran the household, with four kids, and she could not bear even an ounce of family drama. Mom, exhausted by her day and the commotion with Ritu, went to her room just across the hall for the short fifteen minutes of rest that her stressful life would allow her, but she could not put her mind to ease. Dad would be away for about two months this time, and she hoped that next month he would come back with better prospects for a more profitable year. Mom's mind grew more worried day by day that Ritu was of marriageable age, and they needed enough money for the wedding and dowry.

Pushed down by Mom's overpowering voice, Ritu retreated into quiet outrage that could only be noticed in her blazing eyes, her mute voice having betrayed her. Looking down at the floor, I quietly walked out of the room; from the corner of my eye, I could see a small tear that had slipped down Ritu's cheek. Feeling a pang of guilt but relieved that I was free from her accusing grasp, I ran downstairs and found my brother Jeet studying in his room.

"What do you want?" My sixteen-year-old brother was lying on his bed, his head propped on his hand, surrounded by different books and papers about biology. He had pushed his black turban slightly off his forehead to relieve himself of its weight while he battered his brains with the functions of the pituitary gland. The room was small and split into two, one side lined with bookshelves stacked with science books and car magazines and with a poster of Einstein. The other side was covered with posters of Metallica and Bollywood actresses. That side belonged to Jaspreet, Jazz, our eighteen-year-old brother, who was usually never home. Jeet asked why I was there, but he knew he'd heard the voices from upstairs. When I said nothing, he said, "Why do you wear Ritu's things, Mir, when she hates it?"

"Jazz is such a pig!" I declared. "Look how messy he leaves his side of the room; he's such a loser!" In vain, I tried to change the subject.

Jeet rolled his soft brown eyes at me and rubbed the light beard on his disapproving face.

"It's not a big deal if I wore it, Jeet, and it's in fashion, and I didn't break it or anything!" I exclaimed in my defense. "Besides, I am hoping you'll be on my side."

Jeet flipped his textbook closed and crossed his legs, sitting upright, as I plopped on the bed next to him. "I am on your side. Just try not to get Ritu so upset. It's not fair to her, and you know that. You know the difference between right and wrong, Mira, and you shouldn't try to get away with doing wrong. Look how upset Mom is. I have so much biology homework, and the SATs are around the corner, and you guys are so loud upstairs I can't concentrate."

Jeet had a gentle way of explaining away even the smallest of my mischiefs. "I do feel bad about what I did." I smiled sheepishly at him because I knew he always forgave me. "Sorry we disturbed you. You don't need to stress so much. You are already medical school material, and you're almost there, just remember." With my head bobbing up and down and my hands mimicking the climb of an imaginary train up a high mountain, I said, "You're the choo train climbing over the tall mountain that said he can, he can, he can, he can, and you can too, Jeet!"

Jeet and I laughed at my childish pep talk till we fell back on the bed.

"All right, Mir, go and find another hiding spot—I've got

work to do."

I smiled as I left, feeling more encouraged. Jeet and I could not be described as stacked spoons; however, Jeet and I, fork and knife, made the best team to win an argument against Ritu and Jazz in all controversies.

Since my brothers' names were so similar, to avoid confusion, we called Jeet by his name, and Jaspreet, well, he liked us to call him Jazz. I thought it was because Jazz was ashamed of his Indian name, like it wasn't cool to have a name that most Americans could not pronounce or spell. Their names were still similar, in my opinion, and by design, as Mom and Dad's intentions were to have their two sons have this special connection with their names, but I think that backfired. Jeet and Jazz were nothing like each other; they were like night and day. A name doesn't make a connection or forge a bond; it is the soul that does that. They were brothers but did not share their thoughts and dreams with each other. Jazz isolated himself from the family and didn't share what he did with his friends outside the house. It wasn't hard to guess that he smoked weed and went binge drinking with his friends from the way his clothes stank, and his eyes glazed. Jazz cut more classes than he attended and barely passed every year.

Like the flip of a coin, of the same flesh and blood was Jeet, utterly unlike Jazz. Conscientious, sensitive, and responsible, Jeet was on his way to fulfilling Mom and Dad's dream that he became a doctor. Our parents believed that becoming a doctor in the US was a fast-track way of reaping financial rewards and gaining respect and esteem from society. Although Jeet had once disclosed to me his dream of joining Dad's business and working side by side with our parents, for fear of their reaction, he was unable to reveal his ambitions to them. When I told Mom and Dad what Jeet really wanted to do with his life, they dismissed it as a silly idea and a waste of Jeet's potential.

Jeet shared a room with Jazz, just as I shared a room with Ritu. We only had three bedrooms; the fourth one had been converted into a television room. Mom insisted she wanted to keep the small formal living and dining separate and impeccable and where we sat only when we had company. Privacy for children wasn't a common and familiar notion to Indian Punjabi families; it was something overlooked and considered by adults to be unimportant and unnecessary. Children, brothers and sisters alike, were supposed to be close and open enough to share everything and make sacrifices for each other. I heard Mom's voice in my head: "What is the need for privacy? What are these children hiding? Who needs privacy from their parents?"

Jazz, however, insisted that if he couldn't get his own room, then he wasn't going to be home. He brought shame to the family, Dadiji, our grandmother, said. He did what he wanted despite the consequences. He constantly fought with other boys in school, played hooky from class, and was the nightmare of every teacher. His bullying didn't end at school. He constantly threatened Mom that he was going to cut his hair and stop wearing his turban (his beard was already buzz cut) if they didn't get off his back about passing the twelfth grade. We are Sikh, Mom reminded him, so cutting one's hair is against our religious and cultural traditions, and therefore, long hair is kept tied and adorned with the crown of a turban; it made her ashamed how Jazz insulted his identity. Both Jazz and Jeet, although Jeet would never admit it, felt estranged from American society because of their turbans. Most Americans called it the "thing" on their head or the "hat," and they could not tell the difference between Sikh turbans and the ones worn by other religions. Jeet accepted the name-calling and blamed it on the ignorance of people. Not

Jazz—he wouldn't let anyone get away with making fun of his appearance. When boys at school said that Jazz looked like a terrorist, Jazz answered them with his fist.

Dadiji always said that people were heavily involved in the rituals of their religion and had forgotten the wisdom and spiritualism embedded in it. She taught me that the Guru Granth Sahib, the holy book of Sikhs, is the living word of God. The virtues of a clear and honest heart, charity, and honest living, the most basic of what is required to lead a spiritual life, is how Sikhs should aspire to live our lives. However, there were some who only pretended. They were donkeys wearing a lion's (Singh's) skin, fooling the world and themselves, but they didn't fool me. The donkey in our house was Jazz. Dadiji always said that he was that rotten apple that had fallen from a good tree. Like the other donkeys in our temple, Jazz was a fake who pretended to be a good Sikh by keeping his turban, but he was lacking in good deeds. He and his friends would hang outside the Sikh temple, the Gurdwara, during the religious service to gossip, backstab other people, and flirt and exchange phone numbers with the girls. Jazz had been known to date several girls at one time, one from the Gurdwara and another from school. This was not to say that these girls weren't up to anything bad themselves, but Jazz could not be trusted. Perhaps, because we didn't try to understand why Jazz acted the way he did, we were partly to blame for his failure.

My humanities teacher encouraged me to base my research paper on the historical context of my religion for one of our class projects. Mom said she was proud of me for being so passionate about our roots, but she still thought that writing a report about things that I was too young to understand was sinful, even though I got an A on my paper. This was what I wrote:

In Sikh history, having uncut hair served as a sign of nobility and was a gift from the tenth Sikh Guru (Incarnate of God) when he baptized the Sikh army, called Singhs, or Lions. The uniform for battle consisted of five items, including the turban and the sword. Why is this so important? In 1600s India, only the nobility and royalty wore turbans, as a sign of their higher rank in society, and a sword was only carried by the warrior class. The Gurus, leaders of the Sikhs, created an army that allowed the common man to be raised above the confines of a strict, class-conscious society by bestowing upon them the same turban and sword. The Gurus gave people a true sense of equality—in the eyes of God, we are one.

The Sikhs were the first to break class barriers and treat all people, including women, as equals within and outside of India. This uniform formed a conspicuous identity in the face of religious intolerance and genocide by foreign rulers that had plagued the subcontinent for hundreds of years. This outward-facing symbol, the turban and sword that the Gurus bestowed upon the army of Sikhs hundreds of years ago, aimed to help them defend themselves and others from genocide by the Mughals (Muslim conquerors) and to preserve Indian culture from being obliterated. If it was not for the martyrdom of the ninth Guru, who chose to sacrifice his life in order to protect the right of every human being to freely practice their own religion, specifically to protect Hindu culture from obliteration by Emperor Aurangzeb, India may not have been the democratic nation it is today.

While honoring the sacrifices of the Gurus, and continuing the tradition of the Singh army, Sikh civilians in a time of relative peace today carry on this martial uniform more as a cultural tradition and a physical form of their Sikh identity. The turban, therefore, not only is like a crown but is a symbol of righteousness.

I left my brother's room in desperate search of another haven before Ritu came downstairs looking for revenge. I quietly tip-toed down into the basement where my family had built an all-purpose room from a laundry area. It was now a sitting room with a television and couch; a dance floor, which was unveiled with the removal of a piece of carpet during parties; and a prayer room separated by long white sheets. It was here that I had my famous teen birthday parties full of friends and my allotted two sleepovers per year. Countless hours in our dungeon of a basement were spent ironing, listening to religious hymns, and watching Bollywood movies. I rushed to put on my chunni, my headscarf, and turned the light on in the prayer room, or Guruji's room, as we called it. Just in time—the ajar basement door with a splash of light spilling out underneath it had been spotted.

"Mira, are you down there?"

"Yeah, Mom, I'm doing sukhasan!" I yelled back.

"Thank you!" My mom treated the evening prayer on the Holy Guru Granth Sahib as another chore that had to be done, so when I did it instead of her, she always thanked me like she was thanking me for making her chai or for ironing the clothes.

When I came up from the basement, I saw Ritu had come down from her room. She was calm. I guessed that when she saw that I was praying and Mom was cooking, she immediately knew that her argument against Miss Goody Two-Shoes, the name she called me, would not work. I too knew that the coast was clear—Mom was satisfied with my work, and Ritu had accepted defeat in our battle. My appetite even returned with the thick aromas rising from Mom's spoon that was her magic wand. Masala (spiced) chicken and matar paneer (cheese with peas) were my two favorite dishes. Mom made fresh rotis (bread) on the hot tawa (cast-iron pan), and we kids devoured it while watching TV in the living room.

Later that night, Jazz came home without having called that he was going to be late. I was upstairs in bed, but I could hear them and could easily imagine the scene. Mom opened the door in her floral nightgown and slippers. Silent but angry, her eyes peered closely at Jazz's eyes. Jazz attempted to look away when she broke down crying.

"What, Ma? What'd I do now? Why you cryin'?" said Jazz.

"Why are you coming home so late, at eleven o'clock, smelling like beer and smoke? You think your mother is stupid? That she doesn't know anything? You and those boys from high school—what mischief you get up to!"

"Just leave me alone, Ma. I'm sick 'n' tired of you and everyone at that fuckin' school treatin' me like I'm no good." Jazz forcefully entered through the front door, pushing past Mom, and disappeared into the dark hallway leading to his room without saying another word.

Mom fell back against the stairs crying and talking to herself. "If your dad was around more often, he would give you a good beating for troubling me so much. You're going to kill me one day!" She wailed into her arms.

I snuggled closer in my blanket, listening to Mom's anguish. I couldn't get up to comfort her in case she scolded me for being awake so late. But I felt pain for her and in a small corner of my chest almost felt pain for Jazz.

Chapter 3

1995

The year that my uncle, Kinchan-chacha, got married was the year secrets began to surface in our family. Although it was only the start of April 1995, the dark clouds began to loom; the leaves fluttered in the wind and then went thrashing down to the ground. Yet we ignored these signs, as we might have those of a coming rainstorm. All I could see was what I wanted to see, and it was spring in all its glory; buds were blooming around us, the air was warm, and I could sense the happiness in everyone.

I was so excited for my uncle's wedding that was set for June. We were very close. When he lived with Dadiji, after she moved to New York from Punjab, India, my popping by their house became common. We kids ate there if our parents were out of town. I felt at home there even if no one was home. Kinchan-chacha was included in every family birthday, anniversary, and celebration. I remember Kinchan-chacha helping us get ready for bed; he would make us all drink hot milk because he said that this helped us sleep and kept our stomachs clean. My uncle was rosy-cheeked and gave me big bear hugs and baby-talked to me, calling me one of his favorites.

Plus, finally, this was the first family wedding that I wouldn't be too young to enjoy. I was almost fifteen years old. I was ecstatic about all the lovely new clothes I would wear, about the festive singing we'd do, and of course, about the dance performance I would be in! Ritu and two of my aunts and I were going to perform a dance for Kinchan-chacha's wedding and had to rehearse every day after my school and their jobs were over. My Dadiji went shopping in India to buy the new bride's trousseau and of course some lenghas, long Indian skirts with crop tops, for us nieces. Ritu had a special one made for her in a lavender color with gold and silver embroidery all over, while my cousin-sisters, as we sometimes called our cousins, and I were left to choose from three ballooned skirts. I took the orange one with gold embroidered along the hem, and my cousins took the parrot green and the fruit punch color.

One afternoon I sat at the table in my great-aunt's house doing my homework and waiting for the other girls to join me for dance rehearsal. My great-aunt had a young servant brought from India, a boy of fifteen, he must've been. He annoyed me with his eager smile and shining green eyes. He came swiftly into the room to ask me in Hindi if I wanted something to eat or drink. You see, he couldn't speak English, so he bugged me more. No, I answered in a harsh tone with a frown. The more I hated him and expressed my dislike, the more he liked me, and he tried to serve me something every ten minutes. Finally, my sister and aunts arrived, laughing and chatting as they came into the living room.

"He's so cute and fair," said Ritu to my aunt. "Get us some juice," she said to him.

How could they think this servant was cute? He was a servant, and I couldn't possibly think of him as equally cute to the boys in school I thought were cute.

"Let's start the rehearsal!" I shouted.

"Excited, aren't you, Mira? Which songs in the mix do you

want to dance in?" asked my younger aunt, Nicky.

"I want to do the one where she's celebrating the coming home of her lover."

"I think Ritu should do that one; it would suit her age more," said my older aunt, Pammi.

"Oh, why don't I get to do the nice girly songs? I always have to be the comedian and act as the drunken man in every dance!" I fussed.

"Now, Mira, if you want to dance with the older girls, then you have to cooperate, OK?" said Pammi-auntie.

I obeyed with a gentle nod and a sullen face. I wanted to be in the dance and in the limelight at the reception so badly that I couldn't risk losing my chance. We played the cassette tape and began to choreograph our own steps to the songs in the mix. We twirled and lip-synched the words, making expressions with our eyes. We practiced for a good three hours, until it was finally time to go home.

Ritu drove us home, inquiring all the time about one of her sweaters, in case I had hidden it somewhere. I denied all her allegations. As she made a surprising turn away from the direction of our house, she rather abruptly seemed to dismiss the topic.

"Where are you going?" I asked.

"I must stop by school to pick up a book from a friend. I won't be long; just wait in the car," she instructed.

As we drove onto the Hunter College campus, where Ritu was a senior, and parked in front of the big brick library, I saw a tall and cute guy run from a black sports car into the library. I could follow my sister's eyes, staring first at the car and then at the young man who jumped out of it.

"I'll be right back, Mira. Sit here and don't move," repeated Ritu uncomfortably.

Ritu swiftly walked through the same door of the library as the tall guy had. I sat there and waited. After twenty minutes, my impatience, not to mention my curiosity, got the best of me. I slowly and cautiously got out of the car, just in case Ritu was to return—then I could jump back in. Not seeing her, I began to walk quickly toward the library door. Inside the brightly lit building, I paced up and down the tall bookcases looking for Ritu and having the feeling that I would find her with someone.

"Mira!" Ritu called out from behind me.

My head jerked around, and I saw Ritu sitting with the tall and good-looking guy…who by no means looked Sikh.

"Come here," my sister demanded. I rushed over to where Ritu was sitting with a mystery man. "Amir, this is my little sister, Mira."

"Nice to meet you," said the guy.

I smiled and shook his hand.

"OK, I've got to go, so I'll see you tomorrow," said Ritu, touching the guy's hand.

"All right, the usual place at ten," he replied as he touched Ritu's waist.

It seemed to me that their goodbye was a little too comfortable with each other and a little uncomfortable for me.

As we drove home from Ritu's college, I waited for her to say something about Amir. She didn't say a word until we pulled up in our driveway. "OK, I expect you to keep this a secret." Ritu turned to me. "You can't tell Mom or Dad and especially not Jeet and Jazz. If you mention anything, I will kill you, and you can forget about ever touching my things."

I knew that this was the opportunity of a lifetime for me. "Fine, I won't say anything as long as I can wear your clothes," I declared with a victorious smile.

"You little blackmailer, Mira. Fine, you can wear most of my things if you tell me the night before that you're going to wear them, but you can't touch any of my new clothes."

"Done deal," I said, and we shook on it. Then I focused on the enormity of the secret. My eyes opened wide, and I shouted, "So, Ritu, his name is Amir? So, he's Muslim, isn't he?!"

"Shut up! Didn't I just tell you never to mention it even by accident? You know Mom and Dad will kill me if they find out I am going out with any guy, let alone a Muslim guy.

"But why?" I inquired.

"I don't know, Mom and Dad think it's not decent for girls to date and are prejudiced against any guy who's not Sikh."

"That's true. I guess it's because they want you to marry in the same culture and religion because it's what is expected, and even if it was a Sikh guy, I think they would still be disappointed because you know you have to have an arranged marriage anyway."

"I don't need a lecture from you about what's right and wrong, OK!"

"Fine, I don't care if you're goin' out with a guy. I thought he was so cute!"

"Really? Did you think so?"

"Yeah, of course. I think you have good taste. So, what does he study?"

Ritu's voice quieted, and a big smile appeared as she spoke. "Oh, he's in engineering, and he's smart, and he treats me well. He brings me flowers every day..."

"Wow, that is so romantic! I wish I could get flowers every day! Are you both in love?"

Ritu hesitated for a second. "Yeah, we are in love, and we want to get married soon."

"I'm so happy for you, but I think you shouldn't marry anyone until you know them well and love them first and you're sure you want to spend the rest of your life with them," I blurted.

"But you know how Mom and Dad think—they think that because they fell in love after they got married and it worked for them that it would work for us too. I keep worrying in my mind about how much embarrassment it would cause them in society, and they may even throw me out of the house."

"Don't worry. I think they'll be mad in the beginning, but they'll just learn to accept it."

"Let's hope so. Anyway, enough talk for now. Mom might get suspicious about why we are sitting in the car in the driveway for so long," said Ritu and signaled for me to open the door. As we entered the house, I felt content that Ritu and I were pals again; we were sharing secrets the way we used to when we were little girls. Even Ritu knew that despite our quarrels, she could trust me. We were a team against our parents, who would never understand.

That night as Ritu was massaging her cream into her face and brushing her hair, I lay under the covers trying to hide my eyes from the bright light. I couldn't push all the thoughts out of my mind and had to keep reminding myself that if I didn't go to sleep, I wouldn't be able to wake up in time for the school bus. Images of my screaming parents and Ritu's tears and helpless cries made my heart sink. I so wanted Ritu to be happy with the one she loved, but I couldn't see how it would work out for her. Although I had given her consolation that it would, deep in my heart I knew that she would need a miracle. Why did our lives have to be so repressed and complicated? Why did we have to think ten times before we could do things those other girls did without blinking? Why did our parents control us so much that we felt suffocated? The sheltered life that we lived, what good could it possibly do us? I wondered.

"Mira, will you stop tossing and turning? I don't want to hear another sound from you," snapped Ritu, who was agitated herself.

I knew Ritu was in a world of her own thoughts and fears. She dreamed of how Amir and she had kissed so passionately in the car earlier that day, how his hands caressed her curves, how sultry the air was, and how musky he smelled. It had been an animal instinct that came alive between them at that moment, and they consumed their aching desire for each other. She had done more than she would allow herself, but there was something irresistible about him that she wanted more and more of. I blushed thinking of my sister in this way, but I couldn't help it. Even though I was younger, I understood. Every night, Ritu's dreams for Amir grew more intense, and then she would tuck away her dreams and passions and surrender to sleep.

Things in general felt tumultuous. The US was involved in the conflict in Bosnia, and Clinton was securing his re-election. Besides watching the war on the news every night, I listened to my dad, who was on a kick telling us stories of travel and adventure from his childhood. It seemed that they had had all the fun and we weren't having any. Dad said it was because they had been in India, and times were different. Now, they had to protect their children from the bad influence of Western culture. Anything to do with Western music and dance and fashion could only bring corruption and immoral behavior to his children. I always thought that it was precisely our dad's contempt for these things that led Jazz into rock music and grungy clothes, his way of rebellion. I longed to get away from my mundane life and everyday problems and travel, free as a bird, to meet a handsome stranger who would turn out to be the one, the love of my life, and we would be happily married and would live in a free world away from parental restrictions. He would be my true soul mate, like Mr. Darcy in my favorite book, *Pride and Prejudice*, and I would be as strong as Elizabeth.

Chapter 4
1984

America, land of the free, home of the brave; the nation that embraces the tired and poor huddled masses of the world; the nation where only hard work is needed to achieve the American dream. All that America advertises itself to be is probably true… for the people who are named in the fine print: *American dream for the white and the Christian; for all others, certain restrictions apply.*

Moving to America in the early 1980s wasn't an easy transition for our family, especially Jazz. Jeet was seven, and I was only four years old, so we didn't miss India much. But Ritu was eleven, and Jazz was almost ten years old. Ritu missed her friends, but she managed to keep in touch with them through letters. After a slightly rough transition, she became engulfed in the world of Material Girl Madonna, fashion, hairspray, and lip gloss. But Jazz missed everything about India. He missed stealing the milkman's bicycle every morning, and he missed paying the man with the monkeys ten rupees to see them dance. He missed riding his bicycle to the nearby market to eat pistachio ice cream in the summer. It was the slow pace of life, the homely aromas of his favorite street food, the stream of familiar faces in the market, and the sound of his mother tongue being spoken in the streets that Jazz longed for. America was a large place where he was lost among strangers. Surrounded by alien languages, unappealing aromas, and people who were closed and isolated, he felt unwelcome in fast-paced New York City. After a year or so, Ritu eventually mixed with the other girls in school and adopted the American uniform of jeans and T-shirts, but Jazz was tortured for his turban. He was no mighty Singh here. Jazz bore the brunt of our newfound freedom.

Some of the older boys from the adjacent middle school beat Jazz up after school and then left him alone on the ground behind the school parking lot with his head naked, turban in his hands. Mom and Dad tried talking to the principal about it, but that only temporarily stopped the abuse. Mom tried dropping and picking up Jazz from school, so he wouldn't be hurt outside of school hours, but then he was beaten during lunch and recess. The verbal teasing and pushing and shoving by kids were curtailed by teachers in class, but the following year in middle school they could not stop the older boys who would easily drag Jazz into the locker room and beat him there with fists and racial slurs. Jazz heard it all: "You're not wanted here!" "Go back to your own country!" "You dirty people are taking our jobs!" "You're a terrorist!"

Jazz begged Mom and Dad to let him move back to India and live with our uncle, but they would not part with their son. They considered cutting Jazz's hair, which would have been almost as heart-wrenching for them as sending him away, but then the Sikh community they were just beginning to befriend would look down upon them.

The beating continued for the first two years. It wasn't that Jazz was skinny and weak and that he could not defend himself; in fact, he was tall, well-built for a young kid, and strong enough to beat the boys in his own grade as well as some of the older boys. But it wasn't what we were taught by our parents; physical confrontations were for the lowly classes and not those who were educated and well-to-do. Our father always taught us that problems could be solved by reasoning and discussion and not fighting. Mom and Dad agreed that it would be wrong for Jazz to stand up for himself and stoop to the level of his bullies. I now wished they had thought about our background, and what we as Sikhs stand for, and not about society. I was too young to know back then, but Jazz was fighting injustice almost like our Sikh Gurus had; instead of pacifism, our Gurus embraced war in the face of tyranny, and strangely, so did Jazz, but perhaps because he lacked guidance from our parents, he took it too far in the wrong direction. Unlike the Sikh Gurus who fought courageously and fairly and risked their own lives for the sake of justice and righteousness, Jazz fought the discrimination he faced with cruelty and hatred and for the sake of revenge.

Jazz would come home, hiding his bruised face from Mom, and then hide himself in his room. If he wasn't watching Rocky or kung fu movies, he just sat on his bed staring at the blank white wall with a solemn face and fiery almond eyes that glowed with hate and anger. He became very quiet and after a while stopped telling our mom and dad what the kids said to him and what they did to him in school. He didn't participate in any school activities, and he never made any friends; his confidence had died. He slowly began to distance himself from Mom and Dad and never spoke to them unless he was spoken to. He refused to play games with his brother and sisters and stayed home when we went to a family friend's house. He slowly shed his docile and timid garb, losing feeling for everyone he knew, even his family, and becoming cold as ice. The signs of his metamorphosis were always there, but we didn't pay close enough attention to notice them.

After three years of living in Queens, when Jazz was around thirteen, he gave himself to the aggression snapping and cracking inside of him like ferocious fire. His anger was finally released, manifesting itself in gruesome punches and sharp kicks he threw at the unsuspecting bodies of every boy who had beaten him. The school principal reported his behavior to Mom and Dad, and they tried desperately to make him stop, but he mercilessly continued. Not only did many kids become afraid of Jazz but over time the same bullies who had beaten him began to befriend him. His new friends shared with him cigarettes, beers, and their taste for rock music and bullying others, their hatred of people, their anger, their frustration. For the first time in America, Jazz felt accepted and part of a group. Being accepted was all that mattered, even if it meant being a troublemaker in school and alienating himself from his family, his culture, and who he was.

Around that same time, my parents were able to afford a small house on Ash Lane in Manhasset, Long Island, where we moved in the late 1980s. The move came too late for Jazz, though. He lost too young what could not be replaced; only the deep scar in his heart was proof that something sweeter had been there. He only had a faint vision of its memory; he could no longer feel it or live it. Too much had happened. Mom and Dad thought a change of scenery and schools would bring a change in him, but it made him worse, more determined to challenge and oppose the American system, the place he loathed, the country that had robbed him.

Suburbia was an isolated place compared to the city streets of Queens. There were no more busy intersections, highway noise, kids littering the sidewalks, and immigrant women pushing their laundry carts to the nearest Laundromat. Long Island held forth its charm, cleanliness, and neat houses with neat green gardens. Doors and windows were left open on a summer's day with no sign of danger. Children biked even after sunset. Abundant rows of trees lined the streets, blue skies offered blessings with a bright hue, and the sun shined upon the chosen people who lived underneath it. They traveled only by car, they spoke with a strong Long Island accent, all their children attended summer camp and had activities after school during the year. And, frankly speaking, they were all white. Gone were the Latinos and the Indians and the African Americans and the Chinese. Left, right, they were all white faces, well except for ours. We were the only nonwhite family who lived on Ash Lane. Ironically, the prejudice we had faced in Queens, a place inundated with immigrants, was not overtly directed at us on Long Island, a segregated place where we, a minority family, stuck out like a sore thumb. Our neighbors were graceful and welcoming, and their children were kind and accepting and became our friends. The community accepted us, and we were grateful for it. But nothing prepared me for the changing of schools.

Chapter 5

1992

My school experience was luckily not violent like Jazz's, but it was a roller-coaster ride that never calmed or slowed down until it was finally over. Being accepted by other twelve-year-olds in middle school was a harder task than I could have imagined. It was not enough to wear designer clothes, have your hair the same cut as Jennifer Aniston on *Friends*, have your mom on the PTA, and talk about your skiing trips and trips to the Caribbean. You needed more than that to be popular at our new school; your parents had to be rich, and you had to have an attitude. The income of parents here was triple that of the families in my previous school in Queens. My first and only friend showed me how fat with money her father's wallet was when I visited her house on a play date.

I was so far from any of that that my mind was often plagued simply with the thought that someone might notice what I was eating for lunch. At least in Queens I could eat my stuffed parantha (bread stuffed with spiced potato) with the other Indian girls, who knew exactly what I was eating and envied me for it. On Long Island, my lack of grilled cheese, Fruit Roll-Ups, and juice drinks aimed a beacon at my immigrant status, starkly revealing in the process that my mom wasn't in the know and neither was I. There was no chance of popularity and a very meek chance for any level of acceptance by the "cool" kids. I was unpopular and often preyed on by the other girls like a bird caged with a bunch of cats. They jumped on any chance to tear down what bits of dignity I had left. It took many years for me to secure a small group of friends and make my insignificant little nest in preppy land.

One afternoon, as usual, all the school's kids, from fifth to eighth grades, were waiting in the gymnasium for the school buses to take us home. It was a hot May Day, and everybody was a little irritable. That's when Jennifer Ackman came up to where I crouched alone against a wall with my book bag waiting for my bus letter to be called and shouted enough so surrounding groups of boys could hear, "Mira, I love your hairy legs!" Everyone, including my crush, turned to examine and laugh at my indeed hairy legs that I had been trying to conceal all day with my arms or book bag.

My mind raced with disgust for Jennifer and myself. *How could I let Jennifer catch me off guard like that?* I would have to give a comeback that would shut Jennifer's mouth but at the same time did not anger her, because then my school life would really be over.

"Thank you!" I exclaimed in a defiant tone with a strong and rigid face and a thin smile that hid my inner tears but left me weak and insecure about myself. I was like a beetle using its hard shell to protect its soft body.

Frustrated at her failure to make me cry, Jennifer made a face, turned around, and left without saying another word. I swore at that moment I would go home and shave my legs, and it would be worth getting into a fight with Mom. Mom believed that a twelve-year-old girl in the seventh grade should not be allowed to remove hair from her body because she was only a child and it would somehow rob her of her innocence. She had mastered the art of telling dramatic stories about how shaving my legs at an early age—and wearing tampons (I had started my period two years earlier) and makeup—would destroy my chances of having a fresh beauty on my wedding day. Tampons were especially forbidden because they didn't just take away the glow—they nullified virginity. She proclaimed that if I followed her guidance, I would shine as the swan among my duckling friends who wore makeup and dressed up so much that they would lose that unique youthful beauty in their coming of age.

I quickly made up my mind that I was not going to let all these tall tales stop me from surviving high school with some decency. If I kept these hairy legs and long braids and no makeup, I would lose the few friends that I had. After school, I sneaked one of Ritu's razors into the shower and shaved my legs and underarms, then "borrowed" a pair of Ritu's shorts and a tank top for the next day. In the morning after my bus arrived at school, I ran into the bathroom, changed into my stolen clothes, and applied some lipstick and blush that I had taken from Ritu's makeup drawer. This process lasted more than a few months, but it didn't solve one big problem I had.

I hated my long, thick hair that Mom braided every morning into a tight rope that only she could rebraid if opened. Really, I hated just that braid. I wished I could let free the hair I knew would stop every boy in his tracks, if only they could see its lustrous waves. All the boys in home economics class loved to tease me by tugging and pulling on my braid, wrapping it around their necks. When one of the boys took the rubber band from the bottom of my braid and put it into his pocket, my twelve-year-old brain realized an opportunity.

"Hey, Mira, if I don't give this back to you, would your hair unravel by itself?" asked Justin, whose short dirty-blond hair rose in spikes frozen in the air by an abundance of gel.

This was my chance to show off my long hair! "Yeah, it sure will—if you dare me!"

"We dare you to open your hair!" a few boys gathering around exclaimed.

Slowly, slowly, I unbraided the rope, stringing along with the excitement of the boys, whose eyes grew larger with every ripple that came unloose. The large crowd of boys encircling me caught the teacher's attention, and that was when the trouble began.

The teacher, Mrs. Strictner, was like her name implied, strict in all matters, especially when it came to boys and girls mixing in class. At my moment of teenage glory when my hair was fully open and the boys', and girls', mouths were gaping at the wondrous sight of lush, silky locks tumbling down to my knees, Mrs. Strictner grabbed my arm and pulled me out of the crowd. "Miss Mira Singh, I am sure your mother wouldn't like it if she found out that you were disrupting my sewing class with this obscene show of hair!"

"Oh, please, Mrs. Strictner, don't call home about this. It won't happen again!" I pleaded, almost crying.

"Well, I can't let you prance around your classes all day long like this causing further disruption, so I'm just going to have to braid your hair back myself."

We were all shocked when Mrs. Strictner roughly braided my hair out in the hallway for the remainder of the class period. Although I did not get reported to my parents for my unacceptable behavior that day and my mother did not realize that my hair had been rebraided, my disappointment of being limited and different resonated for years after. I would never be allowed to let my hair down, and of course, the unmentionable was my desire to cut my hair so it could look pretty and stylish like the other girls'.

Years earlier, Ritu had astounded me when she encouraged me to trim the split ends of my hair, as she did. I had shamed Ritu for cutting her hair when she knew it was against our religious traditions. But as a teen, the answer to why we kept our traditions began to feel less clear to me. When I was a little girl, life seemed simple: there was good, and there was bad; there were rewards and punishments; life was black and white. With each passing year, truth seemed less absolute and more fluid, like my faith, which continued to remain my loyal companion, but which morphed over time. My young hands prayed for liberation every evening, for a universal enlightenment that was far beyond the scope of a twelve-year-old brain, one that would bring together my modern life with the spirituality that still resonated and kept me steadfast. Religious knowledge alone could not produce an iota of true understanding, I now realized; experience through samadhi (conscious meditation) awakened new eyes to God and the universe. Only time could reveal the complexities of life, the way a peeling onion reveals both layers and tears. Back then, youth kept me blissfully ignorant of pain; mental agony was reserved for grown-ups. The cocoon around me had formed like a wrapper, tight and almost impermeable. The pain of metamorphosis was yet to begin, and I, like all before me, was ignorant to its beginning.

Chapter 6

1995

It was finally June, and the wedding festivities for Kinchan-chacha started with the prayer ceremony, to bless the couple a week or so before the wedding, as is customary. Sikh religious ceremonies are rather peaceful: the holy scriptures are read by the head priest, and hymns are sung by the procession; a sweet devotional offering called prasad is passed to everyone at the end of the prayers; and then, of course, langar, a savory meal, is distributed to all present. The day after the prayers is officially party time with song and dance, and women decked out like Indian village dolls gather for the mehndi, or henna ceremony. The red dye symbolizes the transition from being an unmarried maiden to being a bride and wife; it is the color of marital bliss. All the girls in our family called a professional mehndi lady to draw intricate tattoos on our hands and feet. The bride, of course, had the most intricate and beautiful mehndi of all, but the rest of the girls still fought to have the second-best.

"Renu-auntie, won't you make my mehndi a little more detailed and finer like the older girls'?" I begged as the mehndi lady was filling in a large leaf painted on my palm.

"Now, baby, I have twenty other girls to do and only three more hours. I just can't spend so much time on you. Now, you want only one hand done or both hands?"

“Oh, I want both hands, and I wanted you to make a squiggly on my arm,” I whined.

Ritu stepped in, “Mira, you’re hogging Renu-auntie. Let someone else get their mehndi done too!”

“I’m almost done here; you keep the next girl ready—and I don’t want a fidgety little one like this one.”

I gave Renu-auntie a nasty look. I was as still as I could be while the mehndi spout tickled my hands with continuous sweeps of paint.

“OK, you’re done. Next.”

I examined my hands. My mehndi wasn’t intricate at all. Instead, Renu-auntie had made me two quick flowers and leaves with little dots on each finger while the other girls who were fanning their hands dry by the fan had gotten beautiful paisley-shaped twirls with the initials of their lover hidden in it.

As Ritu sat down to have her hands covered with the red dye, the music started to play, and the older women began to dance in the living room. Dadiji came in and joined the circle by clapping and moving her head side to side. I jumped into the dance by folk singer Malkit Singh, shrugging my shoulders and stamping my feet to the music, conscientious not to let my wet hands touch my mint-green silk salwar kameez. In a few minutes, all the girls were on the dance floor, and we danced in those beautiful trousers-and-tunic suits, and as our hands dried, dried bits of green mehndi fell to the carpet and were squished by our feet. When we got tired, we all rushed to the stove in the kitchen where Dadiji was heating some oil. The darker a girl’s mehndi came out when it dried, the more love she would share with her husband. The old secret to making one’s mehndi darker and last longer was to rub off the dried bits of the henna with some mustard oil over hot gas. Since my mehndi always turned orange instead of red, I rushed to heat my hands over the stove. After all, I wanted my future husband to be madly in love with me—like the Bollywood movie I had recently seen where the man was so much in love with the girl that he took a knife and etched her name on his arm and did it without flinching as he bled uncontrollably.

That same night was the sangeet, or the night of music and dance. My excitement was beaming like stars in my eyes, and my cheeks glowed red with happiness. Everyone dressed for the event that was to take place in Taj Palace, an Indian restaurant and party hall in the next town. For some reason, Indian families, including our own, could never be dressed for any occasion on time. I carefully ironed my salwar kameez, the pants, the shirt, and then the matching scarf. It was a beautiful rust color that made my complexion look fairer. I was not yet allowed to wear makeup, but I did manage to steal a bit of blush, black eyeliner, and clear lip gloss. I lined my wrists with matching red glass bangles mixed with gold ones, tied my hair back in a long braid, and slipped on multicolored Punjabi shoes, which, by the way, can be worn on either the left or right foot.

Mom came to our room where Ritu and I were dressing and said, to our delight, that now that I was a little older, I could wear a very small Bindi on my forehead and Ritu could wear some real jewels. I got to wear my special occasion gold earrings, and Ritu wore Mom's gold-studded necklace with matching earrings. Mom looked like a queen; I had always admired her looks and her graceful walk. She was tall, medium built, with golden skin; she was beautiful. People always said that I looked so much like her. She wore a light-pink-and-gold sari with a five-string pearl necklace that was studded with multicolor stones, matching dangling earrings, and a thick pearl bangle. For a woman who had four grown-up children, our mother looked young, especially because she dyed her white strays with henna and wore a deep-toned lipstick. We always noted, standing at a party, that our parents made a good match in their stature and grace.

I was ready before Ritu. She always took longer, for she had tons of makeup to apply and hair to do. Mom would always object to Ritu using so much makeup, but Ritu would only nod and continue to wear it. Jazz had put up a fuss about going, and he was being forced by Dad to wear a proper shirt at least, if he was not going to wear a tie. Jeet wore an old three-piece suit since he was saving his new suit to wear at the reception party and, as usual, was dressed and ready without a fuss, his turban tied, his light beard brushed and tied under his chin, his finest cologne sprayed, and his boots polished, and when I got downstairs, I found him reading a science book while waiting for the rest of the family.

"Ritu, Mom, can you guys' hurry? I don't even feel freshly dressed anymore!" I shouted from the bottom of the staircase.

Mom came, her heels clunking down on the wooden stairs.

I pretended to be falling from boredom.

"Mira, stop acting silly. You'll dirty your salwar pants before you get to the party and stand up straight before I give you a good punch in the back. You really are ruining the beauty of your height."

Mom had been trying to straighten my posture as far as I could remember. I straightened for a moment, and then my shoulders went slouching down again. Another fifteen minutes zipped past, and Jazz was dressed and looked presentable.

"Hey, Jazz, I recognize you now," I said with a grin.

"Oh, shut up, Mira!" he yelled.

"Jazz, I don't want you speaking to your sister that way, and don't cause any problems for me tonight. I want you on your best behavior!" said Mom.

"Yeah, and who's gonna make me, you?!"

Trouble dawned in my mind. Dad got up from the sofa.

"How dare you speak to your mother like this. Is that what they teach you in these American schools? If you don't apologize right now, I'm going to grab your ears and drag you to every Indian party and take away any spare money you get, and you can forget about going out with your crazy friends and forget about me ever buying you your own car!" Dad's face was red hot. Jazz just loosened Dad's grasp from his ear, walked into his room, and shut the door hard. "Don't you dare bang your door at me! I'll mend you in a minute, bandha banja! Become a man, or I'll beat your skin off!" Our parents threatened to beat us whenever we did wrong, but they never did; it was just a tool their parents had used to make them obey when they were children. Besides, it was very rare for our dad to be threatening—that was usually Mom's department—but Jazz was a special case. As Punjabis say, "Aflatoon!" In other words, a pompous or mad person, who in our case only our dad could control.

The rest of the family was quiet. I especially felt guilty for bringing trouble before a party. When Ritu came down, she was still smiling with the satisfaction of how she looked so dolled up. Her smile soon faded as she saw there had been yet another argument in the Singh family. All of us piled in the car, an old Mercedes, of course—what Sikh didn't drive this symbol of high status in the community! The ride to the restaurant was quieted by the argument, and I even resisted whining about my shirt that was caught under Ritu's leg in the back seat that was tight for the four of us.

When we arrived at the restaurant, we were greeted with overjoyed smiles and overdressed women. Mom and Dad faked their smiles until they seemed to forget the incident at home as they congratulated my uncle and the rest of the family and apologized for arriving so late. Jazz's expression remained serious and unhappy until he spotted the pretty young girls on the dance floor. Ritu and I gladly began our quick greetings to the old bags (the older aunties)— "Oh, Sat Sri Akal, Auntie. How are you?"—and skimmed the hall for our friends. Jeet dreaded big parties and remained quietly behind my parents, smiling boyishly at everyone and speaking to no one.

Tender mint chicken and succulent lamb kabobs were being served by dark-skinned men in white uniforms buttoned up into Nehru collars. A separate table had been set up where vegetarian potato patties and spicy chickpeas were served covered with a sour tamarind sauce. The roaring laughter of the men who were gathered around the bar ordering Black Label whiskey could be heard over the loud bhangra music being blasted by the DJ.

Soon the DJ announced the entrance of the bride and groom to have their first dance alone on the floor. "Lady in Red" started to play, and Kinchan-chacha and his soon-to-be wife, Reeya, danced shyly. Other couples were urged to join them on the floor, and more soft music played. Finally, once again the bhangra started, and Ritu and I jumped on the dance floor. Almost immediately, Ritu was surrounded by her friends, and I was knocked out of the circle. I fled the dance floor in a desperate search for my friend Deepa. I spotted her mother from a distance, Bindu-auntie, with her beautiful pair of white plums heaving over the bar as she smiled at my dad! I had once overheard Mom and Dadiji talking about Bindu-auntie. Dadiji had said something about how she was always wearing low-cut saree blouses to flaunt her abundant breasts. She had a fair and sweet-looking face, but we should not assume an innocent one, Dadiji had said. The rest of the allegation against my friend's mother I could not hear as Ritu hit me from behind and dragged me away to another room. Now, at the wedding, I flinched, watching her and Dad together; I was relieved when he turned away from her and left the bar. I was glad that he wasn't extending his conversation with Bindu-auntie and scanning her famous bosom any longer; after all, a daughter is possessive of her father, for at least her mother's sake.

I was glad when I found Deepa near the snack table.

"Deepa!" I shouted.

"Hi, Mira, you look so nice! Ah, wearing a bit of makeup! My mom made me rub off my lipstick—it's so unfair!"

"And now," we heard the DJ boom, "will everyone clear the dance floor, please. Kinchan's nieces will be performing a special dance for us."

My heart felt like it was going to jump out of my chest. I was so nervous. All those weeks of practicing, and this was finally the moment.

"Mira, line up quickly," whispered Ritu.

My head was spinning. Suddenly, I didn't know what to do. Once the music started, my limbs automatically did what they were programmed to do, but my mind remained blank. At the end of the dance, everyone cheered and clapped. I breathed a sigh of relief and felt proud as the compliments came rushing in. "Oh, Mira, you are such a great dancer." "Mira, we loved the dance." "You are one of the best dancers I've ever seen. I've been watching you all night!" I was in bliss and quite full of myself.

Our drive home was not as quiet as the ride to the party. Mom and Dad were talking about how well the party went and how much fun they had. They laughed about the same old people in the community and how they always met at big parties and talked about the same things every time. Ritu and I continued to talk about the success of our dance and all the compliments we received, while Jeet fell asleep and Jazz rolled his eyes at every comment we made and rubbed his forehead, which surely was spinning from the tequila shots he got the bartender to sneak to him—after all, he was almost twenty-one. All in all, we were as happy as we could be.

The wedding day the following morning was more hectic since we had to reach the Gurdwara, the Sikh temple, for the groom's baraat by ten. After the usual yelling and screaming that mom had to do to wake us up and get us dressed, we piled up in the car and left home at ten. We reached the Gurdwara as Kinchan-chacha was getting ready to mount his white horse. As is customary, the bride's family was already present and waiting on the Gurdwara steps to greet and welcome the groom and his family. The dhol man that Kinchan-chacha had called to play music for the baraat's arrival started to bang on his drums and sing his folk songs while the horse walked slowly toward the entrance steps. Our whole family, including my grandmother, uncles, and aunts, started to form a dance circle; each of us, when the name of our relation to Kinchan-chacha was sung by the dhol man, jumped into the middle of the circle and danced. Ritu, our cousins, and I jumped in to dance when they called for the groom's nieces. The dancing continued for the next half an hour until my uncle climbed off the horse as we all readied for prayers.

The priest stood and prayed between the two families that were being joined that day. The priest then signaled that the milni ceremony should begin. *Milni* means "meeting" and signifies the joining of the two families into one new one. The fathers of the groom and bride bestowed a garland of flowers and dollar bills around each other's necks and embraced. The bride's family was responsible for buying these garlands and giving each family member on the groom's side an envelope with money in it. After the fathers embraced, the brothers, the uncles, and the cousins embraced. Usually, only the males participate in the milni ceremony, but in some families, females do as well. Once the families joined, we all followed the groom into the Gurdwara for a brief breakfast before the wedding ceremony started.

Ritu and I carefully noted Kinchan-chacha's shoes. Ritu and I were not about to miss out on one of the best playful traditions of Sikh weddings. The goal of the bride's sisters and cousins is to steal the shoes of the groom on the wedding day so that after the wedding, they can tease him and negotiate with him the price of returning his shoes. The groom's side is to make sure that the shoes are not stolen by the bride's side and are safely hidden so that the groom doesn't have to pay for his shoes. As soon as Kinchan-chacha entered the Gurdwara, we noticed that our new auntie's brats were following our uncle closely, their eyes glued to his shoes. Ritu and I rushed after Kinchan-chacha down the stairs to the shoe room.

"Kinchan-chacha, no! Don't take them off yet!" I yelled.

But he had taken off one shoe already, and at that moment, Reeya-auntie's younger cousin grabbed it and ran out the other side of the room.

"Mira, catch her while I get the other shoe!"

I went running as fast as I could after the chubby one who was already up the stairs leading to the parking lot.

"Girls, stop this foolishness," complained some of the older women who had become caught in the battle of the shoes.

"Oh no, you won't," said a cousin of Reeya-auntie, smiling at us.

Later, Ritu would tell me that she was so intent on saving that other shoe that before Kinchan-chacha had a chance to slip it off, Ritu grabbed it herself off his lifted foot, and—*bhramp!*—Kinchan-chacha fell to the floor! She was embarrassed but said, "Sorry, Kinchan-chacha, but you do understand this shoe situation is a life-or-death matter!" Our uncle only laughed as my dad and others helped him to his feet.

I was just returning to the temple, huffing and puffing, as Ritu appeared in the parking lot, hugging the shoe to her chest. "I couldn't get it in time!" I cried. "That girl passed it on to the boy cousins, can you believe it? And they ran so fast, I couldn't catch up with them."

"Mira, can't you do anything right? What's the point of having just one shoe!" Ritu opened the trunk of our car quickly and locked the shoe she had in it just as one of the bride's cousins came up behind her. "Too late, I don't think you guys will get anything from this wedding!" boasted Ritu, her attitude taking a 180 from what she'd dished out to me.

"We're not worried! You've not got the other shoe yet," said the bride's cousin and kept walking. We followed her; the wedding was about to start.

The Darbar, or main hall, inside the Gurdwara was already crowded with family, friends, and guests from abroad. Ritu and I found a place to sit on the floor near the front of the room behind Kinchan-chacha. Mom gave us a look of disapproval for our lateness. The priests were already singing hymns of celebration with gusto. Finally, our new auntie, Reeya, was brought in by her brother. She looked so pretty dressed in a dusty-pink-and-silver brocade outfit with a long, heavily embroidered veil. Although her face could be only slightly seen, it was obvious that she was fair and had rosy lips and large black eyes. Everyone turned to look at and admire the new bride as she walked toward Kinchan-chacha. As the couple walked around the Holy Guru Granth four times as hymns were sung, tears rolled from my grandmother's and mom's eyes. I had never imagined that Kinchan-chacha's wedding would make me so emotional. I felt like I was choking, trying to keep the tears back. Once the wedding was over, we all went to kiss and congratulate the new couple and take pictures with them. The afternoon lunch was catered in the Gurdwara itself, and everyone ate till they felt they were bulging out of their outfits. Most of the guests had left by two in the afternoon, and only the family remained, taking more photographs.

Kinchan-chacha was now frantically looking for his shoes. "Girls, girls, bring uncle's shoes now; it's almost time for the Doli to leave," demanded Reeya-auntie's mother of her children.

"We only have one shoe, Mommy. Ask Uncle's nieces where the other shoe is."

"We're not letting you have it, if that's what you think. You will get paid for only one shoe," I blurted out rudely.

"Come on, girls, let's resolve this issue," said Kinchan-chacha. "How much do you want for one shoe?"

"Well, let's see, we're the five of us cousins and nieces together," spoke one of Reeya-auntie's older cousins, "so we want $200 each. That's $1,000!"

"No way! Don't give them that much money, Kinchan-chacha. They are greedy!" shouted Ritu, swinging the shoe she'd retrieved from the trunk in her hand.

"Come on, girls, don't you think that's a bit much for just one shoe?"

"No way, Uncle. We worked hard to steal it! Now, pay up, pay up, pay up!" They started cheering.

By now, impatient to continue with the day, Reeya-auntie's mother interjected, "Just compromise, OK? Give these girls $500 total. One hundred each, and you girls are not getting any more than that, you hear!"

"Say no, Kinchan-chacha." Ritu and I tried to dissuade him, but he was prepared with the money, and he agreed to his new mother-in-law's terms. So, the other girls were paid $500, and we were forced to surrender the other shoe.

Reeya-auntie's Doli, or what is known as the going away or giving of the bride from her parents to the groom's family, was the final tradition on the day of the wedding. She had changed from her wedding outfit into an outfit that my grandmother had bought for her. When she was ready to leave, sad songs were sung by the women in her family as they symbolically gave away their daughter to the groom and his new family; they would be her new family henceforth. Reeya-auntie cried a lot and hugged her parents' goodbye before sitting in the limousine with Kinchan-chacha, and they both waved goodbye as they went off for their first night in a hotel at an undisclosed location.

• • •

I could not fall asleep right away that night. I kept thinking about what it would be like when I got married. What would I be wearing? I knew—a lovely pink because I looked pretty in pink. Who would my husband be? I could only envision a young, strong, handsome shadow. The shadow didn't have a turban, weirdly enough, so I tried hard to envision one with a turban—yes, of course, that would have to be. I could not marry a non-Sikh or even a Sikh who did not wear a turban because Mom and Dad would not like that. And, of course, who would steal my future husband's shoes, and would I cry when I had to say goodbye to my family? Why do we have to make that break from our parents so definitely like a line etched in stone? After all, wouldn't I be living in the same city? Oh, I would never want to move so far away from home like poor Reeya-auntie. It must be very hard on her and all brides who must move countries. Perhaps that was a tradition I could live without. My thoughts were beginning to make no sense at all as sleep engulfed me.

• • •

The next night was the reception, the last event of the wedding. As the groom, Kinchan-chacha had to organize it. Like the sangeet night, this party was full of rich foods, loud music, dancing, and the same people. The only difference was that Kinchan-chacha was now a married man. The three-tier wedding cake was cut to soft music, and everyone had a chance to feed a bite to the new couple. They danced their first dance to a slow Hindi tune, and slowly all the other couples joined in. I wanted to do a slow dance too, but of course, it would be totally inappropriate if I asked one of the boys to dance with me in front of everyone. It was OK for girls to dance with girls and boys to dance with each other, or a girl and boy could dance together if they were already related, like two cousins or a father with his daughter. However, dancing with a boy who was single and unrelated to her was only for the very gutsiest of girls who did not care whether the whole town talked about them and made-up stories of their dating even if it was just one dance. I was never that brave. I preferred being the good girl whom all the grown-ups approved of. I was never the black sheep, never the rebel. We left the party feeling happy for Kinchan-chacha but a bit melancholy that the wedding was done and there were no more parties to look forward to.

But I would soon learn that Kinchan-chacha's wedding had set the stage—the real drama was yet to unfold. Clouds of tragedy had not yet loomed over the Singh household. We still had a couple of years of simplicity and happiness to come. Perhaps, if we had been less naive about our possible fate, we would have been less vulnerable to it.

Chapter 7
1998

Exhausted and drained from the events of the past couple of months, I heard my alarm clock ringing in the distance, somewhere amid my dream, but my body was unwilling to make any movement, almost paralyzed.

"Mira, wake up! Miraaaa, shut off your alarm!" Katy croaked sleepily.

As I slowly opened my eyes, I saw the large Gothic church through our window and heard the bustling of traffic on the streets. "Oh, I'm sorry. I was so deep in sleep," I said, fumbling to find the off button on the clock on top of the desk behind the headboard. The disturbing ringing ceased, and I reluctantly swung my bare legs around and onto the floor where my fuzzy bunny slippers awaited my feet. I pushed myself to embrace another unwelcome day.

"I have a ten o'clock lecture today, and I haven't done any reading for it, Kat."

"Tell me something new, Mir."

I dragged myself to the bathroom. Just as I finished toweling off from the shower, the room phone rang. "Oh, Katy, if it's Dev, please tell him I haven't returned to school yet," I begged with my hands clasping my wooly, cream sweater hanging between my elbows.

"You can't keep avoiding him like this! He's called here so many times, and he's probably found out you're back!"

Katy answered and then quietly gestured to me with her thin hands still holding her socks to take the phone. "He sounds really sad," she murmured.

I took the phone from Katy with a slight roll of my eyes. "Hi, Dev, how are you? It's good to hear your voice too. I'm OK, still hanging in there. Ahh…" I let a deep breath out. "I don't know. I have classes all afternoon. Mm. All right, at four o'clock where? OK, OK, I promise I will this time. Yeah, same here. Love you too. Bye."

"I don't understand why you are alienating him," Katy said. "I'm sure he would understand."

"Oh God, I don't know. If I tell him everything, then what if he thinks that my family and I have too many problems and he doesn't want to have anything to do with me? You know how much I care about him, and I don't want to lose him, but at the same time, I think I should break up with him. I'm not sure I can handle a relationship right now. And you know my parents would never accept him, and I just can't pile another set of worries on them."

"Well, if you keep him in the dark about your life, you won't have to initiate the breakup," she said while pulling her socks to her bony knees before throwing on her jeans.

Throwing my head through the soft bundle of wool of my sweater, I knew Katy was right. I had to gather enough courage to tell Dev the truth about my family, and the truth about our impossible future together.

• • •

After my aesthetics in philosophy elective, which I spent at the top of the big lecture hall as far away from the professor as possible, I took a break for lunch before my metaphysics lecture. As I ate my sandwich quietly in a corner of the Loeb Student Center, I thought about Dev and me, about how we met and how we fell in love. Thinking about Dev was a welcome distraction from my usual thoughts about death, and somehow it lightened the burden of pain I carried.

• • •

The NYU Sikh Club party was at the Violet Café across from Washington Square Park with a DJ pumping bhangra music into the night. When my friends left our conversation circle to dance to a song I didn't like, my gaze wandered the space, and just as it fell on the door where they were collecting money and handing out tickets, a guy I had never seen before entered, and my subconscious said, *Wow!*" I could hear myself think it, and then I remembered to start breathing again. He was tall, probably close to six foot two, and had a muscular build with tanned skin and a soft look in his almond eyes. What just happened? There had been only one other time in my life when I had been left with a frozen body and a thumping heart at the sight of a man, and that had been when I was a little teenager with a high school crush. This was different, more intense.

Oh my God, he was looking at me, so I turned around quickly, an involuntary reflex. I must have looked like such a loser standing by myself. If he'd arrived just a minute earlier, he would have seen me talking with friends. I felt a light tap on my shoulder, and when I turned around, I saw it was him! I audibly gasped. *Breathe, Mira, breathe.*

"Hi, my name is Dev. Are you Mira?"

He knows my name! How does he know I exist? He came up to me. Me? Why? Of all the beautiful girls dancing in this place, why me?

I must've been wearing a look of astonishment and utter shock because the next thing he said was "I didn't mean to come off like a stalker. I just saw you the other day leaving the Sikh Club meeting, and they told me you were the secretary of the club. I mean…I was interested in buying a ticket for this party, so they told me I could speak to you, but I couldn't catch you in time."

"That's OK." I quickly rushed to save him from his explanation, and to distract myself from staring at his smile, which was so alluring. Of course, I knew he wasn't interested in me; it was to buy the tickets. Of course. Why else would anyone so breathtaking know my name? The thought was a little depressing, yet it relieved me enough to allow me back into reality. I squared my shoulders, smiled, and was ready to move toward my friends on the dance floor, when he started talking again.

"So, what year are you?" His voice was deep. Even under the loud music, it made my stomach bubble. His Indian accent was tinged with an American accent, making him sound sexy.

"I'm a freshman."

"Oh, I'm a sophomore," he said. His hair was cut short except for a soft-looking flap curled at one side of his face. The dholi supporting the DJ began banging his sticks harder on his dhol. Dev crouched a little to speak to me in my ear. "I'm studying at the Stern School of Business. What about you?" I could smell his scent, fresh but enticingly masculine. Musk with the slightest hint of cinnamon, as if I had only imagined it.

I swallowed what little bit of saliva was left in my mouth before I answered. I leaned close to his face, and with what little voice I had left around my breathlessness, I answered, "I'm a philosophy student."

His eyebrows arched a little, and he leaned back a little to give me a good look.

Is he amused? What's wrong with being a philosophy major?! Fine, be that way!

"Is something weird about that?" I scowled at him. I turned my face and waved to my friends on the dance floor, who were by now smiling and giving me the "oh my God, who's he?" look.

"I'm so sorry. I didn't mean for you to take it that way. I am actually very impressed. Philosophy! You must be smart."

"Oh, thanks." *Hmm...impressed by philosophy? Well, that's a first.* Most guys just thought I was too much of a bookworm to be of any interest. But forget about that—his strong jaw, and the way his muscular chest flexed under his shirt, and his smell, and the loud music, and I was beginning to feel that familiar sense of discomfort under the male gaze... I was feeling dizzy.

"I'm sorry," I blurted out, "but I have to leave."

A flash of disappointment stole the smile on his face. "Oh, so early?"

"Yeah, I'm not a late-night type of person, so...it was nice meeting you, Dev."

"The pleasure was mine," and he reached his hand out, and when I put my hand in his, a sudden rush, like a wave of electricity, flowed into my body from my throat down to my abdomen. My face felt hot and red. There must have been some effect on him too as he was still standing frozen, holding onto my hand firmly like he was never going to let go.

I broke away and hurried to my friends on the dance floor, leaving Dev behind.

"Who is he?!" They all snapped at the same time.

"We are leaving right now!" I demanded.

They protested but followed my lead. When we walked out, I felt Dev watching me. His presence was too much to endure.

I couldn't contain the anxiety and excitement I felt, so I had to flee.

"OK, Mira!" Katy and Leila leaped on me as we walked down Fifth Avenue to Tenth Street. "Who was that hot stud? And why the hell aren't we back there with him?"

"Well, if you stop salivating over Dev, I will tell you!" I growled back.

"Dev, ooh, I like his name. Dev, Dev…"

"Will you cut that out!"

"How do you know him? Come on, seriously," urged Katy.

"Well, I don't know-know him. It was the first time I'd laid eyes on him. He knew *my* name and just started talking."

"Wow, that's awesome! He's into you!" yelled Leila.

"Leila, you think everyone's into me," I said. "He only knew my name because he wanted to buy tickets for the party, and they told him he could buy them from me, but he couldn't catch up to me that day, so, anyway, it isn't like he is into me."

"Well, he is into you enough to come over and talk to you," said Katy.

"Anyway, you girls just get excited every time a guy talks to me, and it's never anything."

"That's not the guy's fault," barked Leila.

I gave her a shocked look. "What's that supposed to mean?"

"It's just that there have been so many guys who've been interested in you, and you blow them all off!"

"What? Like whom?"

"Hmm. What was that cute guy from Switzerland's name? Yann! He was so into you, and you didn't even give him a chance. And how about the Indian guy in your class? He's always buzzing around you like he wants your nectar."

"Ha, Leila, you're dirty!"

She kept going. "Oh, and the other American guy from our class, and countless guys from the Indian Society, and when we go out clubbing, you always get attention from the cutest guys… who you then give fake numbers to."

I stopped walking and turned to Leila with my arms folded across my chest. "What the hell, Leila, are you my freakin' private investigator? What, do you keep a journal on how many men I don't have interest in?!" I'm mad, and Leila and Katy can see it.

"Well, you did ask me to explain what I meant," Leila said in a quiet voice. Leila could be such a dodo sometimes.

"We are going to drop the man talk. Is that understood, ladies?" I said with a stern voice and adamant face.

"Dropped," Leila and Katy said in unison with their hands up in the air like they didn't want me to shoot my glare at them.

That night, I lay awake thinking about what Leila had said. It was true; I did blow off most guys who approached me. I wasn't sure what they saw in me. Yann looked like a Greek statue come to life. He had come to NYU from Switzerland to study business at Stern, and he happened to take some early civilization classes with me. At first, I pretended that I didn't notice his flirting, but then he made it clear to me that he was interested. He confronted me about how I was so closed and narrow-minded, that I couldn't face the truth, and that I shunned men without giving them a chance. I blamed it on my being Indian—oh, that was always a good scapegoat to avoid non-Indian guys. I told him it was my culture and that I was traditional. Ohhh… how I regretted doing that. The truth was that I was too scared to start a relationship with him not because he was not Indian but because I was afraid of the attraction, I felt for him. It was easier to run away from it, so I did. And I did the same for the handsome American medical student who was so into me and

I into him that when I spoke to him, I would get shivers down my spine. But again, I blew him off. And I did the same with the Indian guys!

It was my mother's fault! She didn't allow us to have any relationship with the opposite sex, not even friendships. Now, there I was on my own, in college, and afraid, lacking confidence, and having no experience, not the slightest clue how to interact with a guy.

But I could not ignore that zing, like I had been zapped by a lightning bolt, from Dev. A guy who was breathtakingly gorgeous but whom I didn't even know except for our short conversation. I was just being silly. How could this guy I met once become anything long-term and serious? I'd probably never speak to him again. He was at Stern, and I was at CAS, the College of Arts and Science; we probably didn't have any friends in common; and he was probably not even Sikh—his hair was cut. He just couldn't be the one. I tried to stifle the feeling of excitement in my chest with negative thoughts about him, and eventually, after great deliberation, I fell asleep.

Chapter 8

Oh, shit! My class started twenty minutes ago! I threw what was left of my lunch in the garbage and ran to class. I took notes on the professor's lecture about the mind and body. Was I simply my mind? How could that be? (And with my mind solidly trapped between the tragedy and Dev, I sure hoped I was not only that.) In modern Western philosophy, some have called the brain the source of our consciousness. Descartes said, "I think; therefore, I am." I disagreed. I told my professor earlier in the semester that Sikhism taught me that we are more than the mind, because we can trick our mind—we can observe our mind thinking; therefore, we are beyond the mind. We are the smallest iota of the all-encompassing consciousness that I like to think of as God, or Guru. Yet we don't recognize that we are that consciousness and nothing else, nothing different, nothing separate.

Professor James was not acquainted with Eastern philosophy and somehow couldn't wrap his head around it. I could not fathom how a professor at NYU with a PhD couldn't understand what I understood so well and lived my life by. He made the mistake, like countless others, of believing that we are all different and separate because we look different and are not attached physically to each other. Not true. The whole world and everyone in it we treat like the "other," but really, we are all one and the same. One big reflection of an infinite pile of shattered glass, yet all most people see is our tiny image in one broken piece, unable to ascertain the larger view.

Dead people too. The body of the one I was missing may have been gone, but his consciousness, or atma, or soul, had immersed into the cyclical universe, and his consciousness would keep recycling itself in different forms or bodies until it realized that it was in fact, the paramatma, the universal soul, infinite God. I knew that I was not Mira—that was just the name I gave to my vessel of a body. I knew my loved one was not separate from me; his spirit could be felt in my heart even now. Even at this moment, as I sat pretending to listen to the professor's ramblings, I knew that he didn't just, *poof*, vanish from the face of the earth. His energy, his life force, remained. I didn't know if he had taken another form yet or if he had relinquished into infinite paramatma. All I knew was my sadness was due to my not being able to see his form or interact with it; it was not because he no longer existed. He existed! My mind was screaming, *He exists! He still exists!* My screaming found no voice; it was lost in the vacuum of silence and numbness that enveloped my being. I suddenly jolted awake at the sound of the students standing to leave their seats. No damn professor of philosophy was going to be able to convince me that he was dead. Strangely, considering my troubled half-awake state in class, I left more confident and feeling slightly liberated from the pain and anger.

One more class before I had to face Dev. I didn't want to talk, and I didn't want to tell Dev everything that recently happened in my family. I was shut tight like a clam that could not be forced to open. *Oh, Dev, how will you understand? You won't, is my fear.* Dev was the only man I had ever confided in, other than family. Dev had given me something no one else ever had.

He made me fall in love.

How amazing it felt to be in love—a gush of urgency, emotion mounting to an endless peak of excitement. I usually could not contain the happiness Dev made me feel, and I burst into smiles even when I was alone just thinking of him. He was beautiful, like a god, simultaneously masculine and divine, and I blushed when I thought of it, he'd told me I was the most beautiful woman he'd ever seen. He talked about first noticing my eyes, large and dark, yet soft and sultry, framed by long lashes. He talked about my long, black, wavy hair that fell in silky folds to my waist, a deep contrast to my golden skin. I knew my hair was my prized possession. But we weren't drawn just by looks; there was chemistry between us. With him, I felt the way earthen clay mixed with water by the loving hand of its creator must feel, becoming a new, better shape.

Although we knew each other longer, Dev and I got together as boyfriend and girlfriend officially only two months before I went home for the funeral. It took me time to enter our relationship, but Dev was finally able to bypass my beetle-hard shell to my underbelly where my soft and vulnerable emotions lay. How did he find the small opening to my fortress? I didn't know, but now he was inside me, and nothing I could do would cleanse me of him.

Our love flowered the way the multiple folds of a rose slowly open day by day, nourished by the earth, rain, sun, and bees to ultimately reveal its seductive scent, its peak of beauty before its petals wither and the degeneration of its short-lived life ensues. Our every day and every moment were spent with one another, or at least thinking about each other. Even marriage crossed my mind. The only fear was that Dev was Hindu, and I was Sikh, and while Dev said he loved Sikh women—we had strong, feisty spirits, he said—I knew both our parents would never accept our relationship, especially now that Ritu was back home. I tried not to think about the consequences of our relationship and instead got further pulled in by its gravity.

My current dilemma, however, was to tell Dev what happened. I had ignored Dev and not given him my home number or address for months while I was at home after the funeral. But I could no longer keep secrets. Not opening our hearts fully to each other was like committing a sin in our relationship. Dev once said that to me. Dev was my friend, my love, my confidant—he was my world. I would tell him today what happened to my family. I would cry in front of him and let him console me. So, I had decided to tell him, but only if I could gather the courage. I gulped down my last sip of Snapple iced tea and went on my way to English lit.

We were reading the novel *The Plague*. It moved me, but its message seemed so devastating that it crushed me every time I thought about it. The novel was like my life—there was no hope, and there was no such thing as hope in the future. As I sat in class, my eyes filled with tears, and I could not wait to run from my seat when class ended.

I returned to my room where I lay watching the clock turn its hands toward my meeting with Dev. My old, happy spirit was dampened by the burdens I carried; my shoulders collapsed under their weight, and I hunched and curled into a tight ball. My thoughts again drifted to the funeral. All that my family had endured in the last few months… How could I possibly reiterate it to Dev? He couldn't possibly know what we were going through. The drama unfolded repeatedly in my mind. Rewound and fast-forwarded…

Chapter 9

The sun was setting rapidly that cold January evening, and most of the crimson leaves that were left over from autumn lay crisp on the corner with the broken twigs that the wintry winds had slashed from the trees that stood quietly on Ash Lane. The houses on that quiet street on Long Island were lit up, and the shadows of the families who lived inside them could be seen behind drawn sheer curtains. There was only a dim light remaining from the final ray of the sun in the living room. None of us got up to turn on the lights. What use were lights now when the shadow of death had permanently darkened our lives. The living room that was once spotless now lies dusty and untidy. Magazines and unopened mail were on the floor; flowers that once flourished withered in brown water in a crystal vase. Beds were left unmade; food had not been cooked in the kitchen in a week; the garbage slouched stinking in the corner.

What had happened, no one could say. How it happened, we knew, but how we could have let it happen, we did not know. Lost in a trance of disbelief that the shifting tides of life could bring such a sudden loss, we felt a burning hole sear through us all. Flashes of seas of people dressed in white, as is the Indian tradition, clouded my mind. Family, friends, neighbors, and community members from our Gurdwara filled the funeral home. Women wailed as they met my parents and walked past the coffin. My mother looked like a thin ghost. The Ragis' sang hymns of how the world is a temporary place, and our bodies are like wood that burns in the flames of cremation, and our hair is like straw that will also burn away. The only thing real about us, those Sikh musicians sang, is the soul and the deeds of our life etched within it. Those deeds and our devotion to God are what will protect us and bring us happiness in the next life. After the hymns were sung and the prayers done, people stood to meet us and express their condolences. Mom had fainted once earlier that morning from the sheer trauma of loss, but now she stood silent, and her tear-stained face and hollow eyes made her almost unrecognizable. My father was the stronger one, at least on the surface. He shook people's hands and thanked them for coming to grieve with them. I could barely speak when women hugged me, and men patted my head or shoulder and nodded in mutual understanding. Ritu tried to console Mom, who was beyond reach.

This was one of the few funeral homes on the island that also performed cremations. They told us to say our last goodbyes before they closed the coffin and took it to the cremator. I had to. I could not lose this chance for goodbye. I inched up closer to the coffin. It wasn't him. The life within him was gone, and with it, life had taken the glow from his skin, the warmth from his body, the beauty from his face. What remained was cold, swollen, just painted to look like him. The sheer touch of his hand by mine caused me to shudder; I brushed his forehead with my lips.

"You are young. You will move on from this," said Bindu-auntie, whose bosom emphatically rose up and down as she tried half-heartedly to console me, and two other aunties reiterated her sentiments. I looked away, wishing that people would stop coming, stop asking, and stop telling me how to feel.

They don't know how I carry the guilt of his death, how my mind races with a million scenarios of what could have been different, and how all I wish for is to go back in time.

Hindsight is twenty-twenty, they say. Should've, could've, and would've plagued my mind. I tried to untangle myself from that mental web, telling myself I was stronger than this and should stop running away; come face-to-face with it; look it in the eye like a grown-up would. Stop feeling sorry for myself. Stop being afraid of what might happen. Stop giving up and keep moving on.

But I despised hearing their phrases and false condolences in my own internal voice. "You have to move on." *No, I don't have to move on,* I told myself. I didn't have to dismiss what happened, forget why it happened, and pretend that nothing had changed. That was not what it meant to be an adult. *Damn these people in our community!* I'd like to have said it to their faces, but it was the funeral, and people said things because they didn't know what else to say, and of course, Mom would never approve of my snapping. I could only shout it in my mind, *I'm living life, not moving on* because *I'm a goddamn grown-up!*

Anger accumulated in my head, buzzing like a hive of bees whose nonstop chatter made me deaf to my surroundings. The growing pains I was experiencing were not the leg cramps that would rouse me from sleep in the middle of the night when I was younger. My pain now was *the* test, *the* rite of passage into the adult world that demanded sacrifice. A human sacrifice. This test was thirsty for blood and hunger for more than flesh—it consumed spirit. His body burned, but so too was my soul engulfed, by death, and its suffocating grasp became the markers of our tragedy. All the while I persevered, carrying my sorrows in the hollow of my chest like I wore a crest on the pocket of my blazer. Thin folds of pain, like the golden threads of the crest embroidered onto the dark woolen cloth of my jacket, were intricately interwoven with the delicate fibrous tissue of my heart. A badge of my survival, lifelong proof that I went through darkness and came out still breathing, still standing, still living. "Becoming grown-up is painful," Dadiji counseled me earlier the day of the funeral, "but time is a healer."

But time was passing, and I was not healing. Wounds don't heal with time; they are buried into the deep shelter of our being, and all the while, we pretend that we don't feel them. The disease and the cure are the same knowing the difference is our liberation. I hid my jumbled thoughts from the families who came to give their condolences and who stole peeks of my downtrodden face from the corners of their eyes. Rumors were going around that he was pushed, and it had not been an accident. We kept quiet about the circumstances involving his death, and although people were very curious to know the truth, they could not push us to talk this close to his death. There would be many questions to come and many rumors to hush, but for now, we let people believe what they wanted to. I hoped that they would disappear and that I could be hidden from their gaze.

My head remained down until the commotion of Mom's loud wails dragged me out of my soliloquy. Mom had thrown herself over his body to hold him once again. Dad gently took hold of her and shifted her off the body. Ritu stayed back. Death was not something she could look in the eye, so she pretended that she had not seen anything. It was the only way she knew how to deal with it. Dadiji had sunk into a chair, and for the first time, she looked extremely frail, old, and beaten by life. She could only say to those who came to call upon her that God should have taken her instead and not such a young boy of only twenty-one years, in his prime. She must've said it a hundred times, probably hoping that eventually, it might come true. Kinchan-chacha and Reeya-auntie looked very sad and were extremely worried about my mom's state of mind.

It was time to close the coffin as goodbyes had been said and the funeral procession needed to be completed with the cremation. The man who managed the funeral home, along with Dad, Kinchan-chacha, and a few other men close to the family, held the coffin on top of their shoulders and brought it outside to what looked like a steel chamber. They slipped the coffin into it. They asked if my father wanted to push the button. It wasn't like in India, where they built a funeral pyre with logs and sticks and carried it to a beach near the water and burned the dead body on top of the wood.

In New York, there was no such legal way of honoring the old tradition. The cremating was done by an electric burner, which did its job in a matter of seconds. My father slowly and reluctantly pushed the button. The loudest of moans and tears echoed long after the body was gone.

"Why do you burn and not bury the body?" Katy asked me after the funeral when she came to pay her respects to my family. I said that we believe that our soul becomes very attached to our body since it is the vessel that carries the soul, and over years of our life, the soul identifies with the body as itself. However, once the body dies and the soul becomes detached and suddenly sees its body dead, it lingers like a ghost. Therefore, the body is burned quickly so that the spirit may leave the site of its body in peace and continue its journey. If the body is buried and left to very slowly decay, the spirit continues to linger around it in unrest. Katy thought it was very interesting, but the thought of burning a loved one was still hard to fathom.

Our sorrow lingered for days after the funeral. "Whoever wants dinner can get it from the stove in the kitchen. There is rice and some chickpeas that your Dadiji left for us," said Mom, who remained still in her seat.

No one moved from our seats. We could not really hear her words; they sounded like echoes in the distance, and of course, we could not eat. Our stomachs were already overstuffed with agony. The tears hadn't stopped rolling from Mom's eyes. Dad's face was dark and sullen now; he too had shed many tears and wails, just privately in the bathroom. We stared into the beige carpet on the living room floor, still and unblinking. The turn of events had frozen the emotions inside us, making our minds and bodies numb. An overwhelming sense of loneliness and loss engulfed me; the world seemed like a prison. Those who escape the bounds of its walls are free only at the painful expense of those who are left behind. I sat staring out the window, watching the sun disappear behind thick, violet clouds, thinking, *could life be so hopeless? Could love be in vain?*

Dad's eyes were brimming with tears as he looked at Mom. "Kamal, it wasn't your fault. It's nobody's fault. It is what Waheguru had destined for us, and we cannot escape our destinies. We must have committed some terrible sins in our past lives that God is making us pay for them through our innocent children."

I ran to Mom, and I sat in her lap and hugged her chest to chest like a small baby needing to smell their mother's scent for comfort. All I could see when I closed my eyes in Mom's embrace was his face, cold and unfeeling, and his ashes floating in Roslyn Harbor. In our tradition, the ashes were not saved but set free in a river, the Ganges, if we were still in India, and the soul is then also free from all entanglements of life and is blessed and made pure by the holy waters. I supposed his ashes could have been sent to India, as some older people often request theirs be, but he belonged here with us and not back in India.

We were all crushed by the unexpected loss, but the most inconsolable was, of course, Mom. No one could feel the tremendous loss as she could. It felt like a part of her body had died, like she was no longer whole.

What Dad said caused her eventually to rise and leave the room. We were all going about our daily tasks like zombies, dragging our dead spirits along with us to work and back, but Mom had been days without sleep and proper meals. She was dehydrated because she refused to drink anything that would make her feel better. She wanted to feel the pain; after all, what was mourning if it didn't hurt? She felt guilty enjoying anything and it would be a long time before she felt that she deserved to be happy again, to live again, to enjoy things in life again, even the smallest of things like a cup of English tea.

Chapter 10

As I later heard the stories, Mom lay in her bed the night the letter about the organ donation arrived. Her thoughts drifted back to the day Jeet was born. Her eyes were closed, and she could see him, but he was in her belly, and she was being taken to the hospital by Dad, with a little Ritu holding her hand and Jazz, a toddler, wobbling behind them.

After nine months of carrying him and fourteen hours of intensely painful labor, no pain relief, he was born at midnight, weighing in at eight pounds and four ounces. The doctor announced that he was a strong baby boy. And he was. She fell in love with him at first sight and cried. Dad was overjoyed at the birth of another son and gave her a big kiss when he entered the delivery room after the nurse brought him inside with the good news. Then he took him into his arms and pronounced that he was the luckiest father on earth. Dadiji declared that her grandson was a prophet, a king, the likes of the Gurus, because he was born at midnight, such as the Gurus had been, and only very special and saintly souls are born at this hour. He was meant to do many things in his life; he was destined from birth.

The following day, Mom was released from the hospital, and as she carried him in her arms in the back seat of their new Fiat car, the sun shone bright and hot through the car windows. Her little baby boy was squinting, and perspiration leaked down the sides of his bald head and forehead to his cheeks. Mom softly wiped the sweat off his face with her fingers and cupped his head with her arm to cast shade above his face. She could feel the burning of the sun on her skin, but how wonderful it felt to hold her baby and protect him. How perfect that moment felt as she gazed into his rosy new face. All in life was perfect in that moment, all was happy, and she never wanted it to end.

The scene in the car looked as clear in Mom's mind as if it had only happened yesterday and brought a small, faint smile to her face. But years had passed, years raising and nurturing him, and now he had disappeared in a flash, just like that. Mom's tears were now racing down her cheeks, down her long neck, and into the crease of her bosom. Dad had come into the room.

His wife's crying made him feel helpless and frustrated. He could not do anything to bring him back, nor could he take away her pain. He carried a weight on his shoulders that she did not have to, and that was that his words had led to his son's death. If he only hadn't forced him to leave, had himself instead left in his anger, his son would be alive today.

"Excuse me, Mr. and Mrs. Singh," Dad heard the police say, once again, in his memory, "we would like to ask you a few questions about the death of your son." The policeman who had met them at the hospital after Jeet's fall had been young too, very tall and broad in his uniform. "We know this is a difficult time for you, but it is necessary and won't take too much of your time."

Dad nodded quietly and walked off with the officer.

"Now, this letter that you gave the police has been confirmed by the investigators to be a suicide letter by your son. However, we want to make sure that when your son left the house, he did not leave with anyone else."

"No, he left early in the morning, and no one saw him leave. I believe that he was alone," Dad had answered.

And you say he had no enemies? Was not involved with anyone in any conflict?" inquired the officer who was peering down into Dad's drawn face. "Could you please describe to me again how and under what circumstances did all of this happen? Were there any problems at home?"

After the police left the hospital, another troubling issue arose for our family. The doctors managed to revive Jeet. Well, not really him, but some of his organs. Whether or not to donate his organs, which were still functional and had not been damaged by the fall, was a question we had never anticipated. At the first mention of the idea, Mom shook her head and cried out that no such cutting would take place. However, as the head of the family, the final decision was up to Dad, and after hearing everyone else's opinion, he would decide whether to donate or not. Dad spent hours and hours debating in his mind.

As a devout Sikh, he believed that the soul was an essence of God, a small part of God, like a drop of water is a tiny part of the vast ocean. His religion taught him that when the soul leaves the body, the body no longer possesses that energy, that essence, and therefore is like the dust of the earth.

His son's body was to be cremated anyhow, so why couldn't he donate organs to another child in need? After all, the parents of that child would always be thankful, and his son would be giving someone else the chance to live. He knew his son would want that, in fact.

All this was right and true, but once the step was taken, he knew that it was irrevocable. Could he live with the decision? Dad's mind was spinning with different thoughts, his heart pounding loudly in his chest and his breath racing. He stood outside the hospital ward where his boy lay and watched people enter and disappear into the elevators, the doors shutting behind them, and then a new flock of people would materialize as the doors would reopen and exit into the corridor. As he watched people come and go, he thought more intensely about the ramifications of what he was about to do. Mom and Dad would have to understand that by donating their son's organs, it would not mean that a part of him would be alive in someone else or maybe in multiple people. Their son was not his body, was not his organs; what contained his "essence," his "aliveness," was not those things at all. What was him was now gone from their immediate lives. His soul would have to reenter the cycle of births and deaths as an incarnation of some other animal or maybe, if he was blessed, then as another human form, maybe in another time. This would have to be Dad's final conviction if he were to donate the organs.

After long hours of contemplation, Dad shared his decision to go ahead with the donation. Mom exploded into uncontrollable howls and tears. After the donor staff had administered a lengthy questionnaire to Dad and taken his blood for purposes he could not remember, the family was given some time to say goodbye. In the end, Dad had to forcefully untangle Mom's hands from their son's, as she was reluctant to leave her son there alone in the room. "He is not here, Kamal. He is with Waheguru. Now, let's go." With those words, he dragged a wailing mother out of the hospital room where the body of her once-living son lay.

No one talked about the donation until a letter came in the mail. Dad recognized the name and the seal on the letter and opened it while he ignored the remaining mail. The letter thanked our family for our most generous donation at such a difficult period in their lives. It informed us that donor matches had been found for his heart and eyes. Dad informed the family of this news, that Jeet's heart was given to a boy of sixteen who had suffered from heart problems since he was born and was now saved from heart failure. The other was a woman who had been involved in a terrible car accident that had damaged her eyes; now his eyes had given her the ability to see the world again.

Most of the family was happy, as happy as one could be under the circumstances, to hear the news. But Mom was not comforted by this news. Her son had been carved like a Thanksgiving turkey, leaving him with no dignity, and now Dad wanted them to celebrate.

She retired to her room for the rest of the evening and was lost in her own thoughts about her son's birth, when he was whole in every possible way. She had ignored the sound of Dad steps coming up the stairs, and as he entered their bedroom, she kept her eyes tightly shut as she feigned a deep sleep, desperate to be undisturbed. He lay down behind her and brought his arm over her waist, shielding her, if not to give comfort at least to receive it. She was repulsed by his touch; she was in agony and wanted only to be left alone to mourn her son's death in the deepest of grief. She took his arm off her waist and turned onto her stomach, burying her face so he could not see her expression. He knew that it was a very hard time for her, and she would need time before she could be his wife again and perhaps give him what he needed, some comfort and reassurance about their relationship.

Chapter 11

Dev was sitting on a bench at the northeast corner of Washington Square Park, waiting for me. As I drew close, he stood and gave me a long, hard hug. "I have been so desperate to see you. Why have you been avoiding me?" he began quickly. "Is it something I said or did? Do you think I'm moving too fast again? You don't love me anymore? What is it?"

I tried to calm his anxious face. "It's not that. Of course, I still love you. I love you always," I said, holding his face in my hands.

We sat down on the bench together, just looking at each other.

Finally, he said, "You make me nervous when you hide things from me, and I can't tell what's going on in your head. I don't want you to leave me again. I couldn't take it again." Dev seemed to spill his insides in a sudden flood of words. Unfortunately, my fear choked my skills of verbal expression.

I looked into the distance. Under the mist of lost thought, I noticed the bare trees swaying in the wind, the puddles covered with leaves, the black concrete glistening in the sun while people of all colors and dress bustled past. As I centered myself, Dev stroked my arm and reminded me of that night in the club, when he first spoke to me. He hadn't been interested in tickets to the party; he'd found out who I was after seeing me in the library. He'd sought me out at the Sikh Club party, for me. I was the shyest, most guarded person he had met, and my seemingly casual attitude in the face of his charms had unnerved him, so much so that he'd forgotten to give me his number that night. Yet the electrifying current he felt when we shook hands told him I was as into him as he was into me. I left him wanting more, and he wasn't about to give up on me. Not that night, and not now.

That got me.

"You're right," I finally said, "and I'm so sorry that I've kept this from you. It's just that I've been so upset about it myself, and I'm…I'm ashamed to tell you. What will you think of me and my family if you know what has happened…"

"What has happened, Mira? You're going through a difficult time with your brother's death, and that's very normal, but why have you pushed me away? It's not your fault that your brother died. Why are you blaming yourself, and why don't you let me console you? Please don't shut me out. You've been through a lot. Don't go through more without me."

His voice was laced with so much desperation that I cannot hold my immense sorrow in my small frame. "Well, what I'm about to tell you is going to make both of us unhappy for a long time, and I'm so scared that you might not want me anymore after you find out." My chest heaved with pain, and my nose ran.

"Here, take a tissue and please don't cry; you know I become helpless when you cry. I don't handle tears well. Please don't cry. It hurts me too much to see you like this, baby."

I slowly wiped my face.

"Please consider me worthy of your trust, Mira. I promise I will never judge you; you know that. I love you unconditionally."

Feeling a bit reassured, I simply nodded. "It's both my

brother and sister. I'll start with Ritu because I don't think I can handle talking about my brother right now. Well, remember I told you my sister got married almost a year before we met?"

"Uh-huh, yeah, is she OK?"

"She's not. Her marriage has broken up, and she's come home." Dev was silent, but his face spoke of sympathy. "And not only that, but things have become ugly between the families."

"That's terrible. I'm so sorry to hear that."

"And they mistreated her, and when my parents confronted his parents about it, they denied everything and said that it must have been something she did or said."

"That's just plain unjust. I'm glad that your parents stood up for your sister and got her out of there."

"Yeah, but it's my parents' fault in the first place—they forced this upon her. They thought that marrying within our own religion avoids long-term problems between families, but that's not true."

"I'm not sure what you mean, Mira."

"It doesn't matter, I'll explain another time about that, but our problem doesn't end there. You see, it's a great shame for my parents to have her home, and poor Ritu, even though she is so embarrassed to be sitting home after having such a grand wedding in the whole community. Whenever we have company at home, she hides in her room because she doesn't want anyone to know that she's back for good."

"But why? I don't understand. It didn't work out, so why should your sister and parents be embarrassed? They should tell everyone what happened, and they will then support your family."

"They wouldn't, Dev! I wish it were so simple, but it's not. Everything is—"

"Mira! Dev!" My words were cut off by cheerful shouting. It was Maggie, a girl in Dev's entrepreneur class. She was waving and coming over to us.

"I better go before she comes. Let's talk about this another time."

"No, I'll tell her to go away."

"No, no, forget it. I'm getting upset talking about this. I promise I'll tell you the whole story tomorrow. And it's getting dark already, and I should get back now and do some work. I swear I'll fail all my classes if I don't get working."

"Don't go, Mira. I can tell her we'll meet later for the project."

"I don't want her to see me crying like this—just understand me!"

"Oh, but I want to see you tomorrow for lunch where we won't be disturbed. You promise, and we'll talk for hours."

"Yeah, I'll see you then."

We briefly kissed, and I waved bye to Maggie who was only a yard away when I turned my back to them and walked down the path to my dorm.

Chapter 12

Mira left with words unspoken that Dev wanted desperately to hear.

"What's the matter, Dev? You look distracted," Maggie said.

"I am. Do you mind if we talk about our project later?"

"OK, sure, we can meet at the library and finish later this week?" suggested Maggie with a confused but hopeful look.

"Absolutely we will. Thanks for understanding. Bye."

Maggie left Dev still sitting on the bench. His mind was racing. He was frustrated by Mira's swift departure and continued questioning himself. What was the mystery around her brother's death that was haunting her? He knew she was sincere, but God only knew, women were complicated. Her mind was troubled, and she didn't trust him enough to share her problems with him. Maybe he was not worthy of her closeness. She was too good for him, and he prayed that she still loved him. He could not live with himself if he ever hurt her. He only knew that she breathed life into him, and without her, he could never be happy; he would rather die.

"She's reverted to being the same girl clammed up in her shell, the way she was when we met at the party. I don't know how to console her, especially if she won't let me," he muttered to himself. To bring her into a relationship with him and to get her to open up had been so difficult already, but he had enjoyed every moment of their closeness. Now, it felt like they had backtracked instead of moving forward.

• • •

The first time Dev had laid eyes on Mira was days before the Sikh Club party when he was studying at Bobst Library for a test. He was hardly interested in economics—in fact, it was making him sleepy—and Anjali, his girlfriend, soon to be his ex, was about to meet him in the lobby to go for dinner. There was a sudden noise like a thud of books had fallen to the ground from the bookshelf.

And there she was: tall, thin, with long, black, wavy hair that fell like silky folds down her waist, a deep contrast to her golden skin, which glowed. Her face was flushed pink with embarrassment, and she was very slowly and quietly picking up the books and restacking them. Her mouth twitched, and she batted at her hair getting caught in her long, dark lashes, still mortified from her clumsiness, and it was when she looked up that he felt an unfamiliar ease sweep over him. She was gazing at the clock on the back wall, totally oblivious to his fallen jaw, to his sitting in the corner at all. Her eyes, it was her eyes that his eyes were locked onto. It was as if he could see through her eyes; they were clear and innocent. She was like an open book, almost vulnerable. Her skin was flawless; her cheekbones shone with a glow and a natural hint of rose, and her lips were full and in perfect proportion.

He found himself just staring and feeling anxious about his reaction to this girl. Was this what they called love at first sight? He had dated many girls with hot bodies and pretty faces dolled up in makeup, but he never felt anything like this, especially never for a girl so simple looking. She wasn't even wearing any makeup or revealing clothing. In fact, she was wearing a loose

T-shirt that did nothing for her thin frame, and the only way he knew she had a shapely figure was from her fitted jeans.

Suddenly, she was done and picked her bag up to leave. He jumped up after her and then stopped in his tracks, realizing that Anjali would be waiting for him downstairs, and he didn't want to see her yet. Besides, who was this girl, anyway? Forget it—he wasn't about to follow her.

He sat back down, and thought, *What the hell!* Anjali and he were overdue to be over! She was another one of those girls he spent time with. But she was getting greedy, always talking about his money and how she wanted him to buy her this and that and take her to the hottest spots in the city. He was a generous guy and loved to spend lavishly on his women, and most women were with him for this reason, but it was getting too irritating and boring with Anjali. He would have to tell her tonight before dinner that it was over.

Dev stood up and found through the window down to the lobby the mystery woman, and a guy from the other end of the lobby was rushing to meet her. *Oh, shit! He might be the boyfriend.* No, wait, she seemed to be blowing him off. Her body language looked disinterested; she seemed to further herself as he tried to get closer. *Now what the hell is he doing?*

Dev grabbed his backpack and ran to the elevators. When he stepped out of the elevator into the lobby, he saw the guy had dropped something, what looked like it may have been an earring since he kept touching his ear and indicating he wanted her to help him find it—the little prick. Dev was feeling flustered about how she was getting under his skin. He needed to find out who she was, and he wondered where she was from. Hmm. She could have easily been Middle Eastern or even Indian. It was hard to tell by just her face; if he knew her name, that would be a hint. Not that he wasn't interested in non-Indian women, but he preferred Desi. She was a student here, though, so maybe he could ask his friend, the library clerk, about her; he must've checked her in when she came in.

By the time Dev walked across the vast lobby, he saw that she had left the prick hanging, fixing his earring in his own ear—what had he wanted her to do, help him put it on?! Dev passed him and knocked his arm purposely.

"Hey, man, watch where you're going."

The guy was Indian, so she might have been Indian or Pakistani. Indian skater boys like him usually chased Desi girls; they never went after white girls they knew they couldn't get. A smile came to Dev's face. At least his mother would approve. What the hell? Where was this coming from? He didn't even know the girl, and never had he cared about his mother's approval of his girlfriends. The thought was unsettling.

Carl, at the library desk, had been watching the little conversation about the earring, so he knew well which girl Dev was after. "Oh, yeah, she's a pretty one. I see her come in all the time; you can't not notice her," said Carl.

"Listen, buddy, do you know her name?"

"Oh yeah, the first time she checked something out, I noticed, and I never forgot it, but how you gonna help me, my bud?"

"Carl, don't forget, I've put you on the guest list of every happening club in New York City. I think you owe me this time."

"Sure, you're my bro, her name issss...Mira Singh."

"Mira. Mira. Thanks, Carl! Catch you later!"

Her name sounded...oh so sexy. Yes, she looked like a Mira with those sultry eyes. Singh... So, she was probably Sikh. He liked Sikh girls, and he had dated a couple of them in the past.

He knew what he had to do next: find out when the Sikh Club met.

Anjali met him outside the library, babbling about the new gossip she had heard from her friends. He pretended to listen; his mind focused on getting Mira. The same evening, at his favorite Italian restaurant, Anjali made her scene over dinner, as he had expected, but he had bought her a little gold charm bracelet as a goodbye present, which she of course took on her way out. He didn't bother running after her; he continued eating his meal, his thoughts preoccupied with the new girl. He planned to make a few phone calls to his turbaned buddies and find out if they knew of Miss Mira Singh and if he could catch her at a club meeting, granted she belonged to the club. Narinder Singh was Dev's good friend, and he knew he could count on him to keep the information he was seeking quiet and private.

Dev always did a little research on the girls he went out with. He needed to make sure anyone he dated was safe. Considering his family's businesses all around the world in steel, textiles, and now the growing computer software industry, he needed to make sure that the Bala name would not be tainted with any rendezvous of his. From what Narinder knew, Miss Mira Singh was completely safe and innocent, as her eyes had shown him. She came from Long Island, and there was a big Punjabi community there. She did not have a boyfriend, although many of the Sikh guys had been interested in her. She was conservative and didn't even have too many girlfriends, but just a few close friends, mostly hanging out with her roommate, Katy. She didn't drink alcohol or smoke. She was clean in terms of her past; in other words, she had no past, as far as Narinder knew. Hmm… so, she was basically unlike all the other girls he had been out with, who came with a record of how many previous boyfriends they had had and lots of irritating, chatty friends who always stuck by them. This was one girl who didn't know him, and this would give him a chance to impress her not with his flashy car, the new M3 parked in an underground lot in the city, or with expensive gifts but with his true self. Narinder had warned him that he knew she didn't like people who showed off and bragged about their money. She was simple, and for some reason, simple looked good to Dev right now.

And, yes, Narinder said, she was secretary of the Sikh Club, so Dev decided to approach her at the next meeting. Unfortunately, the gathering was over before Dev could reach it after squash practice with his buddy, Nick. Damn, she was crossing the street below them by the time he got into the meeting room in the student center.

"Narinder, I told you to stall her!" Dev grumbled from where he stood by the window.

"She was in a rush, and I couldn't stop her anymore. But listen, I have the best plan," Narinder excitedly exclaimed. "Chat her up at the Sikh Club party this Friday. She's selling tickets, but you could just buy them at the door too."

"Yeah, how am I just going to walk up to Rubin Hall and ask her for tickets? Forget it, I will have to wait till Friday. Shit! I hate waiting, especially to see her again."

Club parties were lame at NYU. They were held to raise money for the club. A cheesy DJ and no alcohol and no food was the scene. Still, for some inexplicable reason, many students showed up. It took him all of two seconds to spot her in the Violet Café that Friday. She looked hot! Unlike the day in the library, she was wearing a fitted, sleeveless top with tight jeans. Her hair was half up and half down, with a few strands straying at the side of her face. And she was wearing makeup—smokey eyes with a hint of lip gloss. She looked breathtaking, and suddenly their eyes met. He could feel his heart racing, but she turned and looked away. He wasn't going to back down now. He was here for her, and he was going to make his move.

Chapter 13

The concrete path leading up toward Rubin Hall glistened with the sedimentary rock embedded within it. I didn't have the stomach to turn my head to see Dev and Maggie chatting in the park. I continued walking slowly past the Washington Muse; Dev and I had spent romantic moments walking along the narrow-cobbled alley that was home to scores of budding roses outside the professors' small brownstone offices. The intoxicating fragrance lured in those who might otherwise pass by the barely visible path, and I closed my eyes briefly to absorb its passionate calling. I continued walking steadily, only stopping at the traffic signal, and longingly gazed into the Rose Café across the street on Fifth Avenue, where Dev and I had sat and drank coffee, talking for hours about our dreams of the future. My heart sank, fearful of Dev's reaction to my family's situation. I didn't know who I was anymore; how could Dev possibly understand me when I had lost myself? I thought about how welcoming this same sidewalk was only months ago, before Manny entered Ritu's life, before my brother disappeared, and before I met Dev. I was open to the world, open to the city, and my future at NYU seemed bright. Those days of exploration, of the city and of ourselves.

The campus of New York University is spread within the artificial magnificence of New York City, and the more we experienced the city, the more we became a part of it—and it indefinitely became a part of us. Along with my new college friends, I absorbed the fast pace, the assertive walk, and the curt talk that made people living and working in New York real New Yorkers. I embraced a refreshing and new sense of freedom and confidence in my first year at NYU. I learned that there was a vast world and endless opportunities that lay ahead of me, making my previous life on Ash Lane seem small and confined.

• • •

The day that Mom and Dad dropped me off at my dorm was the most emotional. After I was signed into the dorm and we had carried my luggage into my room, Mom cried, and Dad expressed his uneasiness leaving me alone in a dorm full of young men and women. It looked as if my other two roommates had already been in the room and chosen their beds and desks, so I took the remaining seat. We were just about to sit down and wait for one of my roommates to return when a young woman appeared at the door and was startled, seeing us.

"Oh, hi, I'm Julie."

"I'm Mira, and these are my parents," I replied with a smile.

"Nice meeting you." Julie shook all our hands. "Have you met Maria, our other roommate, yet?"

"No, I haven't. We just got here."

"Oh, she's really nice, don't worry."

"So, where are you from, Julie?" Dad asked.

"I'm from Corning in upstate New York, and Maria is all the way from Colorado."

The light conversation continued for the next ten minutes, mostly Julie chatting away and us listening. Dad gave me a warning in Punjabi before they left that Julie was very clever and I should be careful.

I spent most of the afternoon unpacking, setting up my computer, and chatting with Julie and Maria. Julie was a petite redhead and "very Italian," as she described herself, and Maria was a chubby American with West Indian heritage. They seemed to have connected well already—both had arrived a week early, which we were allowed to do, for socializing, but Mom and Dad had made me wait for classes to start—and they talked privately a lot. Both were searching for part-time jobs. NYU was an expensive university, and most students could not afford to attend without scholarship and financial aid. Mom and Dad had assured me that my education was the most important thing, and they didn't want me working, as it might distract me from my main goal, which was to become a successful lawyer.

As the days passed, I realized that Julie and Maria were resentful of the fact that I didn't have to work to support myself, that my clothes and shoes were nicer than theirs, and that I had my own computer instead of having to depend on the ones in the library and student center to do my work. I began to feel left out of their conversations at dinner, and they never asked me to come out with them to explore bars and clubs in the city. I made a few friends in class, but they were commuters and went home after class. My first week at NYU, independent and free, didn't seem as exciting as I had anticipated it to be.

On Friday, my dorm floor had an open-door day where everyone on the floor would leave their room doors open and anybody from the floor could come in and meet each other. It was a social exercise in the first week of freshman year to help students make friends with the people living around them. Not many people stopped by our room, but Julie and Maria were room-hopping together, of course not inviting me to come with them. Feeling a bit frustrated, I decided to take the first courageous step to making friends and went to meet some on my own. I ignored the room on my left, which had three boy occupants, and instead I knocked on the doorframe of the room on my right, which was occupied by two girls, according to their names, outside the door. Only one girl was sitting in the room, reading a magazine and listening to pop music.

"Hi, I'm Mira from next door."

"Hi, I'm Katy. Come on in. I haven't seen you around before."

"Yeah, my parents wanted me to be home for induction week since there were no classes at that time, so I just moved in this week," I admitted, embarrassed.

"That's so funny because my parents had the same problem. They didn't want me to come here until classes started, so I just told them that classes started last week."

We both laughed, and she invited me to sit down next to her on her bed. I discovered that Katy was an American-born Iranian who had shortened her long Arabic name, and her family also lived on Long Island. She was the only and eldest sister of two brothers, and her parents worked together in business. Perhaps it was our Eastern heritage that made Katy's life and mine very similar. We both felt restricted by our parents' strict rules, and we both felt that life was so unfair to us while being fair to white American girls. I told Katy about how difficult it was to convince my parents to let me go away to study and how I was only allowed to attend NYU and not Cornell University in upstate New York because my brother attended Columbia University, also in the city, and we could both take the train home together every weekend. Katy laughed and shared her story of rebellion, which finally led to her living alone in the city.

Two hours passed before Katy's roommate, Michelle, came in. Michelle was a very petite Chinese American girl with glasses.

She just smiled at me and said, "So, how do you like NYU?"

"Oh, it's really big, but I think I'm starting to get to know my way around," I replied.

"Yeah, it's such a fuckin' drag. Wait till exams start."

Michelle's use of profane language, which continued as we chatted, caught me by surprise since I was not accustomed to using it myself and didn't feel that comfortable listening to it either. When Michelle left the room, Katy turned to me and said, "Ignore her. She thinks she's so cool because she curses in every sentence, and it's getting annoying."

"Good," I said, "I thought I was the only one who felt a bit awkward listening to her."

"Thank God it's just the two of us here. I couldn't handle a third roommate like her."

"Well, lucky you. My roommates seem to gang up on me and leave me out purposely. I barely know them. I don't know why they don't like me."

"Don't worry about them. I'm sure we'll meet more nice people. Say, do you want to have dinner tonight in the dining hall together?"

I was so happy that I didn't have to eat dinner alone in the massive dining hall full of my peers.

Katy and I had instantly clicked, and we both knew in our hearts at that first meeting that we would become best friends, but afraid to scare off our newfound friend, we didn't admit this to each other until months later when we decided to room together.

Over the next couple of weeks, Katy and I met some more friends in the dining hall, Rob, his roommates Chris and "Frenchy" (Matthew from France), and their friend Erica. Then there was Patrick from Ireland and Kathryn from Michigan and

Shirley from Japan and her friend Gene from California. Rob was a white Protestant from Boston, and his pudgy exterior and bubbly personality made him Katy's and my favorite. Erica was eclectic, and Kathryn was just plain old silly. Patrick was so cute and great to talk to, while Gene was very mature, and we had serious discussions about religion and life together. Shirley was always busy studying and usually left the dining hall early. Frenchy spent most of his time trying to impress us with his French accent or flirting with the girls walking past, and Chris was always occupied learning tips from Frenchy about getting girls. Most of dinner was spent chatting and laughing in the dining hall rather than eating. It became my favorite time of the day, when all of us friends sat at an extended table of ten. We became known as the "6:30 dinner family." We were loud, we played jokes on each other, we laughed with food in our mouths, and we left the dining hall happy every night. On most nights after dinner, Katy and I would go up to Rob's room, which was on the seventh floor, one floor below ours, watch television, and listen to soundtracks of Broadway shows, something Rob was very much into.

Having dinner so early in the evening left Katy and me peckish by nine o'clock, so after doing our homework, Katy would call me to go to late-night dinner at Weinstein Hall, where we would indulge in turkey burgers with extra cheese and curly fries for a little extra money off our dining cards. After late-night dinner, we would walk back to Rob's room and sit outside the hall with Erica and Rob and chat with them for hours about pure nonsense. We played silly elevator games where Rob would throw his sock into the elevator just as it was closing when Katy and I would be going back to our rooms, and then we would come up again and throw it back in front of his door and run back to the elevators. The elevator game would go on until three in the morning sometimes or until we were exhausted from laughter. The next morning, Katy and I would wake up to an email from Rob with a drawing of a sock in it, but we would refuse to acknowledge his victory.

In retrospect, where our unlimited energy—that allowed us to go to sleep at three in the morning and wake up early to attend 8:30 a.m. lectures and hang out all day with friends and maintain good grades—came from was beyond my understanding. But as every month of college progressed, we felt our childishness and our energy slowly diminish. Our energy was replaced by a more serious outlook on life, fears of entering the workplace, and the search for a life partner. But for the time being, making new friends and exploring the wild and famous city around us was our only concern.

Living independently in a city like New York was new not just for me and Katy but for most of our friends, and partaking in city events and visiting famous sights were at the top of our to-do list. In October of our first semester, we all dressed up for the annual NYC Halloween Parade in the Village. Communities and organizations as well as groups of individuals marched from Greenwich Village to the Tenth Street New York Public Library, where they dropped the spider from the tall clock tower. The library itself seemed to be haunted with its eighteenth-century winding steps that led students into an underground cellar where they kept the reference books. Katy dressed up as the devil and I as a black cat and Rob as a clown and Erica as an angel, and the rest of them didn't show up or didn't share our spirit to come in costume. The parade lasted a few hours, and we watched the dropping of the spider as we shivered in a huddle on the sidewalk. The Halloween parade opened my eyes to the diversity of

New York City that I had never encountered before in my small Long Island community.

Halloween wasn't the only time where we saw drag queens and homosexual men and women. The annual Gay Parade in the Village the following spring was a pageant of bright colors, open expression of sexuality, and loud music. It was a different world that we had never been exposed to. Katy and I secretly felt that Rob may have been gay, but our hunch never let our friendship with him waver. In fact, it opened our minds to the understanding that although Rob may have been gay (he came close but never openly revealed this to us), he was a good person and a trustworthy friend. The more we attended city parades, including the Annual Sikh Day Parade, the India Day Parade, the Saint Patrick's Day Parade, and the Thanksgiving Day Parade, the more we realized that New York City was a colorful mosaic of people from different cultures, religions, and sexual preferences. And the more we knew, the more we liked being a part of that diversity.

Parades weren't daily events, so the rest of our leisure time was consumed by hanging out in local pizzerias and shopping in small boutiques in the village. Katy and I were introduced to New York City nightlife by Gene and Shirley, who took us to our first nightclub, called Systems, only a few blocks away from our dorm. Eventually, it became Katy's and my Thursday night scene, but the first night I was in for many surprises. It was Shirley's birthday, and after a group dinner at Lemongrass Café where we had Thai food, I was forcefully taken by the rest of the gang to the nightclub. From a distance, I could see a queue of young university students dressed up in the latest fashions waiting to be approved and let in by drag queens who were dressed flamboyantly and guarding the door.

It was time for our test by the queens. Were we cool and hip enough to be approved and accepted into the club, or would we also be turned down by the mere whim of one queen? The queen studied us from head to toe and asked us for our IDs. We didn't breathe a sigh of relief until we all were stamped on the hand, if we were at least twenty-one or if we'd paid the fifteen-dollar entrance fee if we were not. Most of our fellow underage friends managed to have others in the club buy their drinks for them, but Katy and I refused to drink.

The club was a vast and dark room with deep red lights flashing from the ceiling and music so loud it made my heart throb. The air was filled with smoke, and shoulders bumped into each other as people tried to move around. The large room was divided into sections by long cream drapes that swung from the ceiling down to the floor and up again. Within these sections were soft, velvet couches where couples sat and shared much more than conversation and drink. I recognized some faces from around campus, but many were older. We quickly learned that it was assumed that if you were there, you were looking for a fling. With that in mind, random men boldly approached me and Katy for a dance, a drink, or a chat. We declined and tried to stick closely to our gang of friends. To my shock and horror, Gene struck up a cigarette, and Shirley was drinking. They tried to calm me down by explaining that it was only in a clubbing environment that they did these things and not on a regular basis.

Katy sensed from my hunched body language that I was uncomfortable with the whole environment and the people; I was, after all, the "holy" one in the group, as they all joked. I had seen enough and wanted to leave when Katy pulled me onto the dance floor, promising that it would loosen me up. At first, the flashing lights and loud bass of the music made my head spin, but as soon as they played more familiar songs, Katy and I began to sing along and dance more freely. We let our bodies take the lead. Slowly, the rest of the gang joined us on the dance floor, and we all swung and moved to the music. By the end of the night, there was not one hesitant or restricted bone in my body. I felt free and happy. Music and dance had unleashed the suppressed girl.

After that night, dark spaces, drag queens, and unfamiliar faces no longer frightened me. They were a part of the ambiance of the night that Katy and I grew to love and enjoy through our early months at NYU. Although Katy and I delved into what our parents would consider inappropriate if they ever found out, we had set our own guidelines of what was right and wrong. We concluded that as long as we refrained from drinking, smoking, and any other substance abuse and only enjoyed dancing, our actions were innocent, and God would not punish us.

Oh, and the nights wouldn't end there for me and Katy. After clubbing, we would walk back in our high heels laughing about the men who tried to woo us on the dance floor and consume a chocolate brownie and a large can of cold iced tea in Katy's room to quell our long-deprived thirst for girl gossip.

Clubbing was not the only night of entertainment that we learned to love. Rob's influence got Katy and me into Broadway shows and musical theater. Rob happily arranged our tickets to see *The Scarlet Pimpernel*, as he thought this would be a good show to start with since it contained a bit of drama, humor, song, and mystery. After dinner, we all dressed up and took a taxi uptown to Times Square, the home of bright lights and Broadway shows. We filed into the theater and eagerly took our seats. Our tickets were discounted, so we were nowhere near the live orchestra, but we could still see the actors and the props well from the balcony mezzanine. Our eyes remained fixed on the stage as the show progressed and lit up with excitement when the cast burst into song and dance. It was nothing like we had experienced before: the elaborate stage and props that almost instantaneously changed from one scene to the next, the beautiful clothing of the actors, their steps perfectly aligned in the dances, the divine sounds of the orchestra, and the amazing voices that accompanied them. A show is a captivating work of art that is not merely gazed upon like a painting but experienced by all the senses of the viewer. After our first show, Katy and I, and later Dev and I, went on to watch many more, including *Les Misérables*, *Jekyll and Hyde*, *Phantom of the Opera*, *Miss Saigon*, *Beauty and the Beast*, and the *Radio City Hall Christmas Spectacular*.

The *Christmas Spectacular* was a special treat for all of us because we saw it during the last week before we said goodbye for one month for the Christmas holidays. We all had mixed feelings of excitement and sadness since exams were over and Christmas was here, but we would be going home and not have each other's company. Rob, Katy, Gene, Erica, and I decided to exchange Christmas gifts and explore the most popular Christmas sights in NYC before we had to go home: Fifth Avenue and Rockefeller Center. Wrapped up and well snuggled in our warm coats, hats, gloves, and scarves the evening before our last night at NYU, the gang walked down Fifth Avenue, admiring the lavish, imaginative windows of the designer stores. Light snowflakes slowly emerged like feathers dropping from the sky, and we lifted our faces to see if they would settle onto our eyelashes without melting. We basked in the delight of the soft snow and how it rested on the branches of bare trees lining the streets. Rockefeller Center glowed with the faces of happy children and their shrieks of excitement. The white angels stood on pedestals and the largest Christmas tree we had ever seen lit up the sky with colorful lights. It felt like we had suddenly entered a magical land that night, and we took photographs to keep it alive in our memories.

NYU wasn't just about freedom and having a good time; it brought about a dramatic shift in everything I had ever believed in. It was a challenge, a new way of looking at life, a new realization that life could be whatever I wanted it to be. It was the experience that widened the frame of the looking glass of life, and in it, I could see a broadened view of myself in the world. All these changes were internal and gradual, but my parents probably sensed it very early on because after Christmas break my parents almost forced me to leave NYU and move back home to a local college. No doubt Mom and Dad were afraid of what might happen to me in the big city, and Ritu's experience in college had left them more overprotective, but it was too late—I had already leaped into the air, and my wings had begun to flutter in the wind.

"Your dad and I have decided, Mira, that you should move back home now," Mom started the weekend before I was to go back to NYU.

"What? I can't commute. You know it's too far, and I'd never have enough time to attend classes, travel an hour and a half each way, and study," I blurted in surprise.

"We're not asking you to commute," Dad said. "We're saying that you should attend a local college on Long Island like your sister did and live at home."

I couldn't believe what I was hearing. I stuttered a bit before saying, "But why?"

"We miss you so much during the week, Mira, always looking forward to you coming home on Friday, and this way you'll be with us at home," Mom said with a smile.

"Yeah, I understand that, and I miss you too, but that's not a justifiable reason for making me stop my studies midway and making me transfer to a completely different university!"

"Just think, Mira: NYU is so expensive! All that money we could be saving, and Ritu had the good idea that you could buy yourself a nice new car to drive around to college and anywhere else you need to, just like she had when she was in college. It would be better," Dad said.

I gave Ritu, who'd slinked into the room, a dirty look. "You don't understand," I whined.

"This discussion ends here," Dad retorted.

The next day back at school, I hung up the phone with my parents. I gave all my friends the bad news that I may be leaving NYU. They couldn't believe that my mom and dad could force me into such a decision.

"You don't know what they're like. They didn't ask me if I wanted to leave here; they told me I should and why it's better for all of us if I did, and that's that." I started to cry.

Katy said, "Listen, you must show your parents that you're not a kid anymore, that they can't dictate where you study and build your future. This decision is yours, and you must let them know you're in charge of it."

Rob agreed, "You must explain to your parents that you worked so hard in high school to be accepted into this university. Not everybody can accomplish this much, and then to have to leave and go to some mediocre local college is such a waste of your intelligence."

My crying stopped, and I listened intently to their advice. I knew that I didn't have the strength to confront my parents and tell them how I really felt and not ask them but tell them what decision I had made. It was easy for Rob and Katy—they were a lot stronger and more outspoken than I.

That week I prayed well beyond the time they usually took, and Katy said that she wished that she could also pray as much. It was then that I confided to Katy that it was my faith in the Guru that made things easier for me to handle and cleared obstacles in my way. The Guru gave me strength, and I made my decision to stay at NYU, to my parents' surprise.

"We're so happy that you're going to be coming home for good," Mom said. "Everyone thinks it's a good idea, even Dadiji."

"I don't know why this news has reached Dadiji already, but I'm not moving back home, and I'm not leaving NYU." I paused for a moment as my mom and dad became silent on the phone line. "I've decided," I repeated firmly.

"Since when is this only your decision?" retorted Dad.

"Well, it's not just your decision either. See, Dad, I worked so hard in high school, took all the advanced placement and honors classes, and got top grades all so that I could go to a top university, not go to some local college like Ritu. I don't care about having a car. Which is more important, a car or my quality of education? And I know you miss me, but I can't stay with you forever. You're going to have to let go someday. I'm not going to sacrifice my studies and career for this. I know it's costing a lot, but I have half a scholarship, and I am getting some financial aid, and my other loans I'll pay off myself when I get a job after graduation." "We will talk more about this next time you come home," mom blurted on the speaker phone in the background.

My well-thought-out argument and the confidence and control with which I battled through the discussion was enough to quiet my parents. My ears couldn't believe it when the next weekend at home my Mom and Dad decided that I was right in many ways, and they would honor my decision to continue attending NYU. I ran down to the prayer room to thank God that he had helped me overcome this hurdle. This was a small hurdle in retrospect, but at the time, it was the building block of my existence as an independent and free-thinking person.

Chapter 14

1997

A couple of years after Kinchan-chacha's wedding, Reeya-auntie and her Indian kitty friends caught Ritu with Amir in a nearby diner holding hands and kissing. When my parents found out about this, all hell broke loose in the family. Ritu and Amir had been dating for two years when their relationship became public. I knew, from the side trip to the Hunter College library, but now so did everyone else that Ritu's attractive face and figure had caught the fancy of Amir, the bad boy with the leather jacket, black sports car with tinted windows, and nonchalant attitude. Their meeting in the diner was to discuss their plans to elope in Las Vegas and how they would break the news to their parents after.

"Wait till she comes home! I'll rip her hair out from her head! She thinks we're fools that we would never find out of her sinful deeds!" That was from my mom.

Dad growled, "Calm down, Kamal. I am her father, and I will fix her straight. OK, she's pulling into the driveway. Mira, Jeet, and Jazz, I want all of you kids to go into your rooms, and I don't want to hear a sound from you, understand?"

My parents were seething with anger, and they were going to pounce like tigers onto their unsuspecting prey. I stood at the top of the upstairs banister. I could see some of the scenes that would play out below, and I could listen in.

"Hi, Mom! Hi Dad! Sorry I'm late. Master's level is so much harder than I thought. I had some extra work to finish up in the library."

Ah, why did she have to give such a lame excuse?

"Achha? You were in the library? Because we heard that you were at a diner with your boyfriend!" blurted Mom.

Ritu's face turned red, then green, and then blue! She just stared at them with her mouth gaping as if a jellyfish had stung her leg, but she was unable to produce a scream from the pain.

"Get inside!" Mom shouted with a tight lip. Ritu walked into the formal living room, and Mom shut the door behind her. Although I could no longer see them, their voices were as loud as if we were in the same room.

"You've been lying to us. How dare you. How dare you even show us your face!"

"Kamal, chup!" Dad interjected. "Now, you tell us everything. Ritu, who is this boy, how long have you been seeing him behind our backs, and what are your relations with him?!"

I couldn't hear Ritu's voice. I assumed she wasn't speaking. Finally, she said, "His name is Amir."

"He sounds Muslim!"

I heard a smack and then Ritu's tears. Mom must have struck her.

"Yeah, now you cry, and how about us? We are crying at our fate that the Guru gave us such a rotten daughter who would betray her parents like this. We've given you everything you've ever asked for, more money for your Masters, a new car, we allow you to go to parties, buy all the clothes you like, and this is how you repay us for our trust and love, huh?" Mom was losing control, and she was shrieking from the top of her lungs.

"Kamal, sit down. Ritu, now you tell me, is he Muslim, this boy?" Dad asked in a firm tone.

Ritu, afraid of hearing the truth with her own ears, must have simply nodded because next, I heard Mom shriek, "You stupid girl! Don't you know you have to marry a Sikh boy?! If you marry him, he'll want you to convert to Islam and your children will be raised differently. How could you even let yourself get involved with any boy for that matter? That is how I raised you, ah? To chase boys and do indecent things?!"

Around her tears, Ritu tried to speak. "It's not true. Amir loves me and treats me so well and says I don't have to convert." Perhaps she should have stayed quiet.

"How dare you answer back!" Mom shouted.

"It's very common nowadays for girls to have boyfriends. It's not like I have committed any sin."

"Shut up, Ritu!" Mom had had enough of Ritu's explanations.

"Stop it, Kamal; you'll kill her!" shouted Dad. Mom must have been beating Ritu about the head. I ached to run to her and protect her.

"I want to kill her! You don't know, Harbans. She is a liar, a deceitful witch, and she will only bring shame to us. Because of you, Ritu, now the whole Sikh community knows about you and that Muslim boy. Reeya-auntie was on a kitty lunch, and they all saw you holding hands and kissing him. By now all their families know, and by tomorrow everyone for miles will know about your deeds! You have painted your and our faces black with shame. Which decent Sikh family will want you for their son now, huh? People will gossip about us; people will spit at us. Answer me, kal moiee, witch! You're no good anymore! You're tainted! You stupid girl, you've ruined your life, and you've ruined our lives and any chance of a good match for your brother and sister."

Tears rolled down my cheeks as I heard the yelling and screaming go on.

"Now, you are not allowed to leave this house, do you understand, Ritu?" Dad said. "And you can forget about finishing your master's degree and no more friends' phone calls. Everything for you is over. We were recently talking to a family about doing your rishta"—making a connection— "with a very good boy from Boston, and they will be coming to see you this weekend. You are to behave, and if we say yes, you will say yes, and you will be married next month, understand?"

Although Ritu had dared to love against our parents' knowledge, she somehow lacked the courage to face them and fight for her dreams. At the time, I understood that she had to give in because that was what good girls did, but later when the situation stared me in the face, I knew that I was stronger than her. Or perhaps more selfish and stubborn than she was or perhaps more American and the values of self-overpowered my sacrifice for the good of the whole. Or perhaps bigger than our ideals, the Guru had paved my way for me and left her stumbling over the rocks in our paths.

When Ritu came up the stairs into our room, she kept her face down and avoided noticing me. I didn't know how to express the sorrow I felt for her and thought it was maybe best to avoid the subject in case it may embarrass her more to talk about it with me. She was defeated in her battle, a fallen soldier captured by the enemy. Anything I could say to comfort her would only sprinkle salt on her wounds. So, I looked at her silently and just left the room so she could have some privacy to reflect on what had just happened and what might happen over the weekend. As I walked out the door, I heard Ritu break out into a long wail. What was going through her mind at that moment I could never imagine, till it was my turn to be in her position.

• • •

After a week of Ritu dragging about the house, being ignored by Mom and Dad at every turn, the dreaded day came when the Ahuja family from Boston arrived with their son Maninder, who everyone called Manny. It was obvious they were a flashy family flaunting their wealth. There were only three people, and they had driven from Boston in two cars, one a Porsche that Manny drove, and his parents pulled up in a shiny new Mercedes. Manny was dressed from head to toe in designer wear, and his mother's diamonds sparkled from a distance. Mom and Dad had prepared a nice afternoon tea with fresh cake and pastries from the bakery and some Indian savories. Mom had made sure to call the cleaner early that morning so that our house would be sparkling clean before the Ahujas arrived. All our clothes were even picked out by Mom, and Jazz was sent to a friend's house; they didn't want him around at a delicate time like this. Ritu was forced to wear a salwar kameez, and her makeup was minimal.

The previous night, I eavesdropped on Mom and Dad lecturing Ritu on how she was being given a second chance by the Guru to live a decent and happy life and that it was her duty to obey her parents who always had her good in mind. Ritu seemed to bend in obligation.

When the Ahuja family entered, they took a brief look at our small house and turned their noses slightly at the tea set up on the coffee table.

"Sat Sri Akal, welcome to our humble home." Dad encouraged them to have a seat on the couch. "This is my wife, Kamal"—Mom greeted them by pressing her palms together—"and these are our lovely children."

"I thought you said you had four children," said Mr. Ahuja.

"Yes, our other son has gone to study in the library. He's very studious."

Jeet and I looked at each other and smiled.

"These are Mira and Jeet," Dad continued, "and, of course, Ritu."

We all smiled and greeted each other. Manny seemed to be quite pleased with Ritu's looks since he kept staring at her across the table. She, however, was not excited about the prospect of marrying anyone except Amir, so she kept looking away from him and kept her mouth shut.

Kamal began, "You've had a very long trip, Panjee—won't you have some tea?"

"Oh yes, thank you."

For the next hour, our parents spoke about the weather, the business they were in, and Ritu's and Manny's education and upbringing. They said they had a modern mindset, and Manny was given a lot of freedom, being their only child. Manny, his parents proclaimed, had done an MBA and was helping in the family auto parts business.

"Why don't we let the children go sit in the next room and talk on their own for a little while?" Mr. Ahuja suggested.

"Yes, that would be fine," said Dad, a bit hesitant. I guessed that he was afraid that, left alone, Ritu would run Manny off. But I saw the spark leave her eyes a while ago. She was resigned to her fate. It was a part of our upbringing that would not let her fight for her happiness, and she knew she was being called upon to sacrifice herself for the good of the family.

Manny happily walked into the family room with Ritu. After five minutes, Mom suggested that I join Ritu and Manny in the next room. I slowly walked in and found Ritu was sitting quietly on the sofa staring at the carpet while Manny sat on another chair staring at Ritu.

"Umm." I cleared my throat as I walked in. "Hi," I said.

"Hi, yeah, come on in," Manny replied to a bit unhappily.

"So, what are you guys talking about?"

"Oh, we haven't actually spoken yet." Manny laughed artificially. Manny was sitting with his feet up on our table and was reaching for the television remote. I didn't like the look of him. There was nothing soft about Manny's features, nor did his mannerisms or personality make up for his loss in looks. All he had going for him was that he was a full-bearded Sikh, and his father had a lot of money. Ritu was in a trance, so she didn't notice anything at all. My parents were relieved when the Ahujas left our house on a good note.

"I think they were a very nice family, with a lot of money, you know, Ritu—you will never be lacking anything," said Dad.

"Yes, you are so fond of stylish clothes and jewelry, you will fit right in with their family," assured Mom. "And Manny is such a nice Gur-Sikh boy and sounded intelligent."

I knew that Mom and Dad were praising the Ahujas in front of Ritu so that she would think positively about them. Privately, however, they too had their reservations. I could hear Mom and Dad whispering in their bedroom that night.

"What do you think, Kamal? They show off too much about their business and money—that's all they talked about. And their son, they say he's MBA, but he didn't seem so sharp-minded, you know, especially when we were talking about their business. But here's another thought. Why would they want to do their only son's match with our family? After all, they could be receiving rishtas from much richer girls' families. Don't you think that's strange?"

"Yeah, but these small things can be overlooked. Maybe

Manny did not like the girls from rich families. You know his father was saying that Manny really wants to marry a beautiful girl and has rejected decent girls from so many families already. Not just that, but they are worried that he's so picky. He is getting close to thirty years of age, and they don't want to delay the matter. They were snobby, but I think that your cousin had told them that Ritu was so pretty that they decided it was worth coming all the way to see her. They care more that Manny likes the girl, rather than the girl's family having the same economic status. Besides, I found out today from Dadiji that the news about Ritu and this Amir boy has spread throughout our community; she was even urging me not to attend Gurdwara on Sunday to avoid probing questions and embarrassment."

"Then we must do something and quickly before the news spreads to Boston and we even lose such a good family like the Ahujas. We should get Ritu married off next month. I'll call the Ahujas tomorrow and tell them that it's a yes from our side."

The next day, Dad announced to all of us that the Ahujas agreed with the rishta, and the wedding would be at the end of November, which was only weeks away. Jeet and I were shocked to hear the news. Ritu's face lost its color. She remained silent, not uttering a word the whole day, and then finally at night, she took me into confidence.

"Mira, I need you to do me a favor, and you have to promise that you will not let Mom and Dad find out."

"Don't worry—anything for you. What is it?"

"Please give this letter to the mailman tomorrow. Don't let anyone see you because I'm sending this letter to Amir. I had to explain everything to him." Tears running down her eyes, Ritu handed me the letter.

"I will. Don't worry. Your message to Amir will get through

to him, I promise."

For a few weeks after I mailed the letter, we experienced a lot of hang-ups. I think it was Amir calling trying to speak with Ritu, but upon hearing our voices he would hang up.

• • •

The wedding preparations were in full swing, and the house was in chaos. During the day, Mom, Ritu, and I would visit the Indian boutiques to purchase wedding outfits for the bride, ourselves, the groom's mother, and my aunts and grandmother. It was customary that gifts were given to all the family by the bride's parents. Every evening, Mom and Dad would drive around looking for an available party hall. Since they booked so last-minute, they didn't get the venue, the date, or the price of their choice. Jazz and Jeet were given the responsibilities of organizing limousines for the wedding day and finding a good Indian caterer. Mom and Dad were frantic about making a good impression and pleasing their new in-laws. They wanted to amaze the Ahujas by throwing a grand party and wedding. It was always in the back of their minds that if the Ahujas were satisfied with the wedding preparation and gifts, they would reciprocate by making sure that Ritu was well taken care of and happy in their family.

Time was running out; the wedding was only a week away. All the clothes and jewelry had been bought, and all the preparations had been made. Ritu sat quietly in our room as I came up the stairs. "What's the matter? Why are you so quiet?" I asked.

"What? Should I be jumping up and down with happiness?" she snapped at me.

"Well, you know, you did agree. The least you could do is act happy and show your appreciation to Mom and Dad for all the expensive things they've bought you for the wedding!"

"You don't get it. I am being forced to marry Manny. I'm not happy about this wedding. And it's not only that. I find Manny to be a bit strange."

"What do you mean, strange?"

"Well, he says weird stuff sometimes on the phone, like he really puts me down a lot but indirectly. And then he will lie to me about little things that don't even matter. And one day I was just so annoyed by him that I told him I wouldn't marry him, and he just went crazy!"

I sat there looking at Ritu in astonishment. "All these things happened in only one month of knowing him, and you haven't said anything about it to Mom and Dad?"

"No, I did, but Mom keeps telling me that I'm the girl, so I must adjust. No one is perfect, and I can't be so picky. And that men have lots of bad habits like drinking and smoking and that Manny doesn't do any of those things, so I should focus on his good points and not just the bad."

"This doesn't sound good to me."

"Well, then, hear this: When I told him I was going to break off the wedding, he was, like, crying like a baby and kept sending me roses and teddy bears in the mail to make it up to me. But he would never admit his fault. Like, he would never say, 'Yeah, I'm sorry. I shouldn't have spoken to you rudely or put you or your family down like about what cars they drive or their clothes.' No, just flowers and toys like we're kids in high school or something. He's very immature and a bit twisted, a complete narcissist."

"So don't marry him!" I shouted.

"Shh, keep your voice down."

"Ritu, if you know he's not the right guy for you and you don't get along and he has all these problems, then why are you putting up with it? Just don't marry him. It's not too late yet," I pleaded.

Ritu's voice was low now. "No, Mira, it is. All the invitations have been sent out, and Mom and Dad have already spent so much money they can't get back."

"But you're going to ruin your life."

Ritu was crying now. "Oh, stop. You're too young to understand these things. Sometimes in life you must give in. You can't always get what you want. Besides, my life is ruined now anyway. It's best for everyone if I marry him."

"I'm going to tell Mom that Manny put down our family and the cars we drive," I said as I was walking out of the room.

"No, Mira! Stop. You must promise me you'll never mention that bit to them. What good would it do? Just think. If Mom and Dad knew about this, they wouldn't stop the wedding; they would only be more worried about how to please Manny's family. It's better that they don't know, and I'll work it out with Manny later. But you must promise."

I reluctantly nodded.

"Go on now—help Mom set the table for dinner."

As I helped, I kept staring at Mom's face. What would she do if she knew about the problems between Ritu and Manny? Would she save Ritu from this wedding, or would she too be forced to accept circumstances as they are?

"What's the matter? Why are you looking at me like that?" asked Mom.

"Oh, nothing. How are the preparations going?"

"Really well. Dad and I have paid extra for a special balloon drop on the dance floor and special dessert tables for the party. I'm sure the Ahujas have not seen a party like this in Boston. And I have saved the best sarees for Manny's mom so that she can see how good our taste in clothing is."

I swallowed my words. I didn't think that Mom would

understand, she was too wrapped up in pleasing the Ahujas. Besides, her pride would be hurt if I told her what the Ahujas really thought of our family and our things. I held my tongue to prevent things from becoming more complicated for the family than they already were. Looking back, I wished I hadn't kept my mouth shut. Regret was a feeling that I would learn to live with.

• • •

The wedding came and went a lot faster than it took to prepare for it. Ritu wore a beautiful maroon silk salwar kameez that was covered with golden thread and beadwork and Mom's wedding jewelry. She looked stunning. The rest of us were also dressed in new outfits and looked our best to please the Ahujas. Mrs. Ahuja was wearing the latest baby-pink salwar kameez with silver organza material on it, and her short neck was decorated by ropes of diamonds. Manny looked decent for a change in his cream raw silk kurta with a pink turban. And Mr. Ahuja was dressed in a Hugo Boss suit as usual. After the baraat, the milni, the traditional shoe steal, the breakfast, the wedding, and all the photographs, the whole wedding party was escorted in limousines to the afterparty. To my parents' dismay, the Ahujas had seen the balloon drop and special dessert tables at many parties in Boston, but they tried to act pleased about it anyway.

For the first time, we were introduced to the rest of the Ahuja clan, his grandmother, grandfather, aunts, uncles, and cousins. Although some of them were not as rich as Manny's family, they all had one characteristic in common: they were all snobby. They acted as if Jazz and Jeet were outcasts, my parents were poor and pathetic, I was a simpleton, and Ritu could not really have been Manny's choice. My parents tried to ignore their arrogant behavior, but I couldn't help but feel angered about how they commented negatively upon the party hall, the bride's jewelry and clothing, the DJ's music, the cake being too small... The list went on. Although gossip about Ritu and her boyfriend had ceased when people had received her wedding invitation, constant whispering could be heard in the background. When the party was over, I remembered thinking how much I hated our community and the Ahuja family, all for their idol gossip and hypocrisy.

When Ritu's Doli was leaving, Mom and Dad could not hold their tears back. They had not wanted to give away Ritu so soon, but circumstances had forced them to marry her off quickly. I held Ritu in my arms, crying with her. Then Jeet came to sweep her into his arms and take her to Manny's Porsche, where she would drive away with her new husband. Jazz kept a distance but waved goodbye as Manny pulled out of the driveway with Ritu. It would be a four-hour drive to Boston, and we awaited Ritu's call that she had arrived safely. Her call never came, and my parents became a bit suspicious, so Mom called her the next morning. She didn't stay on the phone with Ritu for too long, and she said to Dad, "she says she's fine, but she didn't sound happy. There was something wrong with her voice. I have this bad feeling, mother's intuition."

"Oh, it's nothing I'm sure," Dad assured us. "She's just missing you too."

Chapter 15

In the month after Ritu's wedding, things settled back to normal. Dad made plans to fly to India for business, and Mom was busy managing work here. Jeet was now in his second year of medical school at Columbia University, to our parents' great delight. Jeet had desperately wanted to go to Brown University for business, but Jeet always did what our parents wanted him to do. It was important for Jeet to be good and worthy in their eyes. Now, with Ritu out of the house, and since I had convinced them to let me continue dorming in the city, Mom and Dad asked Jeet to move back home and commute. Unfortunately, Jazz, who should have graduated by now, was still failing his classes at Nassau Community College and causing his usual unpleasantness at home. He had no ambition to do better or make anything of himself. Besides, he hated books and resented that he wasn't as academically successful as his brother and sisters.

It was for Dad's birthday at the beginning of January 1998 that Ritu came home to visit. She said that Manny couldn't come because he was so busy at work, and she apologized on his behalf. Ritu coming alone without even a phone call from Manny was insulting to my parents; a daughter never came home alone the first time after her wedding. My parents ignored this like they ignored everything else when it related to the Ahuja family, so we continued with our birthday celebration and went out for Chinese with Dadiji and Kinchan-chacha and Reeya-auntie.

The next morning, Mom prepared Ritu's favorite breakfast, aloo parantha with mango milkshake. We heartily ate the stuffed potato bread and listened with curiosity to Ritu's stories about Boston. In Ritu's opinion, Boston was a gray and dreary city, and she much preferred New York. Mom and Dad said that with time she would be so used to Boston that she would never miss New York.

Ritu went up to shower while I helped Mom clean up the kitchen. "Mira, will you finish up?" Mom asked, drying her hands. "I'm going to ask Ritu to call Manny and force him to join us for the weekend."

Mom never knocked on our bedroom door before entering. So, as usual, she barged into the room. Ritu was rubbing ointment on her body, and as Mom would tell us later, Mom gasped at the sight of her daughter. "Oh my God, Ritu!" Her face turned white as a sheet. Ritu tried to cover her bare arms with her hands. "What has happened to you?" Mom exclaimed.

"Oh, it's nothing. I went to have my arms waxed, and this lady, she was so stupid, she made my arms black and blue." She put on an artificial smile.

"I don't believe you, Ritu," Mom said, knitting her eyebrows together. "Who did this to you? Did Manny do this to you?"

With a small voice and tears brimming in her eyes, Ritu said, "It was Manny, but it only happened once because we were arguing, and he was holding me tightly."

"That's no excuse, Ritu! Oh, my Guru, why are you punishing us?" Mom wailed and covered her face with her hands. "Harbans!" she shrieked down the stairs. "Harbans, come upstairs!"

Dad went rushing up to our room, and I followed him. Upon seeing the bruises on his daughter's body, Dad snarled, "That rotten bastard. I will call him right now! What does he think? He is treating my daughter like this, huh?"

"Wait, Harbans, we should at least ask her first when this happened and why before we call them."

Ritu had slipped on her shirt by now and put her ointment on the dresser, and Mom held her in her arms, consoling her. "I don't know why," answered Ritu in a quiet voice. "Just, on the first night, he wasn't coming to bed, and it was very late. He was watching television and gossiping with his friends and cousins, and I just called him upstairs a few times to come and sleep, and he got angry with me. He said that if I thought I was going to boss him around in this marriage that I was wrong and that he would put me in my place. That first night after the wedding, he yelled a few times…and…" Ritu's crying resumed. "Since then, any little thing that happens at his work, even if it has nothing to do with me, he takes his anger and stress out on me, and just two days ago when I was insisting that he come for Dad's birthday, he squeezed my arms so tight that I was screaming in pain. His parents ignore me around the house; they don't include me in any activity or any family discussion. It's like they keep everything a secret from me. When they do talk to me, they don't talk nicely; they talk down to me as if I'm not good enough. I feel like the 'other' and not a part of them."

My parents' faces looked tense and unhappy. "We must speak to the Ahujas. Get their number from the telephone diary, Mira."

I had just come home the night before from the city specially to see Ritu, never dreaming of the situation unfolding before me. I went running to fetch Mom's personal contact book.

Dad spoke to Mrs. Ahuja because her husband and Manny had gone out. "Hello, Sat Sri Akal, Panjee Ahuja. This is Harbans calling. Yes, I'm fine, how are you? Yes, Ritu reached home fine. We are calling because Kamal and I are very upset and have discovered black-and-blue marks on Ritu's arms. She says that Manny has done this to her. Are you aware of this?" Dad was silent for a minute, listening to Manny's mother. "How can you say this?! This is ridiculous. We have called you as adults to deal with this issue, and you are telling me it is Ritu's fault!"

Mom was getting angry in the background. "Tell them they can keep their Manny to themselves."

Jeet came upstairs asking me with his hands and mouthing his words, "What is going on?"

I just shook my head.

"Shh." Dad signaled us to keep quiet. "OK, then, why don't you come down here with Ahuja-sahib and Manny and we can discuss this." Dad hung up the phone looking angry. "I can't believe this family. She's telling me that it must be Ritu's fault that Manny raised his hands against her or Ritu's making up stories."

"These are not stories," Mom pronounced. "Look at her body. When are they coming?"

"She said they will come today or tomorrow and sort this issue out."

"Hmm...we'll sort them out," snorted Mom. "I knew there was something too good about this rishta to be true, such a rich family with only one son, and they approached us. They must have known their son had this anger problem and that's why they agreed to marry him to Ritu so quickly."

I took Jeet to the side and filled him in.

"I can't believe this is happening. Is Ritu, OK?" asked Jeet.

"She's been crying the whole time," I replied.

"I was never so happy about this Manny guy, but I couldn't tell Mom and Dad."

"Me too. I didn't like him from that first day he came to our house," I agreed.

"But isn't it strange that he's so educated, and he can hurt a woman like this? I thought that education prevents barbaric behavior like this. I'll go speak to Ritu."

"I want to come with you," I begged.

"Ritu," Jeet said, "we're here for you; you know that. If you just want to talk and get things off your chest."

"Thanks," Ritu replied. "I wish all men were as sensitive as you. Don't worry, I'll be fine. Mira, can you get me some water?"

I went running down to the kitchen while Jeet and Ritu talked some more.

Mom and Dad decided that afternoon that they would only send Ritu back with the Ahujas if their reaction to the whole situation agreed with theirs. When Jazz came home, Dad gave him a briefing. Jazz never liked to involve himself with the rest of the family's problems, so he decided that he was going out with his friends that evening, to our parents' relief. So, we were surprised to see him going up to Ritu's room before he went out, and I tiptoed after him.

"Listen," I heard him tell her from her doorway, "I heard what this Manny guy did to you, so if you need anybody to teach him a lesson, I've got some friends who can turn his head around."

"That's really sweet," Ritu answered hesitatingly, "but I don't think that's necessary, thanks anyway."

"All right, it's up to you, but learn one thing from me, Ritu: don't let people push you around; otherwise, you'll become their slave. You better learn to stand up for yourself, like me."

Surprisingly, Jazz had given her some good advice that was worth considering. But Ritu's morale was weakened. Mom said it was her fate that the Guru had laid out for her, but it didn't answer her question of why the Guru chose such an unhappy fate for her and not for others who seemed less deserving of happiness. If God punishes those with ill intentions or who do bad deeds, then was she such a horrible person that she deserved so much misery? Why were decent people like herself made the victims of a cruel life? Endless thoughts about the Guru and her life encircled her mind. She could not think beyond a larger universal principle; limited to her single human condition, she continued to grieve her fate.

Later that evening, the Ahujas arrived at our house, which had no tea and fresh cakes waiting for them, only stern faces. They silently entered the house, only a quiet greeting escaped their mouths. Dad gestured for them to sit down and asked Jeet and me to sit with Ritu, who was still in her room. So, once again, we took up our places by the upstairs banister.

Dad started, "Now, Ahuja-sahib and Panjee, we have considered Manny as our own son, and we always wanted you to treat Ritu as if she were your own daughter." The pain he felt for his daughter could be heard in his cracking voice.

Mr. Ahuja started with a loud voice, "Your daughter has to improve her attitude, and only then can she be accepted by our family."

"Attitude!" Mom chirped. "I think it's your son who has the attitude problem that he beat up our daughter."

Mrs. Ahuja leaped into the conversation, "Kamal, watch how you speak about my son; it's your daughter who is making up lies trying to blame Manny."

At this remark, Mom could not hold her anger inside any longer, "Lies, achha! Let me show you Ritu's bruised arms, and then we'll see who is lying. Come upstairs."

Mrs. Ahuja followed Mom up the stairs into Ritu's room. Ritu was sitting on her bed with Jeet and me, panting slightly from our swift flight from the stairs, sitting beside her.

"Look, Panjee, look at her arms! You call these lies?"

Mrs. Ahuja seemed to be uninterested in Ritu's injury. "Ritu, listen, if you want to save your parents respect and honor in the community, then you will forget all of this and come home with us."

"How can we forget this?" Mom exploded with anger.

Ritu started to cry.

"What will people say, Ritu, if they find out you just got married and you're sitting in your parents' house?"

"Leave her alone! Come downstairs, Panjee; we don't need to discuss these things with Ritu."

There was more commotion downstairs between the men when Mrs. Ahuja and Mom reentered the living room. Manny was yelling at my dad that he had not done anything wrong and that they could keep their daughter. Mr. Ahuja threatened, "Your daughter is nothing without Manny; your face will be painted black by society if they know that your daughter is sitting at home. If you were smart, you would send her back with us now."

"How dare you threaten me rather than admitting that your son has done wrong and making him apologize," Dad exclaimed. "We are not such heartless parents that we will send our daughter into the mouth of fire just because of what people might say. We don't care what people say and what you say. I want you to get out of my house right now. Our daughter is not going back with you."

"You'll regret this. You will come begging at our doorstep to take Ritu back, you wait and see," proclaimed Mr. Ahuja as they all left the house.

Mom and Dad's decision to keep Ritu at home was unanimous, although they realized that Ritu's marriage breaking like this would be catastrophic if it was not eventually patched up. Mom tried to explain to Ritu that she was better off without them and that she should not let her mother-in-law's threats scare her. "Ritu-beti, we will handle everything for you from now on. You can even finish your last semester at college and get your master's degree." Ritu nodded to show that she was listening. "Let's see what happens; maybe Manny will realize his mistakes and come back and apologize. You'll be fine, OK? Give me a smile now." Ritu tried to smile with her tear-stained face. "Good girl. Now, wash your face and come downstairs."

"I just want to be alone for a little while. I'll be down in a bit."

Mom joined the rest of us in the family room where we were staring at the television. None of us were really watching anything; we just wanted some background noise to escape the uncomfortable silence. As Mom entered the room, our eyes were upon her to tell us some news of Ritu.

"This is going to be a very difficult time for Ritu and all of us," Mom said after filling us in.

"I want all of us to be very sensitive to Ritu's needs right now," Dad explained, "and Mira, I don't want you getting into arguments with her. Also, we are not going to tell anybody else in the family that Ritu is home now; just Dadiji will know. We want to wait and see if the Ahujas will come down to the earth from their cloud and accept their mistakes. Until then, Mom and I have decided that it's in Ritu's best interest that she stay with us at home."

Jeet and I were relieved by our parents' decision.

• • •

Over the following few weeks, we noticed the drastic changes that had taken place in Ritu in the month after her wedding. Her prior self-confidence and composure had dwindled. She had lost all her previous interests like shopping, going to the movies, and meeting her friends. She wasn't the same Ritu; she had changed from a self-assured and independent woman to someone who was timid and weak. A few times, when Kinchan-chacha and Reeya-auntie popped by, Ritu hid in her bedroom. Jeet and I tried to cheer her up with our jokes, and Mom and Dad tried to make her feel more secure by assuring her that they supported her regardless of what was to happen in the future.

Chapter 16

January 1998

It had been only a few weeks since Ritu was home from her initial breakup with Manny. My parents were suffused with depression that hovered like stink around the house, and Ritu's circumstances made us quiet and somber. But Jeet was still alive. And the only problem that seemed permanent was Jazz disrupting the household.

One evening he came home a little drunk, but no one had noticed because he had walked straight into his room without saying a word to any of us. He was looking for his secret cigarette lighter that he had thrown at the end of Jeet's drawer. Jazz was clever and knew that our parents checked his drawers in his absence for cigarettes and lighters, etc., so he often would throw his stuff into the back of Jeet's drawers where they would never suspect anything. As he rummaged through the back of Jeet's bottom drawer, he happened upon Jeet's planner.

Because he had just downed a few beers, Jazz was especially insensitive to Jeet's privacy, and he began flipping through the planner. In retrospect, perhaps Jeet had made a mistake by unlocking the secrets of his heart by keeping pictures and old notes in his planner, but it was too late—Jazz would expose him. Jazz began to laugh at his discovery of the photograph of Jeet and a thin guy with blond hair standing together smiling. He read the first few lines of a note that was written to Jeet from a guy named Jason Turner.

Jason Turner was a young man a year younger than Jeet who was also studying medicine at Columbia. He was not in the closet; he was totally open about his sexuality and proud of it. He dressed in khakis and a collared button-down shirt to class and was known to be one of the top students. How did he recognize Jeet as a homosexual, we wouldn't know, but maybe there was a vibe between them that couldn't be detected by the other students. What else would have prompted him to write Jeet such a note?

> *Dear Jeet,*
>
> *I've been noticing you for some time now. I know you've also noticed me. I can't help but think that the few interactions we've had could perhaps be more than friendship. I think you know what I mean. Don't get offended by this letter, but please let me know if you feel the same.*
>
> *Jay*

The note was written on the back of a scrap of paper ripped from a medical seminar dated November of last year. *What the fuck!* thought Jazz as he kept rummaging through Jeet's papers. Jeet had written a very private letter to Jason, also last November, but had obviously never given it to him. Jeet had been shocked and horrified by Jason's letter. He wasn't sure if it was the fact that Jason had identified him as one of his own that horrified him or the prospect of engaging in a homosexual relationship. He had no one to turn to, no one to tell. If he confided in Jason and replied to the letter, he risked anyone finding out. He couldn't summon enough courage to tell anyone else, as they may have betrayed his secret. Once he came near to telling a guidance counselor, but what if they told his parents? He had nowhere to turn, so he wrote it down on paper and hid it in the darkest corner of his room, thinking that one day he may be brave enough to give it to Jason. He never imagined that his own words may one day betray him.

Jazz flipped through more scribbled letters. Not all were undelivered love letters to Jason; some seemed to be diary entries just for Jeet, like those that confessed embarrassment Jeet had felt at the doctor's when matters of his sexuality came up. Jazz's eyes fell on a letter dated December 21, 1996.

> *Dear Jason,*
>
> *I often hate myself. Who am I if not some deranged and sick beast? Why have I been given this disease that has no cure? If my mom and dad ever knew that I was like you, they would think that I am an incomplete son, that I am lacking something. I wish I could change myself. To fall into their eyes would be to lose everything that matters to me in this world. If they cannot love me, I have nothing to live for... How have you dealt with this with so much confidence? I am in awe of you and admire your courage.*
>
> *Yours,*
> *Jeet.*

Jazz's eyes popped open, his mouth gaping; after a few breaths of shock and horror, he burst into laughter. Laughing and trembling like a drunkard, he walked into the living room holding Jeet's letters under his arm.

"Are you drunk, Jaspreet?" Dad asked angrily.

"Ahh, I may be a drunk, a disappointment to you, your no-good son, but he"—Jazz said, pointing to Jeet—"he's a fag!"

"What the hell are you talking about? You should be ashamed of yourself for talking about your brother like that."

"Well, once you read his letters to *Jason*, you'll be ashamed of *Jeet* for a change. I'm sick of being the outcast; now Jeet will be the disappointment." And he threw the letters at Dad's face.

As Dad read the letters, the secrets of Jeet's sexuality were revealed to him. Jeet's face had turned red, and his palms were sweaty from fear. Mom, Ritu, and I stood puzzled.

"Is this true, Jeet? Did you write this?" Dad's voice grew louder.

Jeet had no answer. He stood still with tears running down his cheeks like a hunted animal exposed in its hiding place by the predator.

"What has happened, Harbans? Why are you yelling at Jeet?"

"Kamal, your son is abnormal; he is a homosexual, a gay man."

Mom stared dumbfounded till Dad explained, "Like a hijra."

Mom gasped in horror.

Ritu and I immediately turned to look at Jeet. Our ears could not believe what we had heard.

"I can't believe it; he's never acted odd or queer before," Mom said.

"Ask him, what does he have to say for himself?" Dad was in a rage. He could not come to terms with the notion that his son, the only son with potential, was now in his eyes abnormal, a mutant.

"Is this true, Jeet?" Mom shouted. "Answer us."

"Yes, I'm sorry," Jeet replied quietly.

"Oh my God, if this was all there was left for me to hear, why didn't the Guru kill me first!" Mom wailed, her tears running like a faucet.

Jazz was still laughing and fell over in the corner of the room. Ritu and I stared at Jeet in shock; our minds had come to a halt as they could not absorb the news.

"I want you out of my house by tomorrow morning! Do you understand?"

"What are you saying, Harbans? Where will he go?" pleaded Mom.

"I don't care where he goes. He is a burden, a black mark on our family. If this secret gets out, how much respect and dignity will we have left in the community? Already we have Ritu on our hands. We will never be able to show our faces to people again. He cannot be my son; he's some sick animal. I want you out of this house in the morning, and that's it." Dad had pronounced his sentence on the criminal.

Mom looked heartbroken at Dad's decision but still could not forgive her womb for such debauchery. She had a look of anguish on her face and left the room.

"How about me?" Jazz was still lying in the corner of the room laughing. "I had to share a room with this homo!"

Jeet, feeling abandoned by his family, went running out of the house without a coat.

• • •

Later, I imagined some of my brother's final moments.

Jeet wiped away his tears and took the long way around the block so that he could not be seen from the house. He walked slowly down the path, purposely stepping on leaves and kicking small stones to the curb. His heart was broken, and every ounce of hope and dignity was shattered. He would do anything to change himself to please his parents, but this was one thing that was beyond his control and choice.

Since he had been a child, he had felt different from the other boys and girls. As he grew older and realized his preferences, he was baffled and upset with himself. He was ashamed of himself and who he was. He wished more than anything that he could change himself, make himself normal. He knew that this would be a secret he would have to keep hidden from his family. But how long could he keep all his emotions and feelings bundled up inside? When he met Jason, he decided to write letters with all his secrets in them; one day, he hoped he would have the courage to give them to Jason.

But now that his sexuality was exposed to his parents, he felt trapped by it. He could never go back to being accepted as their normal son, as the son who would make them proud. Anything he would do and achieve in the future, even becoming a doctor, would not remove his parents' disgust for him. What hurt him most was that his own father wanted him out of the house, out of their lives; he was being disowned. Tears began trickling down his cheek as the path swerved nearer to home. In this life, he was destined to be a hideous and grotesque beast, he thought; only the next life could bring hope.

• • •

Later that evening, no one spoke to Jeet. Jeet did not eat dinner and stayed in his room packing for the next morning. Jazz resigned to sleeping on the sofa in the living room because he said he felt uncomfortable. Mom continued to cry but did not say a word. Dad angrily went to his room after dinner. Ritu lay on the bed just gazing out the window, her thoughts somewhere far away.

There had never been a time in our lives where Jeet and I did not support each other, whether we were to blame or not. I could not let him go now without giving him a few words of encouragement. I knocked on Jeet's door and let myself in when he didn't answer. He was sitting on his bed with his back to the door.

"Jeet, it's me, Mir."

He did not reply but just sat still.

"Listen, Jeet, I know that you are very hurt and upset. I want you to know that it's OK. I still love you..." My words choked in my throat, and tears fell from my eyes.

He turned toward me with a sullen face. "Thanks, Mir. So, you're still my sis?"

I ran to hug him. "You're still my favorite brother." We smiled at each other, and he sat holding me in his arms. "Don't worry, Jeet. It'll be OK. Mom and Dad will soon cool down and forget about this, and they'll ask you to come home again. But where will you go? Do you have a friend at college that you could stay with? Honestly, I think Dad just said that out of shock; he doesn't mean it."

"It's not that, Mir. Things are a bit complicated for me. It's not just them; it's me."

"I don't know what you mean."

"That's OK. You don't have to know what I mean right now. Maybe one day you'll understand. I'll miss you, Mir, and I want you to forgive me."

"Forgive you?" I said, puzzled. "Jeet, I don't think you've done anything wrong. Cheer up. This is America. There are a lot of gay people here, and they are accepted by society, well, American society, but who cares about the Indians who don't accept you. Mom and Dad are just in shock; they will come around and accept it one day. They still love you… They just…"

He smiled at me and released me from his embrace. I took that as a sign to leave and rose from the bed and walked out. Those were the last words he ever said to me.

The next morning Jeet left the house before the sun rose. Mom discovered in his room a letter, which would be considered his suicide letter, that was addressed to all of us.

> *To my dearest family,*
>
> *I'm sorry that I have caused you so much pain. All I ever wanted to do was to make you happy and proud of me, Mom and Dad. I cannot bear the fact that I am unworthy and unclean in your eyes. Please believe that I am more ashamed of myself than you are of me. That is why I have decided that the only way I can save you from being disgraced in the future and save the little dignity left in me is to cut my incurable disease from its root. This root of homosexuality is inseparable from the tree of my life, so I am ending my life. Maybe in my next life I will be normal, and the Guru will give me the chance to be your son again. I am going to miss you all so much, especially you, Mir; thank you. I love you all more than life itself. I hope that one day you can accept me and love me again. Goodbye.*
>
> *Your devoted son and brother,*
> *Jeet.*

"Harbans, Harbans!" Mom shrieked from Jeet's room. There

was so much fear in her voice that we all rushed to see what had happened. We found Mom kneeling on the floor of Jeet's room crying and crushing his letter in her hands. "Read this, Harbans. Go find Jeet quickly. He must have gone to school. Where else would he go?"

Dad quickly read the letter and stood frozen until Mom shook his shoulder. "Go, Harbans. Find him."

Ritu and I grabbed the letter from Dad's hands and read it quickly and gave it to Jazz to read. Our faces were horror-stricken; we didn't know what to do.

"Dad, let's go," said Jazz.

While Dad and Jazz rushed to the car to find Jeet, Ritu and I tried to console Mom. "He won't do anything that drastic, Mom. He was just upset," Ritu assured mom.

"I'm sure they'll find him, Mom; don't worry," I added. A strange sense of fear engulfed me, and it left a bitter taste in my mouth. I was afraid, like Mom, that maybe they had been too harsh on Jeet, and it was too late to bring him back. A couple of hours later, only Dad and Jazz came home. They had found Jeet. Dead.

• • •

Jeet had indeed gone to his university library, as they had all suspected, but it was too late when Dad and Jazz had arrived. Police cars and ambulances had already circled the library. They frantically tried to explain to the cops that they were looking for their son, who was probably in the library. The cops explained that after the accident all the students in the building were evacuated and that no one except the parents of the student who had fallen from the tenth floor into the lobby would be allowed in. A wave of terror echoed in their ears.

Jazz spoke as Dad was silent in shock, "Sir, I think that may be my brother in there."

It was confirmed by Dad and Jazz that the blood-drenched clothes and turban and the smashed watch of the disfigured body that lay in a puddle of blood was Jeet's. The officer began asking Dad questions, which in his grief and guilt, Dad assumed were accusations.

"Officer," Dad spoke in a broken-down voice, "I was very angry at my son after I came to know his feelings... He'd just revealed he was a homosexual, and I told him to leave the house in my anger. I didn't mean it. I never thought he would take such a terribly big step." Dad's voice grew louder as he tried to justify his innocence.

"Mr. Singh, we know that you didn't provoke your son to commit suicide. We are not accusing you, so please relax. We are doing our job, and we must ask these questions, OK?" He gave Dad a look of reassurance.

We were lucky to not have witnessed the haunting suicide scene that Dad told us about later. Nightmares of Jeet rising from a pool of blood continued to rob Dad of his sleep. They filed a police report and submitted the suicide letter. It was a true case of suicide, according to the police, and we were not held legally liable for his death.

Their decision was odd, I thought. There was no one more liable for Jeet's death except for his family. In my court of justice, I would have found us guilty and deserving of severe punishment. It was on that day that Mom and Dad were unconsciously realizing the mistakes they were making as parents. They didn't have to say it to one another, but they knew within their own hearts that their haste to throw their son out of their home was preposterous, since they knew he would have nowhere to go. They didn't think it through; they didn't foresee that their intelligent son would find a way to leave. They let their anger, their superstitions about homosexuality, and their worries of how the shame of it would affect their reputation in the Punjabi community overcome their reason and their love for their son. But there was not a second chance to redeem themselves, no good would come of taking back their words now.

He, our dearest brother, Jeet, had left us. We would never see him and his tall, thin figure, hear his quiet voice. His gentle face and soft expression were now frozen as only a memory that would never grow or age. He would now never again touch his books, flipping through their abundant pages, and never again wear the clothes hanging in his closet. All his things would remain and his scent from his room would soon dissipate into thin air. We could not contain him, his scent, his body, his essence. We could not hold the stuff that contained his life that made him who he was. He slipped through our fingers, and we could never find him again in another. He was truly unique; there was no one like him. Everything he had once owned would no longer be his. In religion school at the Sikh temple, they taught us that people come alone with nothing into the world, and they leave alone with nothing from the world except their deeds and their devotion to God etched on their souls. Jeet had also come into the world with nothing and left with no possession or person. But he had left us a deep scar, a secret that had consumed him and left us covering his tracks.

Chapter 17
1998

The bustling sounds of New York City traffic woke me early in the morning. I could see out of the corner of my eye that Katy was still asleep in her bed across the room. I quietly tiptoed into the bathroom.

"Morning, Mir."

"Sorry, Kat, I didn't mean to wake you."

"You didn't. I've been up for a while."

"I know why I'm not sleeping, but why aren't you sleeping?"

"I don't know. I think it's this noisy city, the city I love, New York, New York. Sometimes it gets to me. I can't relax, always on the go."

Before I could reply, the phone rang.

"It's probably for you, Mir, so now I can use the bathroom." Kat smiled.

I picked up the phone, knowing that it was Dev who was calling. I was right, and we planned to meet for lunch. Still sitting by the phone, I called Katy, who was brushing her teeth. "I'm going to do it today. I'm going to tell Dev everything."

"I'm proud of you," Katy yelled back after the sound of a big spit of toothpaste into the sink. Katy came out, toothbrush still in hand, and put her hand on my shoulder. "Now, just remember, tell him everything the way you told me. Just be honest and let it all out."

"I hope God gives me the strength to do this. I'm so scared of his reaction."

"Well, think about it this way: if he really loves you, then he will accept you and your family as you are and will understand. If he's just having a good time with you, he might think this is all too heavy and serious and he'll alienate you. Either way, you'll know his intentions before it gets too late."

I knew that Katy was right, but I also knew that she understood why I was so hesitant. I loved Dev, but our relationship had not been without its issues of trust.

The hot water beat on my aching neck and shoulders in the shower, and I lost myself under its rhythmic pressure, thinking about how Dev and I had already broken up once. It wasn't long ago that I thought Dev was a fraud.

• • •

A month after I started meeting Dev on a regular basis, by which point I had finally come around to admitting to myself that I liked him more than a friend, our relationship ended briefly. You could call it the "make it a virgin" incident, and not meaning how Katy and I would order drinks at the bar.

I was spinning like a little girl in my dorm room, holding a new silk dress against my chest. "Oh, Katy, Dev bought me this dress. Isn't it beautiful? It looks expensive," I said with my eyes shining as bright as stars. "He has arranged a special dinner for us to celebrate our one month of being best friends and a special sweet surprise in the Plaza Hotel." I beamed with excitement.

"Uh, Mir, what do you mean by a surprise at the Plaza? Why is he taking you to a hotel, and you're going with him?!"

"Why do you look so shocked? We're not getting a room."

"Because I am looking at the most naive and stupid woman

I know!"

"That is so rude! How could you talk to me like that?" I admonished, hurt by her words.

"Listen, I'm sorry, Mira, but in this one month, you've moved quickly from being strangers to friends, to best friends, and obviously to everyone except you, to a couple! Just because you don't call each other girlfriend and boyfriend yet doesn't mean he's not expecting you to start acting like one now. Let me tell you, my darling friend, about the truth of where this is going. He has been patiently waiting for you to take your head out of the sand and understand that he does not want to stay 'best friends,'" she said with a tilt in her head, "*forever*. He wants to take you to that hotel, feed you a very fancy dinner, get you to drink some wine, so you're giggly and tipsy, and kiss you and tell you how he wants to move this friendship into a deep love… and then deflower you!"

I just stared at Katy, and as the blood left my face, I realized she was right. Dev had been trying to kiss me for the last week, and I'd been avoiding it, too scared to indulge in it. God knew how much I wanted to, but I couldn't. If I did and he didn't think I was good, it could kill what we had going on. Kisses aside, would Dev try to bed me? No! I was horrified. He must have known that I would never in a million years lose my virginity before marriage.

"Oh, Kat, he's Indian. I'm sure he knows I can't have, have… God, I can't even say the word, you know, sex," I whispered. "I think we're going to the Plaza to have dessert or a drink. It's such a pretty place, everyone goes there, right?"

"Hmm…I think you don't know much about his past, and I hear he's a real ladies' man." She looked at my doubtful expression and changed her comment to "*Was* a real ladies' man! I think tonight he's planning to charm his way into your pants."

"Stop. This can't be true. I won't go to the hotel with him, and I'll just ask him point-blank."

"Well, you do that, and don't let him persuade you. Do you want me to come with you?"

"No, I'm a grown woman. I can handle this."

"Good luck."

I reluctantly smiled and walked out of the dorm room with my excitement drowned out by fear and disappointment. At least Katy was on my side. She too was conservative about sexuality, and we had made a pact to stay virgins until we got married and, of course, not to drink alcohol when we partied. We both agreed that we liked being "good" and our kind of "bad." Our parents would think clubbing was "bad" of us, but we were still "good" in other things, and we wanted to keep it that way (at least for now). As I walked down the street in my new sleeveless, deep-emerald-green silk mini-dress and high heels with my hair straightened and makeup done, I became anxious about my big date with Dev.

Perhaps Dev wouldn't be interested in me anymore if I didn't sleep with him. Maybe, all this time, he was just being nice to have sex with me, and then he would move on to the next girl. I shook my head in disbelief. No, that couldn't be the sensitive Dev I had opened my heart and mind to. Katy had to be wrong about him. Dev was taking me to Windows on the World at the top of the Twin Towers for dinner, and then we were going to the Plaza Hotel for, ugh, I didn't ask him. I wasn't sure what we were going there for. How could I be so dumb sometimes?! As I approached the restaurant, I could see Dev anxiously watching people around him, waiting for me at the table. Then he found my gaze from a distance and gave me his incredible, delicious smile that usually made me swoon.

"You look beautiful. I love this color on you."

"Thank you." I felt shy suddenly, as if I never imagined before tonight that this man would want more than just my conversation and company.

"What's the matter? Is everything OK?"

"You know, Dev, I—"

"Ah, madam and sir, would you like to hear the specials tonight?"

After the server left with our order, I screwed up my courage and said in a burst, "I'm not sure if I can go to the Plaza with you tonight."

Dev jerked his head back a little. "But why can't you?"

"Because I don't..." I hesitated. Now where was that server? "What are we going to do there, anyway?"

"That's the surprise, my lady," Dev said with a wicked grin and dark eyes, slowly taking my hand to his mouth and planting a kiss.

With butterflies in my stomach and a heavy weight on my chest, I could no longer sit in my chair. I flew up to standing and like fire spit out, "Dev, I will not have sex with you!"

Dev was shocked and looked at me like I just ate a dragon, his eyes in disbelief of what I just said. "Mira, I think the whole restaurant just heard. Can we talk about this after dinner?"

"No, I'm sorry. I can't eat. I must go." I walked out with Dev following closely behind me. We were in the elevator, which seemed to be plummeting down at one hundred miles an hour, making my head spin.

"Who told you I'm taking you to the hotel to have sex with you?" He glared at me.

I stammered a response. "Katy said that this was your big

surprise." I couldn't even look at him, I felt so embarrassed.

He gently took both of my hands in his. "Is it so wrong to want you, Mira? I have done everything in my power in the last month to get closer to you, to have you open to me, to get to know you. Do you think that I could continue like this forever? You have no idea—every waking moment I think of you. All day, I look forward to the time when I will meet you and have a chance to touch you, just a stroke of your hand." He hesitated a minute, closing his eyes, and then a moment later, he continued, "I thought you felt the same way about me. I see it in your eyes even though you don't tell me with your words. I thought we were getting to the point in our relationship where we were ready to at least kiss and then maybe, you know…"

I stood frozen in disbelief. This gorgeous man thought of me all the time. Of me?! And he thought we were ready? How?

"We haven't even kissed, Dev. How could you jump to this conclusion? I can't believe you called me to this special dinner to sleep with me. I can't believe Katy was right. All this time, you… you just wanted me to lose my virginity to you." The tears were about to burst from my eyes, and I could no longer face the sight of Dev as the elevator doors opened. "Goodbye, Dev. I thought I knew you; I thought you knew me, but I was so wrong."

I turned and fled. Dev didn't even try to stop me or follow me. All along I was the naive girl to be conquered, to be bedded. How stupid I felt. I went home that night and cried in Katy's arms. Katy didn't let Dev's shadow near me for a week. I felt I had died inside. I missed Dev so much that at night I woke up gasping for breath. He was my breath, the breath that gave me life. I felt a deep pain in my chest and stomach, and I could no longer endure it. I decided to go home to Long Island for a few days for a change of scenery, but mostly because I couldn't risk seeing Dev, especially not while I was still an emotional wreck. The man I trusted, and, by God, I think I loved just let me go because I wouldn't sleep with him. Dev was a fraud in my eyes at that moment. I wished I knew what our whole relationship had been about. It just didn't make sense to me.

Chapter 18

Throughout the morning lectures, I prayed in my mind. I prayed that the Guru gave me inner strength, and God's own strength, to face Dev, to unveil the truth.

My Guru, please give me the courage to face the events in my life without breaking down. Please give me an understanding of why all these terrible things have happened to us. Make me strong; let these bad chapters in my life be closed. I yearn for peace; make my anxiety melt away. And I bravely ask of you, please do what is the best for us in the future since you are the cause of all misery and happiness; you are the doer that does everything that happens. It's your decision; please make the right decision for me. I leave it up to you to take care of. If Dev is sincere, please unite us; if he is just playing with my emotions, then reveal it to me now because I can't bear to be let down later.

"Excuse me, Mira."

Startled by the professor's voice, I snapped out of my prayer. "I'm sorry, yes."

"The class is over, and all the other students have left."

"Oh, sorry." I was embarrassed and hurriedly left the lecture hall.

It was already 1:30, and I was late for my lunch meeting with Dev. Still, I walked in a daze toward the Lemongrass Café at University Place and Eleventh Street, Dev's and my favorite Thai restaurant. My anxiety was making my chest feel tight and my stomach churn. When I saw Dev sitting at a table in the far back corner of the restaurant, I felt my resolve come into focus. Today will be my test of courage and a test of Dev's sincerity.

"Table for one?"

"No, someone is waiting for me in the back." I walked toward Dev, and he got up to kiss me on the cheek.

"Hi, babe."

"Hi, Dev."

"So, are you ready for your favorite dishes, pad Thai noodles and basil chicken?"

My appetite had dwindled with the horrific thought of Dev's rejection of my story, of me. "I'm actually not that hungry."

"Look, I know you—if you don't eat, you won't have the strength to tell me everything you want to. You'll feel sick. I've already ordered the food, and I want you to eat a little bit before we start talking. And no one is going to save you today because I haven't told anyone where I'm going to be. OK?"

I loved the way Dev pampered me like his small child and made me feel secure with him. I was taken care of by Dev.

"OK," I said with a smile.

"There we go—you're already smiling. It won't be so bad, I promise. If I don't like what you have to say, then I'll just leave you."

I stared at him with a look of fear.

"I'm kidding, oh my God, you look so serious. I wouldn't

leave you for anything in the world. You already left me once, and I never want to feel the way I did ever again." He took my hand across the table. "You know I stayed in bed for days at that time. Narinder was about to kill me—first I give all Desi guys a bad name by letting you walk away just because I'm too much of a scumbag, making assumptions about your experience and what you want, and then I stink up our place by not showering."

I laughed lightly and entertained the idea of eating, poking at the platter of noodles with the serving spoon. "My roommate was about to kill you too. Apparently, she had to thwart a lot of your attempts to see me."

"Yeah, I tried to see you! I love you, Mir. And listen, of course I want to sleep with you! I've been fantasizing about it since the day you dropped your books in the library, and I looked over and saw you."

I blushed. I never looked my best in the library. He probably first saw me wearing an old T-shirt.

"But I'd never push you into anything you don't want. I love talking with you, just being with you more than anything. No, I can't stand the thought of someone else being your first, but that's not why I love you."

We both smiled that inner, knowing smile at each other. The tables were packed as usual with students, professors, and others, yet the hut-like interior gave the restaurant an authentic and cozy atmosphere where, amid the noise, two people could have a private conversation. I began to eat. And then I ate some more.

"Hold on!" Dev laughed. "I think you're going to eat my share as well, so you better take a break and talk."

Feeling more relaxed with some food in my stomach, I began. "Well, I told you about Ritu and her marriage breaking up last time."

"Yeah, but you didn't tell me why no one in the community would believe your family."

"It's because the reason Ritu was married off so quickly was that the whole community, and then my parents, found out she had been seeing a Muslim guy."

Dev worked out the issue in his head and finished the story for me. "Oh, I get it. Everyone would blame a broken marriage on your sister because she was the one who had an affair with the Muslim guy just months before her wedding."

"Yes, bull's-eye. That's the way people think, low about others. They just want something to gossip about."

"But you do know that people will always talk, and you can't live your life worrying about what they think and what they might say." Dev was more serious now. "The same thing might happen when you and I tell your parents about us."

I felt my stomach drop to the floor with anxiety, but my heart refused to cooperate and ached with joy.

"They might not like it, and people may talk about us, but we must be stronger than that; we have to put a deaf ear to gossip. Our love and happiness are more important than what people think."

I wanted to get up from my seat and squeeze Dev; his words made me feel more confident that I could tell Dev about my family. "I'm so glad you understand, Dev; it's so important to me."

"Of course, I understand. I believe you when you say that your sister was abused. I'm not someone who will believe gossip and not you. How could you even think that about me?"

"Well, there's a lot more to stomach."

"Try me."

I took a deep breath before starting the tale of Jeet and Jazz and my father. I gave Dev a little background about the situation in my family. I told him about how my dad was strict and how Jazz was a problem child and involved in bad company. I told him about Jeet and how close we were. How Jeet always loved to be a good son. How he was so intelligent and how he had started Columbia University and how he had the potential to be a great doctor one day.

"So, what happened to your brother, then? You never told me how he died. I mean, I wanted to ask you, but I thought maybe it was too soon for you and you needed more time."

"Well, that's why I couldn't tell you. It's bad enough that my brother has died, but it's tragic how and why he died."

Dev sat with his eyebrows knitted, listening intently. I felt my cheeks turning red and my eyes filling with tears as I spoke. At one point, he interrupted to say, "Mir, there's nothing to be ashamed of."

"I'm not ashamed of him," I snapped at Dev. "I'm upset because we are his murderers." Now my face was in my hands, and I imagined I was crying loud enough to earn a couple of stares, but I couldn't stop.

Dev pulled his chair to my side of the table and held me in his arms. "It's OK, baby. It wasn't your fault."

"It was our fault," I wept. "We allowed it all to happen. I didn't say a word in his defense when my dad was yelling at him. I didn't stop him from leaving the house. I didn't go to my parents that night and try to calm them down and explain to them how wrong they were and how they were hurting him."

"You were in a state of shock, and you could never imagine that he would do this to himself."

"But he did, and we never stopped it. So, do you resent me now, pulling you into my problems?"

"Of course not. How could you think that I would ever resent you? I always want to be there for you when you need me. I'm never going to leave you alone, especially not now."

Hearing his words lifted a heavy weight off my chest that I had been carrying for months. I took a deep breath, and the air was finally flowing inside me, releasing me from the suffocation of the previous months.

"Shh, just relax and put your head on my shoulder."

I rested my head on Dev's strong shoulder and gently closed my eyes.

"Have you spoken to your parents about his death and what you think was wrong?"

"No, we have been so depressed I didn't know how to bring it up, but I wish I could tell them so they would know they are responsible."

"I'm sure they feel guilty and responsible already. That's not what I mean. I think you should tell them in a way where they understand why it was so wrong to punish your brother."

"You know, they called him names like he was abnormal or an animal."

"That's what I mean—try to move them away from that type of thinking and learn to tolerate people's differences."

"You're right. No point making them feel more guilty."

Waheguru had given me the strength to confide in and share the most private details about my family with Dev. And the best part was that Dev not only understood my tragic story, but he supported me and gave me good advice on how to communicate my feelings with Mom and Dad. I took this as a sign that the Guru wanted Dev and me to be together; it gave me faith that our pairing would be for the best. Yet could I tell my parents about us? I saw what happened with Ritu and Amir. I wanted

Dev and me to have a future, but I still didn't know if we could. How could I tell Dev about my uncertainty? I couldn't tell him yet; it would have to wait. I couldn't hurt him now when he had been my pillar of support.

• • •

That night, I took the Long Island Railroad home for a long weekend. As usual, I left my packing to the last minute. I had only thirty minutes till the train, and I was hurriedly packing my dirty laundry to be washed at home when I heard Katy.

"So, you're off to home, eh?"

"Yeah, and I'm late, of course."

"How was the talk with Dev today?"

"Oh, it was so much better than I expected. I'll tell you everything in detail over a turkey burger and curly fries at Weinstein's late-night dinner when I get back Sunday night."

"Sounds good, but at least tell me, is everything OK with you guys? You're still together, right?"

"Oh yeah, and he was so…understanding, and he even gave me advice."

"I knew there was nothing to worry about. Just from the way he looks at you, it's so obvious he's in love with you."

"Oh, really, Katy?" I beamed with an inner hope. A feeling of relief had overcome me since my chat with Dev, and I relaxed my tense shoulders. Unfortunately, feelings of relief and happiness in life are brief. Someone once told me that life consists of only moments of happiness and stretches of struggle. Another struggle was about to begin, and I was once again innocent of the coming future.

Chapter 19

Dad was waiting for me as the train pulled up to Mineola station. He put my luggage in the trunk while I sat in the passenger seat. "So, Beti," he asked as we pulled away, "how was the school week?"

"It was fine, nothing new. I have exams coming up in a few weeks."

"Oh, then you should be preparing for them. You know, your brother—" Dad stopped short, remembering. I saw him take a big gulp to swallow his words. We didn't say anything else to each other for the remainder of the ride. I knew how much dad missed Jeet and realized that I would have to be very gentle with my parents when I spoke to them about him.

The house was quiet, and Mom didn't come running to the door to greet me like she used to. She and Ritu sat in the living room pretending to be busy. Mom was fiddling with needlework; Ritu was flipping pages of a magazine.

"Hello, Mira-Beti." Mom reached up to give me a hug and kiss. "Everything fine at school?"

"Yeah, the usual."

"How's your friend Katy? Did she give you my message that I called in the afternoon? I thought you didn't have class in the afternoon. Where were you for so long?"

"I went to the library to study. I've got exams coming up."

The rest of the night was more general and unimportant chatter. I sensed a strange disharmony between Mom and Dad. I asked Ritu about it. She said that they had had an argument a few days ago, and since then they had not spoken to each other except when absolutely necessary. This supposed fight began to eat away at my mind like a parasite. I'd never seen them like this. Plus, having a tough time made it difficult for me to talk about death with them.

But the dream I had that night changed my mind, and I was adamant about bringing up his death with Mom and Dad the next day. In my dream, I was in a misty place, and my brother and I were sitting in separate compartments of a Ferris wheel that were inside a huge library. He looked the same as he did the night before he died. He was wearing a navy-blue turban and a black sweater with jeans. I was happy to see him, and he smiled at me. We talked for a while, but in the morning, I could only remember the last three lines between us. I said, "Can I come with you?"

"No, Mir, it's not your time yet. You still must go around a few times. Just remember that you must do me this favor."

"I will, I promise."

I woke up with tears in my eyes and sweat trickling down my collarbone. Mom said that family and friends who pass away come very seldom in our dreams. They do so only to give us something, which in dream interpretation is a sign that good fortune is coming our way, or to say something to us to make us understand something we are confused about. All I knew after the dream about my brother was that it made me feel that he was close to me and was watching me. And I believed he wanted me to speak to Mom and Dad about him. I reckoned maybe to relieve him of his guilt or perhaps us of ours.

The next morning, I tried to please Mom and Dad from the start by making my specialty banana pancakes with mango milkshakes.

"Oh, this is a nice surprise," Mom said while walking into the kitchen.

"Well, I thought it would be a nice change from cereal on the weekend." I could hear dad's footsteps walking briskly down the steps.

"Good morning! Something smells good," he said with a smile.

I hadn't seen Dad smile since before the day of the tragedy. I took this as a sign this was the right opportunity to bring up Jeet.

"Kamal, why don't you wake the others up," said Dad, "and they can join us for breakfast."

"You know, before you call them down, Mom, I want to speak to you and Dad about something privately."

Mom and Dad were taken aback by my direct tone. "What is it? Is everything OK at school?

"It doesn't have to do with me; it has to do with…you know."

"Now, look, Mira, I understand that it has been very difficult for all of us to cope with this, and we can understand that it's been hard for you."

Frustrated, I shook my head. "I'm not talking about coping with his death. I want to speak to you about why he died and how you treated him."

"Turn off the stove and sit down," Dad said in a serious tone. "We are very hurt that he hid so much from us, and he committed a sin by taking his own life. We are disappointed—"

"Disappointed?" I interrupted. "How can you say that? It was because of your disappointment in him that he killed himself. If you could have just accepted him as your son when he was so vulnerable, he would be alive today."

Mom started to cry.

"We don't want to discuss this with you, Mira," said Dad.

"*No*, it's important to talk about it. You need to understand that he died because of our lack of understanding and lack of discussions between us."

Tears began to choke my throat.

"Stop, Mira."

I heard my voice getting louder and more persistent. "You don't even know him and how lost he was in all this!"

Mom's wailing grew louder.

"Mira, stop this topic, I said!" Dad shouted.

"You let him down, your narrow thinking; he could've been successful if you hadn't been so strict!"

"Shut up!" Dad shoved a plate across the table.

I stopped. With a red-hot face, I left the kitchen. I could overhear some bickering between Mom and Dad. "She's right—you did kill my son, and now you're trying to kill me," wailed Mom.

"Stop it, now, Kamal; stop it. You must learn to move on with your life. We cannot change anything. He's not coming back, OK? Stop thinking that he's going to come back, and for God's sake, stop your daily crying. I can't take it anymore!"

"It's very easy for you to say that because you're a man; you're not his mother like me. I can't get over it; I'll never get over it. How dare you tell me to stop crying. I'll never stop crying!" Mom exclaimed. "It's as if you didn't even lose your son. It's like you're made of stone."

"You have three other children you still need to be a mother too. You have a husband you need to continue being a wife too.

You have to keep living for us!"

"That's all lies. I know why you want me to stop crying and act 'normal,' to be a wife again—because of your own selfish reasons, for your unquenchable thirst and dirty desires," she seethed.

"Shut up, you stupid woman; our children can hear us."

I made my views clear but shook Mom and Dad to an extent I hadn't anticipated. I didn't want to put all the blame on them, but it was the only way to change their minds. They avoided me the rest of the day, and besides necessary conversation, they stayed quiet. I was upset that I caused so much anger to bubble outward. But what was going on, I could not understand fully; why were they so upset at each other? I could not understand how the death of a child could strain a marriage that had strong bonds for many years prior. Wasn't that what marriage was for, to help us survive the worst storms? Suddenly, the strings of those tightly woven bonds had begun to wither and stretch, leaving them weakened, barely holding on to each other. Mom could not yet come to terms with Jeet's death; somewhere inside of her, she had a small hope that maybe, miraculously, her dead son would return to her. She could not shake herself out of the misery she lay in. I thought of Mom and Dad, and Ritu and Manny, and Dev and me. I was piecing together what it was like to be bound to someone during tragedy. I tried to place myself in my parents' shoes and consider what they might be experiencing.

Chapter 20

Mom's resentment about Dad's quicker resolve to move on with his life and return to more normal living was growing. Dad wanted to live again, wanted to find comfort in his wife's arms, to lie with her the way they used to, to touch her and rise inside of her as only he was privileged to do. But Mom would not allow this. She was not moving back to normalcy. She did not want to live; most of her wanted to die. She did not have the courage to tell her husband this. All pleasures, tastes, and enjoyment had ceased to hold gratification for her. Nothing could fulfill her. She was empty, hollow, and wanted to remain this way without someone forcing her with impatience and anger to get better. She only wished he would give her time. How much time, she did not know. Maybe a lifetime, it seemed.

To Dad, Mom appeared not to even want to try to get better. He felt isolated. His wife never came to him to share her sorrows, to cry on his shoulder; she wanted to be left alone to grieve. Suddenly, he was a stranger to a woman he had spent his whole life providing for and trying to make happy. He almost felt useless as a husband. Dad could no longer bear the burden of Mom's depression; he needed an outlet, a breath of fresh air. He needed to be comforted, to find refuge in welcoming arms, to be fulfilled, to feel something, anything. As I would learn, Dad had begun to contemplate how he would break away from his sorrow and who would help him.

At Kinchan-chacha's wedding, as at Ritu's wedding, my old friend Deepa's mother, Bindu-auntie, with the big bosom, traveled with a cloud of rumors hanging around her like a lingering stink. Because I was only a child at the time, I did not know what the rumors were about, only that many of the women in the community, including Mom, thought negatively of her. I knew now that Bindu-auntie allegedly was having an affair with a man in the community. It was all very hush-hush, and since the man was a widower, no one wanted to point fingers at him. Poor Veer-chacha, Bindu-auntie's husband, was not a very intelligent man and was not aware of the rumors about his wife, nor did he question her actions, but only listened to her and followed her every move. Although everyone knew that Bindu-auntie had no respect for her husband and ordered him around like a servant, there was no proof of Bindu-auntie's infidelity, but as it turned out, Dad was now determined to find out.

It had only been a few months since Jeet's death, and Mom and Dad had refrained from attending any social events. But now, there was the wedding of a very old and close friend of Dad's, and he felt that they should attend at least briefly to give the new couple their blessings, and it would be a good change for them. Mom refused to go, despite Dad's pleading. Ritu and I begged off, though after I learned what happened, I wished I'd gone. So, he decided that he would go alone and pay his respects to his friends and engage himself in society again.

At the party, after a couple of drinks of Johnnie Walker Black Label, he leaned against the bar and surveyed the room. He spotted Mrs. Bindu across the dance floor. She was dressed in a bright-red-and-magenta saree, which was too young an outfit for her forty years, and her bosom lay quite exposed to the wandering eye.

Bindu caught Dad staring at her, and he looked away. Moments later, she was by his side at the bar, asking for a vodka tonic.

"I am very, very sorry to hear about your son, Harbans. It was shocking news."

"Yes, it's been a very difficult time for all of us."

"How are you doing?" asked Bindu while she stroked Dad's right arm and looked straight into his eyes tenderly. It was refreshing to hear someone ask how he was feeling; most people only asked how his wife was holding up. Bindu was continuing to speak, but Dad could not hear her words now; his eyes and mind were focused on her smooth red lips and her bosom that heaved with every sigh and breath. Her eyes smiled at him through long lashes. She was saying as he finally awoke to her voice, "Why don't we go talk in private? Why don't we meet up for a coffee, so you can tell me better how you're getting through this tough time?"

Dad found himself nodding and agreeing to Sunday at 11am at the Barnes & Noble bookstore near the mall. The steps to happiness, or at least to relief, that he had only envisioned over the last couple of weeks were beginning to transpire.

The next day was Saturday, and Dad's mind was preoccupied with his meeting the following day with Bindu. Did she know what he was thinking, meaning, would she be willing…? His mind shoved the thoughts away. Bindu was an attractive woman with a bad reputation, but she also seemed like a pleasant woman to talk to, and she was the only woman, including his wife, who had taken any interest in his feelings and needs.

"Dad, would you like some tea?"

Dad sat on the couch holding the newspaper in his hand.

"Dad?" Ritu touched his shoulder.

"Oh, you startled me."

"I've been standing here asking you if you want some tea for the last few minutes. Are you OK?" She looked more concerned now than bewildered.

"Oh yes, that will be good, thanks. Also, put two glucose biscuits on the side. Sorry, I was just thinking to myself."

That night both Mom and Dad engaged in the dream world as they slept side by side. Except even their dreams were worlds apart. Mom dreamed about her son running into her arms and her quickly lifting him off the ground into an embrace, and they both were happy. She could hear his laughter and see his eyes shining bright. Someone said that he was grown now and hiding in a big closet. Kamal ran with joy to the closet to see her son; she missed him so much. With all her hope filling the rim of her heart, she opened the closet door and saw that it was empty. Heartbroken, Mom felt tears begin to flow, choking her, closing out her breath. Mom woke up gasping for breath and finding her pillow wet with tears. She wiped her face in the dark. Her mouth was dry as she realized it was only a dream. She watched her husband fast asleep, wondering about the space between them.

Dad and Bindu were drinking coffee and chatting happily. A weight had been lifted from his chest. He felt free to take her hands in the bedroom they were suddenly in, and they fell onto the bed together. Bindu's eyes were intoxicating, and her lips invited him to taste her. He grew more excited with the touch of her soft skin against his. Her abundant bosom was gratifying, and her body excited him further and further until they both gasped with relief and fulfillment in each other's arms. He was not in love with Bindu, but he was attracted to her, to what her body did to him, and how she made him feel like a young man again. Her caress and her soft whispering in his ears and her bold moves made her a better and more dangerous lover than his wife. Even more pleasurable and daring than he ever imagined an Indian woman could be. He told her he must see her again, and of course, no one else was to ever know. As they stared into each other's eyes and smiled goodbyes, Dad began to wake, slowly finding himself in a pool of sweat. His dream felt so real; the sensation excited him, but his thoughts had somewhere deep inside frightened him too. If he was to engage in surreptitious activities with Bindu, would he get caught? What if his wife ever found out? He looked over to her, asleep, and wondered what she would do. But then he smiled and shook his head, thinking, of course there was no way she would find out. Bindu would never tell, to save her own face, and her husband was an idiot; he would never guess it.

Mom had always been a trusting and faithful wife; she would never dream of it. After all, it wouldn't continue forever, and no real crime would be committed since he wouldn't give his heart away to Bindu. His heart would always be with his wife; after all, they had more history together. *This is just something I must do for myself,* thought Dad. *Think of myself for a change. I've always thought about the kids and Kamal and what is good for the whole family. When is it my turn to tend to my needs, what I want, what makes me happy? That is the American way, isn't it? Well, we're half-American now, aren't we? So, what difference does it make to anyone but me?* Dad began to center his thoughts of self-inside him. He did not realize that what he was thinking, planning, and doing could only hurt everyone that he loved and cared about. He did not think of his wife, who needed him the most now in all their history together; he did not think of his children, who looked up to him as a figure of perfection, of an ideal and a most intelligent man. He did not think of how it could break their family apart or how big the risk was that he was taking. In the darkness of that night, he thought only of himself and no one else.

• • •

The next day, I took the Long Island Railroad back to the city in the afternoon so that I would have time to settle back in before class the following day.

"Dad, could you drop me at the station at around 11:30?"

"Ah, ask your sister to drop you. I have some important work to get to."

"Important work? On Sunday? Where are you going?"

"Mira, I am your father. I don't need to explain to you where I am going. Ritu will drop you."

"OK, I was just asking."

I went up to my room to get the remainder of my things. Annoyed after my exchange with Dad, I turned my exasperation on Ritu, who was sitting on the bed staring out the window, as had become her habit since she returned home.

"Ritu, you really need to do something instead of just helping Mom around the house and staring out the window all day. It's not good for your health."

"What should I do, Mira?"

"Well, for starters, get a job or something?" I replied.

"I don't know how to get a job, I've just been studying my whole life or working in the house," she replied with a hopeless look.

"Well, go to the library or the bookstore and get some books on how to write a resume and find a job, and personally, I think you should also buy some novels to read in your spare time. You know, to keep your mind busy." I beamed. My idea should surely cheer her up and help her focus on positive things.

"Yeah, it sounds good, but I can't go alone and find these things myself. Will you come with me?"

Not wanting to discourage Ritu's interest, I stammered, "Well, I was planning to take the 11:30 train back today...but I guess I could take the next train. If you can drop me off at the station right after. If we go now, we can even sit down together for some coffee. It'll be like a sisters' day out—it'll be fun!" I jumped up with a smile.

On my way downstairs, I leaned into Mom and Dad's bedroom. "Bye, Dad. Ritu is gonna drop me. See you next weekend. Love you."

"OK, bye, Mira, take care and have a good week, and call your mother when you reach the dorm."

As Dad spoke, I watched him. He was doing more than just getting dressed. He was pressing his beard with hairspray. And did the room smell like cologne? But I had learned my lesson earlier, and I did not ask him again about what kind of work he was doing today.

Downstairs, I hugged Mom goodbye and told her to take care of herself. She smiled and patted my head. "Call me from your room when you reach it," she said.

"OK, I'm not catching the early train, though. I'm taking Ritu out to get some books so that she can keep herself busy. I thought it would help her feel better."

"Good, you sisters need to look after each other."

• • •

Ritu and I were browsing the career section of the Barnes & Noble closest to the train station. Her interest lay in sales or marketing, so we focused on selecting books to help with landing jobs in those fields. This seemed to cheer Ritu, and she was also happy to move on to the fiction section, even looking interested in my suggestion of an old favorite of mine, novels by Sidney Sheldon.

Once again, though, unknown and unexpected negative forces were swirling around us. Some Ritu filled me in on later. But right then, Bindu-auntie was sitting in the café steps away from us, and Dad walked into the store and strode past the aisles where Ritu and I were standing.

"Hi, I'm over here!" Bindu called out to Dad.

"How are you?" Dad asked as he sat across from her.

"I'm well, and I might add, you're looking very dashing today."

Dad felt like he was blushing under her sly look. He thanked her and then said shyly, almost as an afterthought, "Oh, I think you're also looking very lovely, as always."

"I took the liberty of buying us both some coffee. I hope you don't mind," said Bindu, all the while smiling with her eyes.

"No, it was very thoughtful of you," he said as he cleared his throat.

Bindu's gaze was fixed on dad, and she slowly reached her hand across the table and put it over his. "Feel as if I'm your friend. You can tell me what you feel. I am here to share your grief." She beckoned to him as a child does to their pet, purring softly, leading the animal slowly into her embrace.

As she gently rubbed her hands over his hands, dad, who was now terribly distracted, could only hear, "Share, feel, let me..." He suddenly blurted out, "I'm alone. I need a...some company, some female company, you know, to share my feelings with." He looked at her, waiting and wondering if she could uncover the truth of his words.

Bindu was not a novice to extramarital affairs, and she knew exactly what men meant when they spoke in code. She understood men, except for her husband, all too well.

Her own husband, Veer, of twenty years, had only disappointed her from the very beginning in every possible way. Financially, he was not able to support them with the high-profile lifestyle she was accustomed to in her maayka (parents' home before marriage). He was also clumsy and looked like a big oaf. He was much too tall, and his limbs looked like they had been stretched too far. His face was long like his body, and his chin jutted out unnaturally into space. Her parents arranged her marriage to him because she was the second of four sisters, and they wanted to unburden themselves quickly of their older two daughters before it came time for the two younger ones to marry. Veer had a visa to go to America and did not demand a dowry; he thought such a pretty woman was more than he could ever expect for an unattractive man like himself. From the first day of marriage, Bindu loathed Veer; he was not only unattractive and not wealthy, but he was not exciting in bed and not very intelligent, and she felt trapped with him for life.

After a few years, Bindu began to realize she received attention from good-looking men, American and Indian both, who were charismatic and charming. Her flirtatious personality worried her husband, but he did not have the courage to confront his wife. He knew that no one would marry him if she left him. So as the years passed and they had only one daughter, he learned to ignore the flirtatious behavior of his wife and to stop asking where she had been and with whom. He only concentrated on his daughter, the one he lived for and the only person who loved and respected him in their little family.

Bindu was not shocked by Dad's words. She suspected his

intentions when he agreed to meet with her privately for coffee. After all, Indian men and women their age didn't meet alone as friends; they met as lovers. And now Dad, one of the intelligent and good-looking men she had always admired, had chosen her to share his affections with.

She slowly stroked Dad's cheek with her other hand. "Of course, I understand what you're going through, and I would love to spend more intimate time with you. I'm flattered that you chose my company." She spoke in an intoxicating voice and gazed into Dad's eyes.

He could feel his heart thumping in his chest so loudly he thought maybe Bindu could hear it too. He tried to keep his composure, but it was difficult with Bindu's chest heaving and pouring its softness and abundance over the edge of the table. "So, shall we go somewhere where we can be alone?" he asked in a low whisper.

"Absolutely, I'll just grab my things."

Dad stood and turned toward the door, but he stopped short in his tracks, almost frozen. Bindu had come up behind him and wrapped her arms in his and was now leaning against him. "Are you OK? What's the matter?" she was asking him. Her voice was now faint in the distance as all he was focusing on was Ritu's face. Her books dropped from her hands to the floor where she stood a good distance from them but with nothing blocking her view of them.

Ritu, suddenly remembering herself, turned and ran straight into me.

"You almost ran me over! What's the matter? You look like you're going to be sick; you're as pale as a ghost!"

"Let's go right now. I'll drop you off. I must get home," Ritu stammered.

"But I thought we were going to get coffee."

"Well, I don't feel like it anymore. Let's go!" She grabbed my arm and turned me toward the exit, leading me out of the store.

"What has gotten into you, Ritu?" I hollered in the car.

She turned to me and snapped, "I can't talk to you right now."

After that, Ritu and I sat quietly as she drove me to the train station. What could've happened to Ritu in the few minutes that I left her alone? She didn't even buy any of the books we picked out.

Ritu stopped the car at the station. "Bye," was all she said.

"Bye," I repeated quietly.

Chapter 21

After she dropped me at the train station, Ritu could barely drive. She had to pull over for a few minutes. Her hands trembling on the steering wheel, she could not absorb the shock of what she had seen. It was like someone hit her with a bat. It made her want to vomit when she imagined what was going on between that Bindu-auntie and Dad. She was no child, and she knew why they were holding hands. What she wasn't sure about was why, why he was doing this to Mom. To Mom and to us, his children. How could he? She wondered how many times they had met in secret. She was crying uncontrollably now. This was the limit of unhappiness that she could shoulder. "Oh, God, how could you let this happen? That witch Bindu-auntie has been just waiting to trap Dad with her seduction when she knows that Mom is weak," she said aloud. But deep down she knew it wasn't all Bindu-auntie's fault; she knew that the fault, the weakness of character, the scarlet letter of sin, and the blame was her father's. She opened the door of the car and vomited on the side of the road. Her head spun as she shut the door and opened the window for some fresh air. *Thank God that Mira didn't see or suspect anything. I must protect my baby sister from the burden of such a truth. Mira is very sensitive, and this news would completely shatter her.*

Mom could not bear this right now. She was already having

a nervous breakdown over Jeet's death, and she was plagued by constant worry over Ritu's own failed marriage.

Dad was guilty, and now he knew that Ritu knew he was. How could he face her? How would she face him? Oh, this was terrible. What should she do? She couldn't tell anyone because that would jeopardize their family's name and reputation. Although she hated her father for doing this to them, to all of them, not just to Mom, she still could not bear society stamping a black mark of shame on his forehead. She decided: he was a sinner, and it would be best to leave the retribution to God. Only Waheguru could deliver true justice; it was too big a feat for her or Mom. She thought about what she learned about adultery and its punishment from their holy book, the Guru Granth Sahib. The Sikh religion, like other religions, claims that adultery is a sin of lust and deception. The American justice system does not punish adulterers with long jail sentences; in God's justice system, however, the adulterer is one of the greatest sinners, along with murderers and thieves. The adulterer is a liar, is selfish, and is unfaithful to the partner they promised fidelity to. An adulterer is also a betrayer of their children and family. The adulterer's shame is great; the punishment is severe and torturous.

A feeling of pity crept into Ritu's heart. Although she hated her father for his crimes, no matter what, he was Dad, and she still loved him, and it hurt her thinking of all the pain he would ultimately endure, after his death. Even if he wasn't a good husband to Mom, he had been a good father. But then the pain he gave Ritu today moved stealthily into her mind, and again anger bubbled inside of her. She turned on the engine and pressed the accelerator. He would have to face her now. She should not be afraid to face him—after all, she hadn't committed the sin.

• • •

Dad was sitting at the same café table in the bookstore with his face buried in his hands.

"Will you please say something? I've been sitting here for ten minutes. Can you tell me what is going on with you?" Bindu was losing her patience. "Look, if it's something I said, just forget it, and let's go. We were doing perfectly well, and let's not spoil our plans. Come on." She tugged on his arm.

"I'm sorry, but I have to go, and I cannot see you again."

"What?!" Bindu exclaimed.

"I know it's strange, but I just remembered something, and I have to go." With those words, Dad stood up and left a bewildered and offended Bindu alone.

As he walked to his car, Dad could see only his daughter's horrified face in his mind. She surely understood what he was doing there with Bindu, but he hadn't done anything. How would he face her? Any excuse he gave would appear as an obvious cover-up to Ritu. *Now what?* he thought as he revved the engine of his car and drove toward the house. Would she tell her mother? No, she wouldn't, because she was smart and mature enough to know that it would upset her mother too much. But he felt uncomfortable in his skin. The respect of his family was paramount, but now he had trampled it with his own two feet. All the love he showered on his children and all the years of hard work with them were now lost, in just a moment. He guessed this was the work of Waheguru. In one small corner of his mind, Dad was glad that God saved him from committing a great sin. But that thought vanished as he approached the house and saw Ritu's car in the driveway. He knew that he couldn't avoid her forever, but he wished he could.

• • •

Ritu arrived home dreading that her father would be there

waiting with some explanation. She didn't know if she was ready to talk about it. Life had deceived her, deceived all of them, in fact. Her father had deceived their mother, her brothers, and her little sister. The happy times of their childhood flashed before her eyes; it was all a lie. How could he risk hurting them so much? How could he take such a big chance? Things like this broke families apart. How could he take his family for granted over a fling? It was all too wrong.

She wiped away her tears so her mother wouldn't see as she brought Ritu some tea.

"I am not sure if I should tell you ..." Mom started. "But Manny called for you. He sounded very apologetic, though he blamed his mother for babying him, which made him this way... Terrible son... Anyway, he swore he was taking steps to get an apartment, so he could move out of his parents' house, and even spoke to a therapist about his anger issues, but I gave him a good piece of my mind." Ritu stayed silent. "I don't want you to go back to those people. You can't trust them. An apology over the phone is not enough. Once trust is lost, you cannot rebuild it so easily. You and Manny didn't have a relationship long enough to cultivate trust and a deep bond, like your father and I, who have been married for so many years. It will be easier for you to let go, I promise; it will take some time, but you will be happier without him."

Mom's words dug into Ritu's heart like a knife splitting it open. She could no longer hold her tears, and she went rushing to her room. On her bed, she lay crying. Poor Mom—such trust she had built with Dad had just disintegrated in one day by Bindu-auntie.

Ritu thought long and hard. *Men, you can't trust them. After all, if you can't trust your own father to do the right thing, to love and protect your mother and his children always, then you cannot trust any man.*

Life seemed more desolate than ever before. Should she go back to Manny? Manny could not be trusted, but then again, no man could be. There were some positives about him, and maybe over time, she could change the negatives. *What are the positives? He is fashionable and has good taste in clothes, restaurants, and…and…* She couldn't convince herself that he had anything valuable to offer her, yet the chances of finding someone else now that she had been married seemed bleak. Oh, she hated this feeling in her mind like it was stuck in mud. She couldn't move it, and there was no clarity in sight. Every direction she turned, there was something to lose. What should she do? She hated being confused, her mind feeling anxious and uncertain. She wished that God would give her a sign and tell her where she should turn. She wished that her kismet, her destiny, would just take her to where she had to go. Free will seemed a harder task than following a preset destiny. *Why did God give us free will? Why make a complicated life more difficult to endure?*

Ritu fell into a troubled sleep.

• • •

While Ritu slept, small buds of freer thinking began to blossom in Dad. Upset from his time in the bookstore, he went to his wife and told her how he felt. That he felt as torn up as she did. "It was me who told him to leave the house in the first place. If I could go back to that day, I would react differently. I would tell Jeet… I would tell him, 'Do not worry, son'…" Dad broke down, crying into the cup formed by his palms. "We were harsh. We needed to be more understanding, to listen to him. We were too hasty in judging him. It was not his fault."

Both Mom and Dad did not sleep well that night. Mom's

mind drew her again into old baby memories, the long nine months of keeping her son safe in her womb, the happiness of his birth, how he used to cry all night and anxiously gulp down his mother's milk, causing sweat to trickle from his round bald head down into his eyes. With the vision of her round, plump baby and her grief heaving in her chest, she could not help but soak her pillow with motherly tears.

Dad lay with his eyes wide open, blinded by the darkness in the room. His thoughts too were immersed in his son. He did not know his son, and it was his fault that he never got to know his son. He only expected him to be what he had wanted him to be, ignoring what he really was. Why did he not give his son a chance to flourish? He was a failure of a father, and he must be sure to never do this again to any of his other children. What about Ritu? Oh yes, maybe they had been too hard on her, but it was the right thing to do. It was not their fault that Ritu's husband turned out to be corrupt. She would have been happy if Manny were good to her. Dad turned over. Would she have, or would she only be happy with that Muslim boy, that boy from college? He felt responsible for Ritu's unhappiness. These questions disturbed and puzzled him. He was beginning to contemplate the soundness of his beliefs and rules that he had lived his life by and imposed on his children. Perhaps the new times required him to be more flexible with the children; after all, it was a completely different world they lived in than the world he grew up in. Nonetheless, all these new changes were difficult to swallow at once. Maybe with time and some effort he could change, well, just a little.

Chapter 22

The Ahujas contacted Mom and Dad to discuss Manny and Ritu's marriage. It had been two months since Ritu left Manny, and this was the first attempt his parents made to reach out. We were sure that they must be aware of Manny's attempts to reconcile on several occasions by calling and sending flowers and gifts.

"Did they not remember her months ago? Only now they've thought of her?" Mom complained to Dad.

"Now, how can I say that to them on the phone when they've tried to contact us to set things right?" said Dad. "They are coming tomorrow with Manny. We should discuss this with Ritu tonight when she comes home from work."

I had just come home again, it was another weekend, and to my horror, Ritu seemed to have decided to go back to Manny.

"How can you be making the same mistake again with the same guy? I guarantee you he hasn't changed," I warned. "After all, he didn't even try contacting you all these months, and now, just because it suits them to have you back, you're going to go back like their slave."

Ritu remained motionless, sitting on her bed, staring out the window.

"Would you stop making Ritu so emotional?" Mom interjected. "We've decided with Ritu that if they come back in good faith and acknowledge their mistakes, and we feel good about it and comfortable, then she will go back and give it another try; otherwise, she won't. Right, Ritu?"

Her body jolted at the sound of her name, and she looked at us in a sort of trance, saying, "Marriage is not a joke, you know.

How many times will I have to go through this? If I give him another chance, maybe it won't be so bad, I don't know what my other options are."

"See, your sister talks so sensibly."

"Besides, one man is not better or worse than the next: they're all the same. They cannot be trusted, none of them." I noticed Ritu glanced at Dad as she said her last sentence. Dad shifted in his seat, looking uncomfortable. No, more than that—he looked like he had done something ineligible for redemption. It looked as though her words stung and that all there was left to do was for him to stare at the carpet and study its fine, knitted pattern.

• • •

Ritu decided to return to Manny, against all our wishes. She did it to punish Dad, to make him feel guilty for hurting her and for betraying their family. Revenge had clutched her heart, and she couldn't shake it, even if it meant her own self-destruction.

Soon enough she realized what a big mistake she had made. Living with Manny was like sharing a bed with someone you could not stand the sight of. A man she no longer respected. She could not even try to stir feelings for him because she never had feelings for him. There was nothing between them. Their conversations were limited to the mundane, and they had nothing in common. She only wanted to run away. Or, better yet, that she could be a bird and fly away. She was engulfed by resentment toward Manny, his parents, and Dad. The feeling was stifling her, and she yearned to breathe freely. Every night she dreamed of the sweetness of escape and how she would conjure a plan of leaving Manny, her parents, her entire existence, and starting life fresh, going to a faraway place where no one knew her.

Manny had not recently physically abused her, and his parents had backed off somewhat since Ritu and Manny moved into their own apartment. But still, it wasn't the life that Ritu hoped for in her youth. His anger was temporarily appeased and all he really expected from her was to do his laundry, cook his food, and occasionally satisfy his desire. Most of the time, she was thankful he spent time outside the house, making excuses for work, but she knew he was involved with someone else when he didn't come home at night. This time, there was no solace for her in her maayka either. The sight of her father made her uncomfortable, and the grief of her mother made her feel helpless. Finally, against Manny's protests, Ritu secured a job with a small interior design store in their Boston neighborhood.

• • •

Nellie's Interiors was a small upscale shop about five blocks from their apartment complex. Its shop window was decorated with modern furniture, elegant upholstery, and expensive accessories like chandeliers and velvet cushions with studded stones. The owner, Nellie herself, was an interior designer who worked around the area designing people's homes and offices. Her little shop was where she attracted new clientele and kept a small stock of samples. Nellie was looking to hire someone reasonably cheap, presentable looking, young, well-spoken, and with a bit of design experience or at least interest in design. When Ritu saw the hiring sign outside the store, she immediately applied. Ritu had always had an interest in clothes and interior design, and she had some management experience, and it was clear to Nellie that she could handle the job.

Nellie taught Ritu well, and Ritu became well versed with different types of lighting and window dressings as well as names of local furniture designers, carpenters, and painters they suggested to their customers. The job was five to six hours a day, and it helped keep her mind off her dreary life at home. When she was at the store helping prospective clients, her face lit up the way it used to before the days of Manny and marriage. She was confident and enthusiastic and smiled ear to ear when the memory of her unhappiness was momentarily forgotten.

A month into her work at Nellie's, a tall young man with an impassive face walked into the store with an attractive woman inquiring about redesigning their living room as well as a few other rooms in their house. Ritu caught the man, who was named Michael, staring at her every time she looked up. His eyes were an intense ocean blue that loomed large in his chiseled, suntanned face. He had long, dirty-blond hair that slightly flared at his collar. Michael had an extraordinary physique. His tightly fitted T-shirt revealed his perfectly sculpted biceps and a strong, broad chest and back. His well-defined muscles flexed with his every move. Ritu had to steal her gaze away from this God-like figure as he was distracting her from focusing on what his wife was saying.

His wife, Samantha, had auburn hair that fell in loose curls around her shoulders and bright eyes that shone like green apples. She was a well-groomed woman wearing designer clothes from her top to her shoes. She wasn't as gorgeous as her husband, but she had style and spunk.

"Now, Ree-tu…I hope I said your name correctly."

"Yes, that's fine," Ritu replied.

"We would need to order drapes, rugs, upholstery, tables, and of course, lighting for this room. I'm thinking more transitional rather than traditional or modern."

"I think you have wonderful ideas. I can book an appointment for you in which Nellie will come to your home, assess the space of your living room in conjunction with the rest of your home, and then draw up some plans." Ritu was interrupted briefly by Michael.

"I'm sorry, but can you also tell us how much she charges for this visit."

"Yes, of course." A slight flush on her face from contact with those deep-blue eyes. "It's $1,000 for the initial consultation, including the plans that she makes and the samples. Once you place orders with us, that fee will be included in the 15 percent commission that she takes on every order. A budget of anywhere from $12,000 to $30,000 or beyond is agreed to in a signed contract once your consultation is complete. You can always speak to Nellie herself further about any specific questions you may have on the pricing."

"Well, thank you, Ree-tu, you've been most diligent." Michael's smile and the way he said Ritu's name made her blush.

"I just need to take down some of your information, if that's OK?" Ritu was inputting the Kojacks' information into the computer system, but her mind was preoccupied with the intensely delicious man sitting on the other side of the desk. After the couple left, Ritu let out a deep breath of relief and shook her head with disbelief. She had not allowed her mind to drift to even her memories of Amir since she had married Manny—what had made her so drawn to this man? She was amazed and surprised at her lustful feelings. She felt guilty, less because of her marriage to Manny and more because he was a married man. *I could never deceive anyone,* she thought. She felt irritated over how ridiculous her fantasies were getting. After all, not only was Michael married but he did not consider her to be anything or anyone important—just a girl who worked at the design store. That was all and nothing more.

But that night as she lay in bed with Manny, who was fast asleep and snoring as usual, she let her mind, just for a little while, drift into a dreamland where Michael thought Ritu to be beautiful, and he wanted her, and he cared for her, and they shared their passion and love. She was free from all that kept her trapped. She was free to be with Michael in her dreams, if in no place else.

• • •

Nellie was happy that Ritu met with a prospective client and handled her duties well.

"Ree-tu, I want you to accompany me to the Kojacks' home so that we can do some measuring and get a feel for the space. I think it would benefit you to learn from step one how to enlist a new client and then design their home. Besides, I'm going to be traveling a lot for design and home shows, looking for new ideas and trends, and you may have to handle their business mostly on your own. Most of my other clients are at the tail end of their projects, so I'm not too worried about those. So, what do you think? Are you ready?"

Ritu was shocked. An opportunity to design a home with a client and not just hang out at the shop. She couldn't hold in her excitement. "Oh yes, I would love that, Nellie!" Her eyes glistened with hope and new adventure. "Thank you so much for this opportunity."

"Wow, I guess you are happy! I've never seen your smile so wide before," Nellie exclaimed with surprise. "But understand that when you have questions, always call me; don't chance anything. You never want to offend a client. Sometimes they think that your suggestions are not what they want, and that's fine. You and I both know some people don't have the taste for what we might like, but it's all about keeping the client happy, not yourself happy. Do you understand?"

"Yes, of course, I would never impose my designs on someone

else. I would make suggestions and try to gauge what they like." Ritu nodded with serious confirmation that she understood Nellie.

• • •

Two days later, Ritu and Nellie arrived at the Kojacks' mansion. It was set on what looked like about two acres of rolling hills, and at the top of the hill was a very sophisticated brick home that was, like its owners, tidy and cold. The manicured lawn and bushes revealed that the Kojacks also kept their home as well-groomed as they did themselves, but something was missing.

"A lovely home, isn't it?" Nellie peered at Ritu from the corners of her eyes.

"Yes, a fine home," whispered Ritu. She couldn't put her finger on what was bothering her.

They rang the doorbell, and Michael Kojack opened the door. Ritu's heart jumped at the sight of him. *Oh no*, she thought, *this man will be the end of me.*

"Please come in, and nice to see you again, Ree-tu," said Michael with a glint in his eyes when he looked at her. Michael was dressed in fitted jeans with a salmon button-down shirt; a couple of buttons were left open at his neck. He looked fashionable yet relaxed at the same time. *This man could take any woman's breath away*, thought Ritu as she walked in through the doorway in a shy manner.

"Welcome, ladies," roared Samantha from the far end of the grand foyer. She was walking briskly toward them in high heels and a pencil skirt. Her red hair looked a deeper shade today, in harmony with her red lips. Samantha was not relaxed; she was always prim and proper, thought Ritu as she shook Samantha's hand and commented on the beauty of her home.

"Ree-tu and I would love a tour of the house before we begin if you please, so that we can get an idea of the sense of space and feeling in the rest of the home, which will stay intact during the redesigning of your main rooms."

"Of course. Michael, why don't you show the house to Nellie and Ree-tu, while I get them a drink."

"Of course, my pleasure."

"Just water for us, please, Samantha, thank you," Nellie quickly added.

As Michael showed them around the downstairs, dining, living, formal living, library, maid's room, laundry area, magnificently large kitchen, and backyard patio, Ritu noticed how much pain had been taken to perfect each feature in the house, and it looked as if no expense had been spared. The moldings were adorned with different designs, and the solid walnut floors had slats five inches wide, while in the dining and formal living area, there were parquet floors. The doors were also solid walnut, painted white with embellished silver handles. The powder room and the kitchen were bathed in marble and glass. As Ritu was walking a step behind Nellie trying to take in the magnificence of the Kojacks' home, Michael walked by her side, stealing a few quick looks at Ritu.

"I have to say, Michael, that every feature in your home is of top-quality material, and the finishes are top-notch."

"Well, thank you." Michael politely nodded. "Would you like to see the upstairs now?"

"Yes, of course, please lead the way."

"Please, ladies first."

Ritu felt a warm, nervous sensation in her chest as if she could sense that Michael's eyes were on her. Once upstairs, Michael told them to roam freely as he waited in the upstairs foyer. Except for the primary bedroom, which was equipped with a large bed, a flat-screen television, and a dresser, the other rooms were empty. They lived in this five-bedroom, five-and-a-half-bathroom house by themselves. No children. It was odd, mused Ritu, thinking of how her family of six had managed so well with only three bedrooms and two bathrooms all these years.

Her thoughts were interrupted by Michael's sudden appearance as she stood in one of the smaller bedrooms at the backside of the house.

"Hello there..." There was that glint in the eyes again, and Ritu swore his teeth shone a perfect pearl white. "Did I startle you?"

"Oh, it's OK. I was just thinking this room is much smaller than the other bedrooms and about its possible use. Maybe in the future, it could be a good baby's room or a study... "Well, on second thought, it's a bit far from the master suite," and before she could babble further about the room, Michael cut her off.

"We're not going to be having any babies. Samantha doesn't want children."

"Oh." Ritu didn't know what to say but knowing intimate information about them felt somehow wrong. "I'm sorry. I shouldn't have assumed anything. I was just thinking out loud."

Michael walked closer to her. "It's not your fault. Most women think, when they see such a big house, that it will have a family in it."

Gazing into Michael's eyes made Ritu feel that it wasn't Michael who wanted to live in this mansion but Samantha, and Michael could feel what was missing from it, just the way Ritu did when she first arrived: no love and no warmth, no children.

"Oh, Ree-tu! You're in here!" Nellie's screech interrupted Ritu and Michael. "Michael, your home is immaculate. It just needs to be filled, and that's where we come in." She laughed and gave Ritu a poke with her elbow.

Ritu smiled meekly at her and Michael. The Kojacks' home needed filling, but it wasn't empty just of furniture. It had a void in it, same as the void that Ritu felt inside herself every day.

Samantha brought them water and snacks. Nellie measured areas around the dining, living and formal areas, as well as the main suite and one of the large bedrooms upstairs that was meant to become a guest suite. Samantha talked endlessly about what she envisioned for her home, her favorite colors and fabrics, and designers she would like to see. Michael stayed quiet most of the time Samantha talked, and nobody really asked him for his input. Nellie looked up at him from time to time and smiled. Ritu stood listening and taking notes for Nellie. After all, it was her job to make the clients happy and give them what they wanted. In this case, her job would be to fill Samantha's home with couture designs and furniture, not to fill the void in Michael's heart.

• • •

The initial visit went well. Nellie made some sketches back at the design store, while Ritu typed up her notes and started to research different rug designers, curtain fabrics, upholstery, and tables and chairs. The Kojack home was now Ritu's first and biggest project, and she was determined to plunge her heart and soul into it. Endless appointments with her clients filled her days. Her lonely nights were filled with thoughts of Michael. His gentleness toward Samantha's finicky manner; the way his smile lit up Ritu's life. Maybe she was losing her mind, getting lost in someone she barely knew, not to mention a married man. Manny didn't express any of the gentleness that Michael had. When he did try to be close to her, Ritu felt repelled by his touch; it seemed that Manny's object of desire was himself and not her.

Night after night she longed for Michael's presence, his attention, to be desired and to be wanted by him. She dreamed that they had been stranded on a desert island together and had to battle the elements in order to survive. In her fantasy, they would give themselves up to their burning desire for each other and be happy and alone in their world where there was no Manny and no Samantha and no society to judge them. Michael's little smile and few conversations with her filled her gaping heart, only to have his absences disappoint and bring down her day. Were her insecurities masked by her anticipation for Michael's love? Was it his love that she wanted or merely to know that someone like him desired and loved her? She presently didn't know the difference.

All she knew was that her infatuation with Michael was increasing by the day. Her fantasies of Michael spread from nighttime dreaming to daytime thoughts. Every day she hoped that Michael would accompany Samantha to their appointment or just stop by the store to pick up samples. Sometimes a week went by without her seeing him, and then one day he unexpectedly dropped in the store, and she cursed herself for not wearing her most flattering outfit or for not wearing her hair extra special that day. She dreamed of bumping into him in town and having conversations. She tried to identify the silver Audi that Michael drove every time she was on the road, and she held her breath until she could see through the window that the driver wasn't Michael. Her obsession with him was spiraling out of her control. She couldn't eat because thoughts of him gave her butterflies. A strong feeling of anxiety mixed with excitement filled her instead of food, and the reality of the mess she was walking into made her stomach weak. She lost weight as well as sleep. When she woke, her first thought was of Michael; as she showered, ate, worked, and drove, he was always on her mind.

Sometimes she had to consciously try to snap herself out of it and face the reality that what she imagined would never happen. Besides, no matter what her heart longed for, the truth was that it was wrong. They were both married. She was afraid of failing this test God had given her, the same way her father had. He risked everything that was real and good in his life just to fulfill his burning passion. She did not have all that much to lose, but she feared God's wrath.

Her thoughts often drifted to her father. Perhaps she was hasty to judge her own father. She now knew why temptation's ugly head emerged in marriages. People were not all sinners or all saints; they were complicated. She did not know of the intimacies, and the pitfalls, of her own parents' married life. All she knew was herself, that she was an unhappily married woman whose mind and body yearned for escape. This man Michael was her chance for escape. Maybe Dad had reasons. Reasons that she was now beginning to understand. She felt compassion in her heart for Dad and understood that whatever drove him to Bindu-auntie was related to the need for escape, the desire to be needed, to be wanted, and to belong. But why wouldn't he feel that from Mom? She didn't want to think about Mom and Dad and their problems—it was too painful to bear; it was much easier to delve into the thoughts of Michael, where she felt good about herself, even if it was just in her mind.

Yet Ritu's feelings for Michael were not rooted solely in her mind. There was some encouragement from Michael's side that kept stringing her along. During their brief encounters, he stared into her face until Ritu broke into a smile, and he then returned her smile with a sheepish grin. There were those precious times when both Michael and Ritu spoke about general things while being totally engaged with one another. Her ego was fed by his unexpected attention. Ritu hadn't imagined it all. There was something about Ritu that pulled Michael toward her. Yet it seemed to her that he also had an internal struggle regarding her. Sometimes he would ignore her completely and act as if Ritu meant nothing, someone who never crossed his mind. Michael's unpredictable behavior made Ritu feel always on edge and in anxious anticipation of his approval of her.

Occasionally, she sensed that Michael was coming to see her. How was that possible? If she had no connection to this man, then how could she know intuitively about their meeting? Unlike her distance from Manny, somehow, she felt strangely attuned to Michael. But what she didn't know was if Michael felt anything for her in return. The suspense around how he felt was ruining her life; she felt helpless. If she could know for sure that Michael absolutely did not care for her, then she could turn away with her tail between her legs, but as long as he kept surprising her with renewed interest, she could not let him go.

Chapter 23

When her alarm clock rang, Ritu was still tired because of all her dreams. Now she hurriedly showered and slipped on a black shirtdress with a silver-buckled belt tight around her waist. She stuck a hairpin in one side of her locks and let the other side hang loose. She dabbed a bit of concealer under her eyes to mask the dark shadows of the previous night and added a hint of black eyeliner and mascara just on the top lids, some highlighter on her cheeks for that glow, and some plum-colored lipstick as a finishing touch. Ritu examined her face in the mirror. She looked young and fashionable enough, but her face was lacking something—oh yes, a smile.

She had been taught better than this. That was true.

• • •

How did everything happen so fast? One minute Ritu didn't know what Michael was thinking, and the next he had declared his undying affection for her. It happened at the shop when Michael came to collect some samples for the bedrooms upstairs. Their conversation felt a little uncomfortable, but their eyes had a deep, fiery glow in them. They were speaking their feelings with their eyes and only rambling about nothing with their tongues.

When Michael walked through the door, Ritu held her

breath briefly and smiled cheek to cheek over this pleasant surprise. Michael returned her smile with an equally delicious grin.

"I came to pick up some samples for the curtains in the guest bedroom and any other magazine clippings of furniture you may have selected for the room," he said.

His eyes pierced directly into Ritu's, and more than his words, it was his sultry gaze that caught Ritu's heart. "Um, sorry, yes, I have those for you on the desk, and I actually want to send another fabric sample, but it's on top of that shelf. Just give me a moment while I use the step stool and bring it down for you," said Ritu nervously. For some reason, the air about Michael was different tonight, and it made Ritu nervous. As she was sweeping her hand through the booklets of samples, she could sense Michael had come to her side, and as she nervously stepped backward to come down, she lost her balance and fell right into his arms. The most cliché scenario of two lovers meeting, but at that moment, it was completely unexpected by both of them. Michael held Ritu in his arms, her face so close to his. She could smell the musky scent of his cologne, and it made her feel weak. He didn't hesitate another moment and kissed her full on the lips. To Ritu's surprise, she eagerly returned the kiss. Eventually, Ritu opened her eyes to see Michael smiling down at her. She flinched and pushed herself from his arms.

"I'm so sorry. I don't know what got into me."

"What got into you, Ree-tu, is the same thing that got into me."

"I don't understand, Michael. I thought you were not interested in me."

"Not interested!" He grinned with astonishment. "I've been addicted to you since the first day I saw you. Do you think I would ever be interested in Samantha's house designs? God, no!

I only would come along so I could see you!"

Ritu could not find any words; her tongue had betrayed her.

"I know what you're thinking. I'm married, and what about Samantha? Ree-tu, we are not happy. She doesn't even care about me; all she cares about is her house and her clothes, and she doesn't even want to have a family. I feel so alone, and I find in you someone that I could have a meaningful relationship with." Michael's words were like echoes of her own emotions. She had just been kissed by the man of her dreams, and he had just confessed how much he wanted her and cared for her. She was ecstatic but frozen at the same time. "Please say something, so I know you feel the same about me," Michael begged. All she could manage to do was to take his hands in hers and wrap them around her waist and lean into him, letting him hold her. "Oh, Ree-tu, I'm so happy you feel the same way. Sometimes I wasn't sure if you did, but this strange voice in my head told me you understood me, and you would feel the same. I can't tell you how happy I am." Ritu's eyes welled with tears. She felt desire again, after what felt like an eternity since Amir.

• • •

Since that day at the store, Michael and Ritu met secretly in small restaurants tucked away in parts of the city that Michael knew Samantha would never visit. They talked about their childhoods, their first loves, and the loneliness they both felt in their current marriages. Ritu even told Michael about Jeet's death and the trauma experienced by her family. Michael held her in his arms and kissed her passionately, and easily her worries slipped away. They took long walks in the park in the neighboring town and went for long drives in his Audi.

Life was perfect, more perfect than Ritu could've imagined. So, when Michael wanted more, she gave him more. Her passion for him had made it so she could no longer discern between what was right and what was wrong. Spending afternoons in a bed-and-breakfast with Michael on their days off, while lying to Manny that she was at work, had become a habit. Lying no longer impeded her growing intimacy with Michael. All she longed for were the smells of his cologne mixed with his sweat. She relished the sensation of his soft skin that rippled when his abundant muscles involuntarily contracted beneath her hands. His blond hair glistened in the light that shone through the window, and she ran her fingers through its silkiness. Her eyes drowned in the bright blue of his eyes, which caressed her soul like the sea. Her mouth melted into his, tasting his sweetness. She became his after her desire for him surmounted to a point of no return, then released to her greatest satisfaction.

As they lay with their legs intertwined under the cotton sheets, staring into each other's eyes, Michael made his proposal.

"Ree-tu, you know I love you, and I'm the happiest when I'm with you."

"Yes, I know." Ritu giggled with utmost contentment. "So, why do you look so serious?"

"I've decided that my life has completely changed since we've been together for the last couple of months, and I want you to divorce Manny. I can't deal with the thought that you must sleep in the same bed as another man."

"What?" All of a sudden, hope flashed in Ritu—maybe Michael wanted to marry her. Could it be?

"And Ree-tu, I want to buy a nice apartment for you downtown so that we don't have to sneak around in public and worry about Manny finding you. I want you to be relaxed and uninhibited."

"What are you saying?" The happiness in Ritu's voice was

clear.

"I'm saying, will you stay with me?"

"Yes, of course!" Ritu jumped up to hug him. "What about poor Samantha?" Ritu sobered. "Will she get over the divorce?"

"Divorce Samantha? That's not what I'm proposing."

From its highest height, Ritu's heart took a plunge. "What do you mean, then? How would you stay with me and not divorce Samantha?" She could barely speak the words.

"Darling, I mean, Samantha's father is a business partner of mine. If I divorced her, I would lose everything I have, and everything I could give you and us. C'mon, don't look at me like that, Ree-tu, please."

She got up abruptly from the bed, the sheets wrapped around her naked body, which suddenly felt cold and used.

"Please, you don't understand!" Standing naked in all his beauty, Michael stopped her, grasping her arm gently but firmly, and promised that he would do his best to leave Samantha, but it would take time to persuade her to put some real estate in his name and not their joint name. Ritu would have to trust him and give him some time. "I assure you, it's not what you think. I will leave Samantha if that's what you need from me. Ree-tu, please say something."

The tears rolled down Ritu's cheeks. "I'll think about your proposal to leave Manny as long as you promise to leave Samantha."

"Oh, darling," he breathed while taking her in his embrace, "I knew you would come around; you always do. I love you so much."

A small voice told Ritu that Michael wasn't who she wanted him to be. But she couldn't listen to that nagging voice when Michael was holding her and promising her that he needed time to leave Samantha. She had to believe that he loved her and all he needed was some time.

But as soon as she was away from him, the buds of doubt and reality began to bloom in her mind. She was a grown-up, and this was not a fairy tale. "How foolish was I; like a little girl in love, I thought he would do anything for us, for me," she mused aloud to herself on her drive home.

In the grown-up world, people lived double lives because they did not like their realities; they lived half in a secret fiction of their own creation. They lived their lives by lies not just to others but to themselves. In the grown-up world that Ritu now realized she was a reluctant part of, there were no happy endings. Either she had to have the courage to live a life being true to herself or she could be a coward in a life of lies. She was no coward; her sweet time with Michael had come to an end.

She also was no coward when it came to her dad. There in the car, she began rehearsing what she would say to him when she saw him next: "If you did what I think, then I forgive you. If you didn't, it doesn't matter. Because it's your problem, not mine. It took me months of living in hell with Manny and wasting my life with him to figure it out. But I've concluded that I'm not going to suffer for your sins. Whether or not you did anything sinful, it's not my life's purpose to care so much as to carry your burden. I may have made my own mistakes, which I will be accountable for, but I'm done feeling guilty for yours. I will stay in Boston, as I love my new job and my independent life, but I want to talk with you, Dad, and I miss Mom and want to go home and visit."

Chapter 24

I gazed at the dark sky through the narrow window of my dorm room.

"If you stick your neck out any farther, Mira, you'll fall out, and besides, the whole room is freezing with the window open," teased Katy.

"I am just lost in thought as usual." I smiled while pulling myself back inside the room.

"What's bugging you this time?"

"I still don't understand why Ritu went back to Manny. She made up her mind to leave him but then suddenly changed and even went against my parents. It's just weird. I know I'm missing something."

"Listen, you did say that Ritu has a job now and she sounds happier on the phone. Maybe this turned out to be a good thing."

"Maybe," I echoed, unconvinced. "Maybe I should visit her. What do you think, during the spring break?"

"Yeah, that sounds like a great idea!"

"Yes, that's what I think we both need—she will need some sisterly company, and I need to get out of New York and clear my head!"

"Sounds like a good plan! Let's eat, or are you having dinner with Dev again tonight?"

"I'm sorry, but I am supposed to meet Dev. Please forgive me," I said with a sad face.

"Sure, sure, just don't come crying to me if he breaks your heart again because I don't know if I'll take you back," Katy said with a smile. We hugged. "Catch you later, Mir," and just like that, my dear friend was out the door. I quickly brushed my hair and dabbed my lip gloss and put a little blush on my cheeks that seemed to have paled with the wintry air. I threw on my coat and gloves and went on my way to meet Dev at his apartment.

• • •

"What do you mean you want to go to Boston over the break?" Dev sounded less than thrilled when I told him my idea.

"Why? What's the matter? I just want to visit my sister, it's been over a month since she moved, and I haven't seen her," I said.

"What about me? What would I do without you for so long? No, you can't go! I'll miss you too much!"

"Dev!" I laughed. "You are so cute!" And I planted a kiss on his cheek and embraced him, snuggling into his chest.

"I'm serious! I don't want you to go without me—I'm coming with you."

"What? You can't. I'm going to stay with my sister. Where will you stay? And besides, she knows nothing about you, and I can't tell my family about you..." Before I could stop my words, they were already out of my mouth, and Dev was peering down at me, pushing me out of his arms.

"Right, so I see how this is. Are you intending to never tell your family about me?" His tone was dead serious, and I couldn't hide the uneasiness on my face. "Oh my God, I can't believe that I've been played by you!" His volume got louder. "Wow! An innocent girl like you, Mira Singh, is enjoying her love affair, but her boyfriend is never going to exist in her future!" He was standing now.

"No, you don't understand—it's not like that," I begged.

"No? Then tell me when you are planning on telling your parents about me, or at least your sister. She surely is not as judgmental as your parents since she too had a non- Sikh boyfriend in the past!"

I had never seen Dev angry. This was a person I had not met before. I had heard from Narinder that when we had broken up temporarily in the past, Dev had had a bad temper, especially if anyone had brought up the fact that he may have been wrong or pushed me too fast. Dev always had kept that side of his personality hidden from me. He was probably always careful around me so that I wouldn't run away from him, which was always my initial instinct. This time, he wanted to make sure that I had real intentions of staying together.

"You're afraid because your parents will never accept a Hindu guy. Narinder warned me, but I wouldn't listen."

"You're blowing this out of proportion! Calm down!"

"Ok, I'll calm down," bringing his voice down a notch. "So, when are you going to tell your parents about me? I've told mine about you, and they want to meet you. And they know I'm serious about you because while I've always mentioned girls, I've also always told them it's nothing serious. But I told them this time that you're someone special. I was about to tell you that they are planning to come to town to visit me in a few months and want to meet you as well. So, Mira, I, Dev Bala, have made a commitment to you, and now I'm waiting to hear your commitment to me."

My mouth and body could not move. My mind was still. What could I do? My parents would never accept Dev, and perhaps not even my sister and brother would. This would be the worst time in the world to introduce him to them, especially with all the drama going on at home.

"I don't hear anything, Mira."

"I…I…Dev…You…" I stumbled and stuttered but could not bring myself to say that, yes, I would tell my parents about Dev. I knew deep in my heart that Dev was a beautiful dream that I would be forcefully awoken from if my parents ever knew about our relationship.

"Mira, answer me!" he screamed, losing all calm.

"I can't! I can't tell them about you! I can't risk being suddenly married off to some stranger only to be miserable like my sister!" I yelled back with a rush of tears.

I turned to leave when Dev grabbed me by the shoulders. "You can't do this. This is not a game. This stopped being a casual thing when I came back for you, and you took me back. You had that chance after the hotel incident to throw me out of your life because deep down you always knew that your parents would object to me. But you didn't! You accepted my apologies and took my tears and kissed them. Why? I want to know why! So now that I'm in love with you and want to marry you, you're going to cast me away!"

"You're hurting me, Dev; please let go."

His eyes were dark and angry, and his grip was now digging painfully against my bones. "I want to hurt you"—his voice was almost a low growl now— "the way you're hurting me." He suddenly let go of my shoulders and picked up his desk chair and then slammed it hard, back onto the floor. "Just leave now before I do something I might regret!" he shouted.

I picked up my purse and fled his apartment. When I got safely to the street, more tears burst from my eyes. He was right. I had no right to play with his emotions. I had known all along that my parents would never accept him, a Hindu boy, never. My sister could not marry a Muslim, and I would have to marry a Sikh, otherwise another tragedy would befall on my family, and I couldn't bear to see them in any more pain. But what could I do? How could I leave Dev? His words came back to me like a wave of bittersweet emotion… How amazing—Dev loved me, and he wanted to marry me?! I was baffled by his sudden declaration of marriage, but it was a proposal that I could never accept. I loved him, and I couldn't hurt him. I needed to get back to Katy and talk.

Chapter 25

Halfway across the world, in India, Dev's mother was happily surprised to hear from her handsome son when he called out of the blue that morning.

"Hi, Mum, how are you?"

"I'm fine, beta, and you, are you studying at all or just chasing after pretty girls?"

"Oh, I've been studying more than ever before."

"I'm shocked! And what has brought this change in you, my son?"

"Actually"—Dev's mother could hear the grin take over her son's face— "there's this one girl who has become very special to me in a very short period of time."

"*One* girl?" Really? What's her name?"

"Her name is Mira Singh, and she's a year younger than me at the same college."

Mrs. Bala was silent for a short moment and then resumed, "Well, I'm glad whoever this girl is, she is having a positive effect on you. I hope that we can meet her when we come. Your papa and I were thinking of leaving India in a month for business, but we want to see you as well."

"Oh, that's great! I want you to meet her! All right, Mum, I'm running to class, so I'll have to talk to you later."

"OK, sure, beta, you go. Love you."

"Same here."

Mrs. Bala hung up the phone, her expression dark. She had a growing feeling that this girl, the first her son sounded ecstatic over in all his experiences with the opposite sex, would be an obstacle in her plans for him. After all, she was not Hindu but a Sikh, if Mrs. Bala correctly judged the last name. And Mrs. Bala only had one son and had been used to having him to herself for his whole life. Yes, of course girls came into her son's life and girls went, but none of them stuck, and she was happy about that. After all, when it was time for her son to marry, Mrs. Bala had her own acceptable choices for him, of who and what his wife should be.

Mrs. Bala picked up her phone again with her bony fingers heavily studded with solitaire diamond rings to call her assistant, Ramesh. She asked him to come immediately to her side. Ramesh dropped his spoon on his plate on the kitchen table and hurried from his meager three-room apartment, as he did not want to keep his impatient and demanding boss waiting.

"Ramesh, you did not finish your dinner!" called his wife from the kitchen where she was cooking roti for their two children sitting at the table. "That crazy woman—she can never leave you alone. Doesn't she know the workday is over and you are home with your family trying to eat dinner!"

It didn't matter if Mrs. Bala called him at eight o'clock at night or at two in the morning. He was hazar, or attentive and present, at any moment she needed him. After all, his bread-and-butter was the Bala family, and without them, he would have no roof over his head and no food for his family, and no private school education for his two young girls. Ramesh had been a loyal servant to the Bala family for twenty years. He had seen Dev grow from a baby into a young man and seen the Bala empire skyrocket. He knew that although Mrs. Bala was a shrewd and tough woman, she always rewarded loyalty.

• • •

"Good evening, madam," Ramesh huffed as he came running into the twenty-thousand-square-foot mansion that boasted the Bala name on the security gate at the front entrance staffed by three armed guards.

"Oh, good, Ramesh, you're here. I was starting to get impatient."

"How can I assist you, madam?"

"Come into my private office."

"And Mr. Bala, madam?" Ramesh looked around the house questioningly.

"He's busy having dinner with some business clients in Delhi. Besides, this does not concern Mr. Bala." As she sat on her chair in her office, she summoned Ramesh with a tilt of her head to close the door behind him. Ramesh nervously sat down; after all, Mrs. Bala usually kept Mr. Bala in the loop of all her dealings. "I've not called you here to plan an event, organize a charity dinner, or deal with bank managers, etc.—none of that daily nonsense. I've called you here, Ramesh, because I want you to do a favor for me regarding Dev, and I don't want you to mention anything to Mr. Bala about it. I know he won't approve, and I honestly don't want to waste my time and energy trying to persuade him, because Dev is my son, and I control what I allow him to do or not do, whether he or Mr. Bala realize it or not. Do I make myself clear?"

Her voice was so stern that Ramesh almost quivered in his chair, and he knew that whatever no-good deed she was up to this time, he could never risk telling a soul and he would have to obey without question.

"You understand that if you are disloyal to me, you will not only lose this job and everything you have but so will your family."

"Of course, I am forever loyal to you, madam," he said with confidence and a bend and a shake of his head to express his confirmation of her intentions.

"Good. Now let me tell you step by step what you need to do and how this is all going to play out…"

Chapter 26

"Katy, Katy!" I called out for my roommate, but I found myself alone in my dorm room. She had gone to dinner already since she thought I was having dinner with Dev tonight. "Damn," I whispered. I desperately needed Katy to talk to and to cry on her shoulder.

I couldn't just sit here and wait. I had to do something. I picked up the phone and called Ritu as I dried my tears and wiped my nose with the back of my hand.

"Hello."

The familiar voice of family stirred my emotions so that the tears began to flow again. "Ritu," I said in a small voice.

"Hi, Mira, what's the matter?"

"Oh, I'm OK, I just have a little stuffy nose and congestion. I was calling because I wanted to ask you if I could come visit this spring break in a couple of weeks?"

"Ah, yeah, sure that sounds like a great idea." Ritu didn't sound thrilled.

"Is it really OK with you?"

"Of course, I'm happy you are coming; sorry, I was just busy at work. Great, so when do you get here?"

"This week I have a full week of school, and next week I'm off. I'll double-check with Mom, and I'm sure she'll say it will be fine."

"OK, so, let me know when you know your train."

I barely got off the phone in time to get to the bathroom and threw up. Katy found me hugging the toilet, where I was now heaving up nothing, and took me to the student medical center.

• • •

A week passed, and I heard nothing from Dev. I left him messages and emails and even went over to his place to try to talk to him, but no word from him. It was so strange; not even Narinder could get a hold of him, and he had not seen him in class either.

"I just don't get it, Katy—where did he go?"

"I don't know. I'm sure he just needs some space and time to process your breakup."

"We didn't break up," I rushed to correct Katy.

"Yes, you did, whether you like to admit it or not. Telling your boyfriend that you can't ever introduce him to your family because you really will end up nowhere in the future especially after he's told his parents about you and wants you to meet them is breaking up."

"I guess it was the right thing to do, but I didn't want to do it."

"I know, sweetie, but it was either that or you have to step up to face your parents and tell them how you feel about him."

In bed that night, I lay awake thinking about what Katy said. Would I ever have the courage to tell them about Dev? Our school break was next week, and hopefully it would give Dev enough time to calm down and want to talk about his feelings. Perhaps this trip to Boston would give me a fresh perspective, and maybe when we both got back to school, Dev and I could figure out a way to be together.

• • •

Boston was indeed refreshing! It was quaint and historical and had a unique vibe compared to New York. It also felt colder somehow. Ritu had taken a week off work to show me around the city. We spent the days sightseeing and the evenings having dinner with Manny in well-known local spots. The days were fun and full of sisterly chatter about Ritu's work and my life in the city. Unfortunately, dinners by contrast were gloomy and uncomfortably quiet with Manny's unwanted presence. Luckily for us, Manny opted out of dinner on the last night, saying that he was not feeling too well and didn't want to spoil our fun. We expressed our concern and asked him if he needed us to pick up anything from the pharmacy, and then we were on our way to finally having dinner in peace. Ritu took me to a nice Italian restaurant near her office. She said that they had the best brick-oven pizza. My mouth was watering just thinking about it, and after we had ordered our main meal and were sitting with our sodas, the topic that had been on my mind the entire week began to roll off my tongue.

"So, I have something to tell you, and I don't want you to judge me or get upset."

"Wow, we've been together a week, and now you have something so important to tell me? What is it?"

"Well, I met someone."

"Oh."

"Your reply is so quiet, Ritu, like you already know what I'm about to tell you."

"I can guess. He's in your college, you both are in love, and he's not Sikh." Ritu's experience had taught her well.

"Yes, you're right," I said with a sullen face.

"So, who is he?"

"His name is Dev Bala. He's Hindu, and he is studying in the business school, but his family is in India."

"Bala sounds interesting. What do his parents do?"

"I've never really asked him, come to think of it, but I think I heard Narinder, our mutual friend, say that his parents are huge deals in India, like, a big family business. I don't know. You know me—I don't pay attention to these things."

"It's not the same as Bala Industries, the super-rich empire family, is it?" Ritu inquired with wide, bright eyes.

For a moment, the thought of Dev being "super-rich" was amusing. He was just Dev, my Dev. "I don't think so," I said with serious doubt in my mind.

"You never thought of looking up this guy and his family name before?"

"What?! Why the hell would I do that?"

"Because you should know who you're dating, and it's about time that you stuck your head out of the sand!"

"Wow, that was under the belt!" I was offended, and why did everybody think that about me, I wondered, remembering Katy commenting on my naivete.

"Look, I'm sorry. I didn't mean that. It's just that I don't want to advise you because I'm the worst person to give advice. Look at my life. I was in love in college just like you with a guy I could never bring home, and my dreams and heart shattered to pieces. Then Mom and Dad get me married off to this man I don't love and could never love. I can't even be his friend. You have no idea how miserable life is with him, and how alone I was." Ritu stopped, and her face was red.

"What do you mean, Ritu—how lonely you *were*?"

"Ah, lovely ladies, the margherita pizza is ready." The waiter beamed as he put a large round pie in front of us two frozen women. He did not ask if we would like fresh pepper or not but instead quietly stepped away.

"Why don't you have a slice, Mira; this conversation has gone where it shouldn't have."

"Don't avoid me now—what are you hiding?"

Ritu couldn't avoid my stubborn glare any longer. "I had an affair with a married man who's American, and I'm ending it now. If you hadn't come here this week, I was planning on coming home and telling Mom and Dad that I'm divorcing Manny." Before she realized it, she had revealed everything as if she was casually recounting where she went and what she ate yesterday.

I sat in silence for what seemed like an eternity. "What did you say?!" I finally gawked at my sister in disbelief.

"You didn't want me to judge you, so now, you don't judge me. Besides, Manny cheated on me first! You want advice on your love life, Mira? Here you go… Have the courage to stand up to Mom and Dad, and be with this guy, Dev, if he's the one you love, because if you don't, you will regret it like me, and you will do things that you thought you would never do."

After two whole minutes of silence, I finally spoke. "First of all, my situation and your situation right now are not comparable. I broke up with him because I couldn't bear to make Mom and Dad unhappier. You have done the worst possible thing, Ritu."

"Like I said, you are still a child living in your little perfect world, so don't sit there and think you have the right to judge me! You have no idea what I have been through and no idea what I have sacrificed for our family and their happiness. But I'm done sacrificing, and I'm done being played by moral standards that everyone talks about, but nobody lives by, and I'm not going to apologize for the hypocrisy."

"What the hell are you talking about?"

"Look, I've already said too much tonight, and I don't want to burden you with any more truths that you can't handle."

"Tell me!"

"No, and I mean that. This conversation is over."

I said meekly, "Could you at least help me with my current situation?" I filled her in on everything, even admitting how sick I got after making my Boston plans, the night of the breakup. "I'm so heartbroken, it's killing me."

"Oh my God, why do you keep sacrificing your happiness to please Mom and Dad! Don't you see what it did to our brother?!"

"Don't. Please don't. I don't have the strength to talk about that right now."

Neither of us could eat. We could not even look at our pizza that only a while earlier looked so tempting. We had it wrapped and took it home. It was my last night to stay with Ritu, and I could not sleep, tossing and turning, thinking about Ritu's confession. Was it better to make myself happy, and eventually Mom and Dad might come around? I sure would have to take that chance because not taking that risk would mean being unhappy and possibly taking on a sin as Ritu had, and how would she wash that bad karma off her shoulders?

The next morning, I quietly and politely thanked Manny for letting me stay with them. Ritu accompanied me to the train station, both of us completely silent on our way there. I guess she was angry with me for judging her, but I couldn't help it because she was in the wrong no matter what her reasons. But in the corner of my mind, I knew that I would have to forgive her for it, and I couldn't let her keep suffering; after all, she was my sister, and I did love her. Finally, before I boarded the train, I mustered the courage to say, "I think you're right, Ritu. And no, I don't judge you but, instead, fear your fate."

Ritu looked at me earnestly. "Thank you. Go take charge of your life. Be free and love."

With a smile and a long, warm hug, I said goodbye and was on my way back to New York, thinking all along how happy Dev would be when I told him that I'd changed my mind. I wanted to be with him, even if it meant standing up for him against my parents. I was so excited I wanted to call him to tell him the big news, but there was no payphone on the train. Oh well, I would have to wait, but he would know soon enough.

Chapter 27

"Dev, sir, is there anything else I can bring you?"

"No, thank you, Ramesh. But let me know tomorrow if they can fix the modem and dial-up connection. I really need to access my emails. I'm waiting for something important."

"Yes, sir," and with that Ramesh left.

Dev was home, back in India. It had been two weeks since his and Mira's confrontation. He was so upset after he lashed out at her that he didn't know how to control himself. For the first week, he knew Mira was trying to get in touch with him, but he couldn't face her. Not only was he embarrassed about his behavior, but what could her apologies possibly do to help their lost relationship? He knew if he saw her that he would not be able to control himself again; he would never want to let go of her, and it was just too difficult. He was so angry that she would not even consider trying to persuade her parents, after all that he had changed for her, that she could not do this for him.

He wanted to be chased by her for a change, so that first week he kept ignoring her calls and apologetic emails. His mom had unusually called repeatedly, saying that now they would not be able to come visit him after all and that it was better if he came home during his school break. She seemed very sad and to be missing him desperately, and he needed the escape from Mira anyway, so he got on a plane and flew to India. He had been here a week when he realized that there was no email from Mira, and if she tried calling him on his New York number, he would not be able to receive the call, and she did not know his India number. She had no cell phone, so he could not contact her outside of school, and with the school holidays, he knew that she would not be in her room. His cell phone did not work from India... Why was communication so complicated? If only he could email her his India number and write to her that he was not angry anymore and that he wanted to desperately see and talk to her. But India and its damn nuisance technology—sometimes it worked, and sometimes it didn't. The computer in the house was oddly dead, and he told Ramesh to get a new one three days earlier, but nothing. Staff could be so unreliable.

It was so frustrating being unreachable and not being able to communicate with Mira. She probably went to Boston to visit her sister. Perhaps she could not write to him either. Anyway, everything would be resolved once he went back to school the next week, and then he could see Mira and tell her that they would have to fight this thing with her parents together.

"Dev, what are you doing here, beta? Why aren't you out with your friends?" Mum barged, as usual, into the office.

"Hi, Mum, I was just thinking."

A strange look seemed to cross his mother's face, as though she'd had a curious thought. "Ramesh was telling me that you need to access your email account at school and are having a hard time."

"Yes, please handle this for me."

"Don't worry, beta. I've already taken care of it for you. Your new computer is at home, and the technician I've employed will take care of setting up your school account, but just tell me your password and log-in information; it will be kept confidential, of course, and I can have the guy begin doing this for you."

"Yes, you're amazing, Mum! Thanks so much! Listen, next week I must get back to school; the semester is starting."

"I wanted to talk to you about that, darling. Could you not just miss school for another two weeks? It is your dad's big fiftieth birthday coming up, and it would be so wonderful if you stayed for his surprise birthday party!"

"I'd love to, but I can't miss so much class."

"Don't worry. I've already told Ramesh to contact your school and professors and get some assignments emailed to you."

One could never say no to Mum; she was very set in her ways. "OK," he agreed reluctantly.

"Oh, by the way, remember Mona? You guys were very close back in the day?"

"What about her?"

"I've arranged for you to have dinner with her tonight."

"Why?" His face must have revealed his annoyance.

"Listen, Dev, she's not just your ex-girlfriend; she's also a very close family friend's daughter, and she was saying how she hasn't seen you in so long, and besides, her parents and we are going on a short holiday together to the Maldives, so you must be nice to her, do you understand," she demanded with a raise of her one eyebrow.

With Dev being unable to refuse, she walked out with a smile. The wheels were turning, and she was driving again.

• • •

Dev was looking at his face in the mirror as he buttoned his shirt almost all the way up to the collar. He cut himself shaving that morning, and it had been painful to dab aftershave lotion on his chin. Now the tiny nick was hardly noticeable on his soft face.

I wish this mirror would show me Mira's face instead of my own. Why does Mum insist on me taking Mona out? I didn't like Mona much back then; why would I want to hang out with her now?

Since Dev returned to India, even he noticed something in him had changed. Or was it India that had changed? *No way, India is still India,* he thought cynically. The politics were still corrupt, the streets still filled with litter, the cows still disrupting traffic… *And the people, well, at least, the people I have the unfortunate privilege of being friends with, are still superficial and hypocritical.*

Dev had changed, and Mira was the agent of that change, that improvement, he liked to think. He no longer took for granted the extravagant lifestyle of the rich in India, which consisted of dozens of servants who assisted him with every part of his life. Before he left to study in New York, he could not even fetch himself a glass of water; even that a servant would bring for him and that, when he was finished, take away. More than half of his conversations in a day constituted orders to his servants. Living in a dorm at a university in America was at first difficult because it meant cleaning up after himself and having to actually work, but he got used to it.

What school didn't change about him, though, was his entitlement and his extravagant lifestyle. It was an old habit to blow his parents' money on less worthy causes, such as impressing girls and friends. After meeting Mira, his spending came down dramatically. He realized he didn't need money to impress her. More than that, she made him feel real in what had always been a fake life. Him alone, and not what he owned, mattered for the first time. He stopped hanging out with a lot of his old friends, to their disappointment because he was not there to foot the bill for their private tables in the clubs. He didn't want to go out drinking, other than a glass of wine with dinner, and never missed the high of alcohol; Mira was his intoxication. He also discovered that he couldn't "just get" every woman he wanted, because he wanted Mira and Mira was hard work, but worth having. She made him feel and care and empathize, sentiments he'd rarely felt before. She made him see how happy people could be with simple things and how to love and appreciate life. His parents had not taught him these values because they had so much to give that denying him was unnecessary and did not make sense to them. Why shouldn't he have everything they could afford? Now he understood that learning you can't always have what you want is an important lesson in life.

"The car is ready, sir." The maid interrupted Dev's thoughts. "The driver is waiting downstairs."

"Yes, tell him I'll be there in two minutes." Dev grabbed his coat and ran down the stairs.

"You look handsome," Mum called out from the drawing-room. "Don't hurry home. Have a good time. I've noticed you've not been yourself since you've been home. Almost a recluse, no partying. What happened?"

"I'm fine, and I'm getting late. See you later." After a kiss on top of her head, Dev bolted out of the house to the car parked at the bottom of the steps. The driver, Chandan, Dev thought (one lost track when there were so many), opened the door to the back seat.

Dev arrived promptly at the China Garden restaurant in Punjabi Bagh, a posh area in west Delhi; Mum mentioned this was the happening new restaurant. She and Dad had been twice before with some friends, and she thought the food was satisfactory, given that the head chef was not from China.

The polite and pretty waitress showed Dev to his table and

informed him that he was the first one there. He scanned the restaurant's white-linen-covered tables to see if he recognized anyone from his past. He had not visited India in a little over a year. He had been happy to be out of touch and out of mind. He really did not want to be back with the old gang from Delhi. *But this damn Mona—don't know how she turned up in my life again. Speak of the devil...*

Mona walked in fashionably late. "Hi, Dev! Oh my God, you look your same handsome self." Mona leaned in for a quick kiss on the cheek. Before Dev could get a word in, she grabbed his hand and brought it to her chest. "Do you feel my heart racing?"

Oh my! Still the slut, are we? Dev immediately removed his hand from her and put it in his pocket.

She was wearing a skin-tight black dress that fell around her mid-thigh and that had a heart-shaped bustier that accentuated her curves quite well; her red lipstick showed no sign of moderation. In the past, Dev would've been attracted to her and may have dribbled and dabbled with an old flame just for fun. Now he would never dream of it. She looked cheap and tacky and, moreover, desperate. Dev thought of how Mira would never have worn a dress like that.

"I apologize for being late. I know you NRIs are so punctual."

"It's OK—you were only twenty minutes late." Dev wondered if she would hear his sarcasm. He may have been a nonresident Indian, but that was not why he appreciated not being kept waiting.

"I know, but I hate to keep a darling old friend waiting that long."

Dev wanted this evening to be over, so he began to rush along with the meal. "How about we order drinks, and I thought we could order the sizzling Szechuan duck and—"

"Slow down, Dev, let's order drinks and then appetizers, of course, before the duck."

Please rescue me! Dev could do nothing but smile.

Mona launched into a monologue. It was the same old Delhi girl gossip about who was sleeping with who, whose daddy was caught cheating, how Louis Vuitton was opening in Bombay, and how the girls were making a special trip to Paris just to go shopping. Dev realized he didn't know how much he'd come to hate this life, and these people, until sitting across from Mona that evening.

At the end of the night, as they left the restaurant, Mona slipped her arm through Dev's and insisted they go for a little stroll. He refused, to her disappointment, but softened the blow with a lame excuse that the spices turned his stomach sour and he needed to get home.

"Aww, well, you look after yourself, Dev, and we have to meet again because you hardly told me anything about your life in New York."

He could not stand the thought of having to be with this intolerable woman for another dinner. He didn't know how he dated her—the foolish teenager he was.

"Well, maybe if I have time. I'll be leaving for New York soon," he said, trying to get her off him. She was hugging him and swaying a little, probably the effect of having four gin and tonics. Waiting outside for her driver to bring around her car, she caught Dev unguarded and planted a kiss on his lips. "Woah!" He stiffly shot his neck back. "You have the wrong idea about us."

"Why don't you come over? My parents are out late tonight. Besides, they love you, and your parents love me. We can't do anything wrong together."

"You're not listening. I have a serious girlfriend in New York. We could never work out. I'm sorry." With those words, Dev walked off, looking in the restaurant parking lot for his driver. He could practically hear Mona's snarl behind him as she climbed into the back seat of her car and finally left him alone, at least for now.

"Oh, sir, gee, sorry. You should have sent the doorman to fetch me for you."

"That's OK, Chandra."

"Chandan, sir."

"Yeah, Chandan, no problem. I don't mind walking a little."

"Where to now, sir?"

"Home. Please just take me home!"

Chapter 28

It had been two weeks already since school was back in session and a month since Dev and I had any contact. I couldn't concentrate on any schoolwork anymore. I could only focus on the questions that repeatedly swirled in circles around my head: *where is Dev, and why is he still ignoring me?*

"So, I see you're packing to go home this weekend," said Katy.

I was a few seconds too late to respond. "Oh, I'm sorry. Yeah, my sister is coming home from Boston to visit for a few days, and I'm not looking forward to all the drama that will follow her visit. I just can't concentrate on anything... Where is Dev?!"

"I know that you're constantly thinking about him. It is weird he didn't come back to school," Katy agreed.

"What's weirder is that I've written him, like, one hundred emails, and he's not responded, and his roommate says that he hasn't come back to school but all his stuff is still there and that apparently he's having his schoolwork sent to him wherever he is. I can't believe that he's still so mad at me that he doesn't even want to talk, or see me, even if it is the last time, I see him to say goodbye."

"Did you tell him in your emails that you want to make this work and get back together and that you will tell your parents everything?"

"Yes, yes, I did so many times, and I even pleaded with him to give me one chance, but no reply."

"Oh, poor you, Mira, I don't know what to say and how to console you." Katy was hugging me, and it felt good, but it couldn't fill the hole and emptiness I felt without Dev.

"Thanks, Katy, I will see you on Sunday night. Have a good weekend."

"And you be brave for both you and your sister."

I smiled and pulled my suitcase out the door and through the streets of New York City and down the subway steps and finally into Penn Station where I waited for my train for Long Island, for home, for more confrontation.

• • •

Home was the last place I wanted to be right now. But Mom and Dad would hear no excuse, especially since Ritu was visiting from Boston. Ritu was waiting for me in the car when I arrived at the station. We hadn't seen each other or even spoken since my trip to Boston.

"How are you?"

"I'm OK."

"Any luck with your boy?"

"Nope," I said with a sullen face. "He hasn't replied to any of my emails, and, he has not returned from wherever he is. I'm assuming he went home to India; that's what his roommate guesses. How about you? Have you told Mom and Dad about your decision, or have you changed your mind since we last met?"

"Changed my mind—never! I was waiting for you to come home to tell them."

"Why? What do I have to do with it?"

"Well, you could support me by saying you saw how unhappy

and empty our lives were together when you came to visit me."

"Oh my God. I don't want to get dragged into this. It's bad enough that I had to watch it."

"Come on, Mira! How much have I always done for you? Mom always blamed me for your mistakes, stealing my clothes, and getting away with it. I used to drive you to all your birthday parties and nonsense in school. You owe me this!"

"Go, it's a green light!"

Honk.

"Not until you say that you will support me."

"Are you crazy? Traffic behind us is waiting and honking!" I had to agree; under pressure, there was no way I could continue to weigh the pros and cons of getting involved. "Fine, I will, just go!" I yelled. The light was red again, and in the side mirror, I could see a lot of people behind us who had angry faces.

When we entered the house, Mom greeted me with a happy hug. "My daughters are both home, so nice. I have made your favorite, Mira, matar paneer, bhurji style, and rajma, your favorite, Ritu, for dinner."

Inhaling the scents of homemade cheese and peas, prepared Indian style, and red kidney beans for a moment, I almost forgot the household tension.

"And what about my favorite?" came a voice from the back.

"Hi, Dad."

"Good to see you girls home. We haven't been together, all of us, for some time now, so let's enjoy this peace for now."

Oh God..., I thought.

Jazz was reading something in his room, but he came out to meet us as soon as he heard our voices. "Good to see you, little sis."

"Good to see you too."

One brother's smile oddly reminded me of the others for a fleeting moment. That was something new, since I always felt that Jeet and Jazz were so different; it never dawned upon me that they did have some similar facial features.

"Shall we get ready to eat?" Mom called from the kitchen.

It was almost like old times, except for the fact that one brother was dead, Ritu was broken inside and out, and the other brother had turned into somebody else. I set the table as usual, and Ritu poured the food hot from the pots into the serving dishes, while Mom rolled off the last couple of rotis that were swelling with hot air inside them, thin and soft, into aluminum foil to keep them hot.

The food was delicious; one could not deny that Mom's cooking was the best. What a shame, I thought, that such a good meal had to end with such a bitter conversation.

"You seem quiet Mira-beti," Mom said.

"No, I'm just relishing the food since I don't get this in the dorms at school."

Mom seemed satisfied with my answer and smiled.

"So, Mira, you tell us about Boston because since Ritu has been home, she's been like a closed book about it," Dad pushed.

"Ah, Boston, well..." *Should I talk about the fact that Manny and Ritu hardly speak and have no relationship, or should I talk about the affair Ritu is having with some American guy, oh and not to mention the divorce?*

"Mira?"

"Sorry, Dad, I was so busy enjoying my paneer."

Ritu came in to rescue me and simultaneously threw herself overboard. "Mom and Dad, I have something to tell you. You will not be happy to hear it, and I just want to apologize in advance."

Mom put her last bite down on the plate. I imagined that that bite would not be eaten tonight, because after what Ritu was about to tell them, Mom would not be able to finish her meal. "What is it Ritu-beti?" Mom and Dad looked worried. My brother looked at me in confusion.

"I'm divorcing Manny, and I have decided to keep living and working in Boston."

"Heah Waheguru! That's all God kept me alive to hear? Why, Ritu? Why now?!" Mom wailed. "Ritu, this is not a joke. You were the one who decided to go back to Manny against our wishes, and now you are again doing this?"

"I'm not happy with him, we have no future together, and we don't even remotely care for each other. We live the existence of robots. We sleep, get ready, go to work, eat, barely talk sometimes for days, and then repeat. He sometimes leaves for hours. I don't know where he goes and with whom. We have no kids, so I want to be free."

"What will we tell the Ahujas and the rest of the family and community now, eh?" Dad said with a streak of anger and blame.

"Don't blame me—this is all your doing!"

"My doing? What are you talking about?" Dad said.

"Did you know about this, Mira, when you went to Boston, and you did not think of even telling us?" Now Mom was pointing fingers at me.

"I felt really bad for Ritu." I was keeping my end of the bargain. "And I saw with my own eyes what she's telling you. Ritu is very unhappy and miserable with him, and maybe she hoped that she could make it work, but she has realized that there is no helping the situation."

"Taking your sister's side!" shouted Dad.

"Everyone, just calm down!" interrupted my brother with a

roaring voice.

We all kept quiet until Ritu spoke again. "I want a private word with Dad. Could everyone please step out of the room for a few minutes?" I got up to leave with my brother, who gestured to Mom to come out with them. Mom reluctantly got up.

Ritu and Dad were alone for about two minutes. There was no shouting. We barely even heard the murmur of his voice, just hers. When the rest of us reentered the dining room, Mom pleaded with Dad to tell her what Ritu had to say in private. Dad simply said, "We cannot stop her, Kamal; she is a grown woman, and she is right. Staying married to him is a waste of her life. I think we both know now that what people may think or say should be the least of our concerns," and he walked away. Mom stood dumbfounded at his answer. Ritu gave me a small smile. She had unleashed her burdens.

• • •

I was back in Rubin Hall that Sunday night. Katy greeted me with a large envelope. "Look," she said, "there's no stamp on it, like it was hand-delivered or something."

"Maybe it's something from Dev!" I gasped with excitement. I greedily ripped open the envelope. Inside was a folder; anxiety filled my heart as I saw what was inside.

"What's the matter, Mir? You look like you just saw a ghost," said Katy.

I fell back onto my bed, letting the photographs and the note that accompanied them fall to the ground.

Katy picked up the pictures that had slipped from my icy fingers. "Oh my God!" Katy covered her mouth with her hand and, uncharacteristically, swore. "What the fuck is going on? Who is that girl wrapped around Dev, kissing him?"

Chapter 29

A sudden wave of madness took over. "How could he do this to me?" I whispered. I looked at Katy, who was still kneeling on the carpet holding the photographs. All I could feel was rage shooting into my chest. I was finding it hard to breathe. I raced out of the room with Katy following right behind me, calling repeatedly for me to stop. Both of us flew down eight flights of stairs, down into the lobby of our dorm, out into the streets, and toward Dev's dorm. We didn't stop, not even at lights, until we reached the front desk.

"I need to call Dev Bala, seventh floor." I gasped for breath with Katy heaving, doubled over, behind me.

"OK, miss, hold on a second," replied the security officer, who looked highly unamused.

After he called Dev's room, he handed the phone over to me. It kept ringing, no answer. The answering machine came on, and I could hear his smooth voice: "It's Dev, and I'm obviously not here, so leave me a message." *Beep.* "Dev, it's me, Mira. Where are you? How could you do this to me? How could you deceive me like this?" My desperate voice turned into a loud, aggressive roar. "I was going to give us a chance, but you couldn't wait—you son of a bitch!" The sobbing made my message almost inaudible, and the security guard asked me to leave after I slammed the phone down, forgetting that I was in a dorm lobby.

Katy grabbed me by the shoulders and lifted me up from the lobby floor where my tears were forming a small puddle. "Come on, Mir, let's go," said Katy, gently coaxing me to the door.

Outside, Katy was saying something to console me, but I could no longer hear her words. Nothing mattered. Nothing anyone could say mattered. My heart was broken. My mind was heavy with the weight of those pictures of Dev and that girl. My mind kept repeating what I saw. He looked like his delightful self and dressed up so nicely, smiling. She had her lips on his, embracing him with her octopus' arms. There was no mistaking from the background that they were in India. The photographs were taken a couple weeks ago.

The note, oh yes, the anonymous note said, *I wanted to show you to save you.* The handwriting was messy and looked familiar, but I could not think about that now. I could only feel the fire burning in my chest.

"I must go home, Katy. I'm sorry."

"I can't let you go in this condition."

"No, Katy, it's all over. I'm going to be going home for good. I think my parents were right. This place is poisonous for young girls like me. I just got all messed up in it. All I ever wanted to do was be successful in school and my career, and I did exactly what I wasn't supposed to—got mixed up with a guy, and a guy I knew had a reputation with girls and who my parents would never approve of."

"What do you need me to do? How can I help you? Please don't go. Think about all your friends here."

"I'm sorry, Kat, but this place reminds me of him. I couldn't bear to go on here. I'll ask for a transfer to someplace local to my home. But I never want to see that lying piece of shit again!

I can't face him, Katy. I need to be far away from here, can't you see? Besides, everything good I had in my life is broken."

My mind would not be consoled. My brother, whose love was a pillar of support for me, was dead; my sister's marriage and heart were broken; my parents didn't love each other anymore; and the wall of love I built with Dev had crumbled.

The adrenaline that moments before was rushing through my veins had dwindled. I knelt on the sidewalk. By now, everyone on the street was staring at the drama that was my life. I remained quiet while Katy knelt beside me.

"You are running away, Mira. How can you start fresh without facing your problems?"

My response was small, and my voice was defeated. "I don't have the strength to fight this. I've been struggling with too much already. It's proof that Dev was not sincere. There's nothing more I need to talk to him about that I should bother staying here waiting for him to come back. Besides, if he truly cared, he would have responded to at least one email of the hundred that I sent him. He's moved on, and these photos are evidence of that. I don't want to lose all of you, Kat, and I won't. We will stay in touch. Just don't ever give my Long Island details to anyone else. I'm done with this place. Please let me be weak. I just need to feel it."

Katy had never seen me so angry and sad, so she knew I had made up my mind, and she couldn't convince me to stay. She lifted me up from the ground and gave me a big hug, chest to chest, so we could feel each other's hearts beating rapidly. "I won't force you; you've been through a lot. You must do what's best for you."

It took a week to withdraw from NYU and to move out of my dorm room. Katy invited some of our friends for a little farewell party. I knew it was sad, but I could not feel any more emotion. I was ready to move on from Dev, and everyone else.

I applied to Hofstra University on Long Island, which would let me know in a few weeks of my official acceptance to start the following fall term, since it was too late for the spring. Unofficially, they told me that I was accepted, and as soon as I got the official letter, I planned to enroll for summer classes. I wanted to keep myself busy and catch up on any time that was lost on Dev and our unfruitful memories.

Dad came to my dorm to help me bring all my things home. He caught the last bit of my farewell party and could see how sorry my friends were to see me go. "You can always visit your friends; you don't have to leave NYU completely," he said on our ride home. "I know you made this decision for us, your family, but you didn't have to."

"I did, Dad; I had to. It's better for all of us if we stay together. I don't want to be at such a distance when you all need me. Besides, I will be getting a full scholarship from Hofstra, and I can continue the same major there, so don't feel guilty, Dad; it's not your fault."

I stared through my window at the passing images of trees and houses. However, I did not see trees, just Dev and me laughing and kissing. Here I was again, wondering what happened to those moments of love and happiness in my life. But now, I could not feel the love in those memories of Dev the way I used to. Even the old laughter did not make me feel at ease. It was as if I was trapped in an air-tight bubble from which I could see flashes of our moments together but could no longer connect with them. Those wonderful memories of our love and passion had withered so quickly, and I was burying them in the "painful past" box in my mind. I was going to keep that box shut and, yes, "move on."

Dad broke the silence. "So, there's some good news. Jazz got a job with some company from India. I think the parent company is Bala Industries, that huge multinational, but it's still a great opportunity for Jazz—while studying this computer script, he can also work part-time."

I did not hear anything after "Bala Industries." A tear escaped my eye; I could do nothing to hold it back.

"What happened, beti? Why are you crying? This is good news. In fact, it is funny—you should be laughing! After all, who would give Jazz a job? He's so unreliable. Let's hope he doesn't disappoint."

"I'm just missing school, that's all. I'm happy for Jazz too."

"It will be fine. You will do so well at Hofstra, I'm sure." Dad beamed across the car.

We drove the rest of the way to Ash Lane in silence.

Chapter 30

Dev's father's birthday party was enormously ostentatious. His mum spared no expense—from the centerpieces full of orchids and lilies adorned with Swarovski crystals to the multiple musicians, singers, and dancers, to the top-shelf liquor flowing freely. The A list of India, including Bollywood stars, were just some of the guests, who all arrived in their diamonds and designer outfits. Dom Pérignon champagne bottles were given to every guest to take home as a souvenir. His dad made a thank-you speech and invited Dev to come on stage and be introduced to India's highest society. Dev was wearing his black tuxedo, and his dad wore a white tux, just as his mum had arranged for them. It was a little overwhelming, perhaps because it had been a while since Dev indulged in this life. The party was a grand success, and even though Dev was anxious to see Mira, he was glad he stayed the extra time, for his parents' sake.

• • •

"I've booked my ticket to return to New York," Dev said over brunch the day after the party.

His Mum looked up from her coffee, her head still aching from being hungover. "What? You can't go yet!"

"Not so loud, woman," his dad remarked. "My head is still

beating from those damn drums last night."
"Look, I stayed for the party, and now I must go. You have no idea how long it's going to take me to catch up on my work at school." "But, darling, give yourself a few days to rest from the party."
Dev got up from his chair, "I don't need rest, and I'm not going to wait. I leave tomorrow."
And with that said and done, Dev walked to his room to get packed. Dev wanted to buy Mira a gift before he left to apologize for his overreaction and for ignoring her. He knew that if they put their heads together, they would overcome the hurdle of her parents. After all, love conquered all. And Dev knew exactly what she would want for a gift.

• • •

Landing on American soil felt amazing! Dev was finally back, relieved to be home and away from his old life in India. "Please take me to the downtown NYU campus, to 10 University Place," he said to the taxi driver with great excitement.

As soon as he marched up into his room and threw his bag on the floor, he checked his email. He had tons from Mira. He was so happy! He could not even get through all the messages. She was sorry; she wanted to try for them. She would tell her parents; it was all wonderful. "I'm so sorry I kept you away for so long, Mira," Dev whispered to himself.

He picked up the phone and saw the message light flashing: seven new messages. Oh, OK, Narinder, next. Mira… "Where are you, Dev? Please call me." The last message was from Mira, and it was different from the rest. "…you son of a bitch!" Dev put the phone down slowly, missing the receiver. *What did I do to deceive her? What the hell is going on? I must call her now and find out.*

"Hello?" It was Katy's voice at the other end.

"Katy, it's Dev. I just got back from India. I must speak to Mira please!"

"So, you're back," she growled. "You lying piece of shit! Mira's gone, and it's all because of you I've lost my friend. How dare you even call here!"

"What do you mean? What's wrong? I didn't do anything! It was just a misunderstanding—" Dev scrambled to get his words out faster, but Katy hung up.

Dev ran out of the room and went knocking on Narinder's door.

"Woah, man, you're back! I thought you weren't ever coming back!"

"Where is Mira?"

"Can you first come in and sit down?"

"I don't want to sit down. I want to know why the fuck I'm being blamed for something that I don't even know about and why is Katy saying she's lost Mira?!" Dev could not control his rage.

"Dev, calm down and let me explain."

Dev quieted himself. He needed to hear this.

Narinder started, slowly and steadily. "Look, all I know is that Mira was trying to reach you all this time you were away. Suddenly, a little over a week ago, I heard that Katy was throwing a farewell party for Mira in her dorm room. So, I didn't have the opportunity to see Mira, but I bumped into Katy, and I asked her why Mira was leaving, and she said that you went into a wild rage with Mira, breaking up with her before disappearing from this country and were responsible for cheating on her, and Mira had had enough with you. She's left NYU and is gone to transfer somewhere else and has left no contact details so that no one can follow her or try to contact her other than Katy, who is like Fort Knox and won't give Mira's home number on Long Island."

Dev couldn't believe what he was hearing. How did all this happen? "Why would she think I cheated?"

"I don't know, man, but it was like, she was sure. Like she had some proof."

Dev left Narinder's room and sprinted to Mira's dorm. "Katy, I'm downstairs in the lobby. Please, I just need to talk to you one more time," he said in panic on the phone at the security desk."

"Stop calling me!"

"I promise that if you talk to me face-to-face one time, I will stop calling you."

"Fine!" She hung up.

A few minutes later, Katy appeared in the lobby in her pajamas and slippers. "I'm here."

"Thank you. Look, I agree I ignored Mira for a week or two because I was so angry with her. I felt used because she didn't want me in her future. I was crazy with anger, so I fled to India because my parents wanted me to visit them anyway." Each word was running into the next, and everything was half-jumbled because Dev needed to let it all out. "I needed the space to think, you know. I tried to email her, but damn it, I could not, and then I knew she was going to Boston, so I knew I couldn't reach her at her dorm number. Later, I tried, but I couldn't get a connection. Please understand, I missed her and was miserable, and I wanted to come back weeks ago, but I had to stay for my father's birthday."

Katy looked untouched by Dev's pleas. "Sounds like a bunch of excuses. I think you would have contacted her if you really wanted to."

"You don't understand. Communication lines in India can

be so bad—" Dev tried to explain before she cut him off.

"But you know what? It's better that she got to know the truth about what a lowlife scumbag you really are."

"What truth? That's what I don't understand. What did I do?"

"Oh, don't give me this shit. You know you were messing around behind Mira's back. I'm done with this conversation. I'm leaving." Katy turned to go.

"Wait, please, I didn't do anything. I never cheated on her with anyone. Oh my God, what is happening?!" Dev kept rubbing his forehead, trying to figure out what to do. He went back to his dorm to go over the emails Mira had sent, looking for some clue as to how they got to this. He also tried to reach Mira.

The registrar's office would not reveal any current or past student confidential information, such as an address or phone number. The yellow pages listed thousands of Singhs living on Long Island. Which one would be Mira's family? Mira's NYU email was now disconnected.

Dev spent his whole first week back in New York searching for a way to get Mira back. *How could I lose her, just like that?* He started drinking again and missing classes, and he couldn't focus on work. *Could someone have told Mira about his date with Mona in India? That was preposterous. How could that be? How would that information reach Mira all the way from India?* He pushed that thought out of his mind, but how could she be so sure he cheated on her? His mind was puzzled. It just didn't add up. He heard a knock on his door. It was Narinder.

"Hey, man, come on in."

"Dude, Dev, you need to shave."

"Narinder, I don't give a fuck about that. You know what's driving me crazy. Why would she think I was messing around? I was with my parents, for God's sake!"

"Well, did you meet anyone while you were there?"

"I saw one girl who has no ties to America and just for a lousy dinner. She was just an old friend and nothing more."

"I don't know, man. You ignored her for a while. I heard she thought you had forgotten her and moved on; you know. Maybe she just used your cheating as an excuse to break up; girls do that."

"What do you mean?"

"Well, think of it this way: You broke up with her because she was deceiving you by never having the intention of telling her parents about you while you guys were talking about your futures together. So, maybe she took this as an opportunity to break up with you, like you're the one deceiving her, by making up some story that you cheated on her while you're away. Now, you're the bad guy, and she's the poor victim."

"I never thought about it that way. It's so fuckin' complicated."

"I know that's what my girlfriend told me was the real story. These girls, they are messed up. They overthink things and then manipulate us. So, if I were you, I would just let her go."

"It's not that easy, bro."

"Listen, you got to move on with your life. I promise you will meet another nice girl. She wasn't the only one, you know, just the first nice girl you met. Come on, let's go eat."

"I'm not hungry. I'll catch up with you later."

Narinder let the door slam itself closed on the way out.

Maybe he was right. Maybe this was Mira's way of saying that not only were we officially broken up, but I was to blame for it. I realized that we really didn't know each other as well as I thought. I didn't know her home number, the town she lived in, or the full names of her parents. All I knew was "Mira from NYU," and she was gone.

No, I felt more alive with her than ever in my life—this was real love. I thought real love was supposed to overcome every obstacle in life. Maybe that was only in fairy tales. Maybe in real life, love could get lost.

Maybe it was time to move on; maybe it was over. The dream was over.

But no, I won't let Mira get away with this so easily. She would have to answer my questions. She would one day have to make up for the pain she left with me, for the love I lost, for the hole she left gaping in my chest. It won't matter if it takes me five years or ten or more, I will eventually find her. I'm a winner, never a loser.

"Damn it, Mira, where are you?"

Chapter 31

"So happy you're home, Mira. We must stick together in this dark time."

"I'm happy to be home too, Mom. Where's Jazz?"

"Oh, didn't Dad tell you?" And then Mom started rambling on about Jazz's job, just like Dad had.

"That's good for Jazz. I think I'm just tired and want to go to bed."

"No, you must eat dinner! I was waiting for you guys to get home."

I sat down, but the roti was difficult to swallow.

"You are hardly touching your food? What's the matter?" asked Dad.

"Nothing."

Mom changed the subject. "So, you know, Mira, when you spoke to us a few weeks back and we got upset? We were talking, your dad and I, and we thought that you were right."

"What are you talking about?" I asked.

Mom continued, "You see, I never imagined that someone so brilliant and good like my son could also be gay. You know, I just usually imagined these gay people to be into bad company and having diseases. But it's not true. We never realized that even decent people can be gay."

Dad nodded. "We never knew this. We were so set in our old ways of thinking."

If it were not for Dev's betrayal, I would've been happy to hear their words, but at that moment, nothing mattered to me.

"But it was fate that this had to happen, the Guru had decided. We couldn't do anything," said Dad with a sense of resolution.

Sudden anger came bellowing out from my gut. "That's not true! That's not true!"

"Mira, sit down," Mom hushed.

"No, I'm done here, and don't think you can clear your conscience by thinking that the Guru did this. Yes, I understand that we are all destined to die at a certain age, which we don't have control of, but everything else we do is a choice! It's not determined by the Guru. Jeet is responsible for killing himself, and we all are responsible for leading him to that death! We are responsible for our actions—that is karma!"

Mom was crying by now, and Dad was telling me to go to my room. "Please go from here! I did not bring you home to break us apart."

I left for the sanctuary of my room. Ritu had gone back to Boston to collect her things; the divorce papers had already been drawn up. I welcomed being alone in my room, with my own thoughts, finally. I was beginning to understand that destiny was not etched in stone; it was like a sketch that could be erased and changed. The Guru may give us different paths, but it is we who decide which path we travel. The Guru may have given me sorrow, but I was going to decide what to do with it. I was not going to let Jeet, or Dev, or anyone else take away my life, my spirit, my breath, my reason to live and flourish. The spirit of the Universe, God, was continuously flowing through my blood, and nothing from the world could take that from me. I had to keep living, not "moving on" ever, but living with scars. I read once that in Japan, when something is broken, they fix it instead of throwing it away. In fact, they mend the pieces with gold, so that all the flaws may not just be visible but also be uniquely beautiful and celebrated.

I, Mira Singh, was broken but beautiful and would have to start imagining a new future without Jeet and without Dev. I took the remaining loose ends of a ribbon and tied my hair into a loose ponytail. The sun was setting over Ash Lane, and its rays seeped in through the old window, creating dark shadows on the glossy wooden floor. I traced the shadows in the air with my finger and stood up to look in the mirror sitting atop the dresser. The sun's rays made my hair shine a rainbow of red and dark brown, and my eyes sparkled an amber hue. Its glow warmed my flesh and softened my tense shoulders. Childhood stories blazed into life, baking against my tired limbs in the quiet of the room. Shifting back to perch on the windowsill, I smiled at the reflection of the young woman in the mirror. She knew better than I.

• • •

Although Mom and Dad were placating their guilty consciences by blaming fate for Jeet's untimely death, Jazz was battling his inner demons that told him he was the culprit. Jazz was stifling under the belief that he was his brother's murderer. Jazz's guilt, like a thick wax, had smothered his chest and solidified its grip on his throat, and he would wake each night gasping for air and life, the same life he had taken from his brother. After all, if he hadn't revealed Jeet's secret letters to the whole family, his brother would've been alive today.

Returning home after witnessing the suicide scene was more

than his mind could handle. So that same night, while his family mourned at home, Jazz went out to a local bar and got drunk alone. He drowned his sorrows and guilt in his drinks until the bartender refused to serve him. Jazz found himself the next morning in his car, alone and lonely, with repulsive vomit dry and brittle on his face. The reality of his situation sparked the realization that Jeet was dead forever. His long-frozen emotions for his brother and his family began to stir. He could now feel their pain, their agony. How could he have let his brother down like that? Why did he act like such a drunk jerk and read Jeet's diary to everyone? He decided then that he wasn't going to let alcohol poison the rest of his life. He owed his parents more, he thought. He owed them a son they could be proud of, especially now that Jeet wasn't there. He wanted to make up all the years he had wasted to the best of his ability.

Jazz failed the twelfth grade twice, but finally, at Dad's request, the school board allowed him to study and retake two of the Regents exams. It had been over a year since Jazz had obtained his diploma, and he was working in a gas station. He had enrolled in Nassau Community College but had failed multiple classes due to incomplete assignments. Eventually, Jazz dropped out. Although Dad had been urging him for the last year to apply to school, Jazz had tossed the applications away in retort to his father's pressure. However, only months after Jeet's suicide, Jazz enrolled in a vocational training school to learn basic computer and software systems.

Jazz's new initiative and responsible behavior caught everyone by surprise. He was even approached by an Indian company called B Systems that was looking to launch a new software company for industries based in both Asia and America. The man who called him for an interview was someone from India who said they were looking to specifically hire young Indian programmers based in the USA. They specifically wanted immigrants because they could work as the bridge between Indian and American companies. Jazz was confused about why they would consider him, but the man assured him that his name was chosen from his training program and a list of Indian graduates living in the tri-state area. Jazz figured they had him confused with someone else, but he didn't want to lose the opportunity. After the interview, the man who called himself Ramesh gave him a starting bonus and explained how the job also came with some private responsibilities.

For a while, the "ripped jeans sitting low on his hips, exposing his boxers" brother I'd known for years was replaced by a neatly dressed young man who politely wished us good morning, didn't smell of smoke and beer, and said things to his family like "I'm going to my class now, so I'll see you in the evening. If you need me for anything, just catch me on my beeper." Even Dad had to admit his pleasure. "I'm quite impressed with these improvements, son," he said.

But it was hard leaving booze altogether. He missed the relaxation it brought him, how it made him feel loose. Now, he had to face the stresses of work and life rather than binge drink through them. Learning JavaScript hardly seemed to help Jazz's focus. It made him uneasy to be in his room now that Jeet was gone. He felt more alone, yet also like Jeet was watching him. His thoughts kept showing him his brother's body and the surrounding pool of blood. Without alcohol, his visions of Jeet were all too real. Jazz felt weak and was desperate to be numb. He was not strong enough to face Jeet's death or to accept what had happened. He didn't want to go back to drinking, but it was calling him. He wasn't like me, who filled my heart with spiritual guidance, or like Ritu, who filled it with the distraction of living in a new city; he lacked those things, and the only thing that could fill his void was booze.

Jazz got up from his desk to reach the hidden stash of alcohol in his cabinet and promised himself that he would have only one drink, a little bit of whiskey, and then he would sit back down and finish reading the chapter about JavaScript. His hands started to shake as he poured his drink; the closer he got to having it, the more desperate and needy he became. Once he had gulped it down, his hands kept moving of their own accord; his body knew exactly what to do and how to take exactly what it needed. Half a bottle of whiskey later, Jazz was fast asleep in his chair.

Chapter 32

2018

It was early in the morning. The room was still dark and warm, closed off to the rest of the house like a cocoon. The alarm had not yet rung from my new iPhone, which sat atop my bedside table, but I began to stir from the dream world into the reality of the day. I could feel a soft, rolling breath on the back of my neck, my body swaddled like candy wrapped in his embrace. I was comfortable by his side; his presence gave me surety and safety.

In this tender hour, I lay completely still, except for my blinking eyes. A flicker of his face in my dream roused me prematurely. I let out a sigh—why was I still dreaming about him? I had to let go.

The "alarm" in the next room went off. Its ringtone was unique in my life of thirty-eight years:

"Momma, Momma..."

"Mira, jaan baby, go see her. She's crying for you."

"Your arm weighs a ton—I can't move. Please, it's your turn to go see her."

"But she's calling for you."

"Your arm is suffocating me..." My voice trailed off. My husband of twelve years finally released my body so that I could be free to see our four-year-old daughter down the hall.

It was not yet six, but it was a Monday, which meant I had

an hour and a half to get my daughter and me dressed and fed before catching the train to work.

I entered the small, dark room with pink curtains and a dark wooden toddler bed on the far side that rested on a soft vanilla rug embroidered with pink roses. Zenith was already sitting up in her bed, in her snug sleeping bag embossed with pink elephants.

"Momma, Momma, the green monster is under my bed."

"There's no monster, sweetie." I gave her a quick squeeze before I lifted her out over the side bed railing and onto the floor. Before I knew it, she unzipped herself from the myriad of elephants and ran to my bedroom.

"Daddy, Daddy." She was her daddy's little girl.

I followed her and stood there watching them cuddle in bed, and for one short moment, I felt like I was somewhere else looking in at a scene of people I didn't recognize. Our years of marriage had produced something that the world would come to know and love.

The rest of the morning went on as usual: showered, negotiated with Zenith on her choice of clothes for pre-K, and grabbed a protein shake for breakfast as I flew out of the house.

I luckily secured a seat on the overcrowded train on the LIRR. My commute would be only twenty-five minutes from Great Neck to Manhattan. The green-and-blue leather seats were tattered and shabby. I flashed my monthly pass to the conductor without saying a word. I listened to music on my Air Pods and checked my Instagram. My boss's account was there—no way would I follow him. I kept scrolling until my fingers froze on a name I could never forget, Dev Bala. A picture of a man I used to know materialized before my eyes. My heart quivered, and my fingers shook. It had been years since I had seen or heard about Dev. And I had come to terms with how our relationship had ended, at least I thought I had.

• • •

After I graduated from Hofstra and was studying for a master's in marketing at Columbia, I had scrolled through *Times New India* on the internet and seen Dev. I was shocked to see him posing with his parents in front of a modern-looking building. The photo caption read, "New Prince of Bala Industries Dev Bala to Head Software Division." To my surprise, Dev, the only child of a business conglomerate family, was considered royalty in India. He was to inherit all his family's businesses, real estate around the world, and other assets. It all made sense. Of course, a rich playboy would break my heart. I couldn't help but laugh at myself, at how naive I had been. Giving my heart to someone I barely knew. I had no idea about his background, and he had slyly concealed it from me. Although, thoughts of how my life would have been if Dev and I had stayed together did creep into my head. Foolish images of myself dressed to the nines, waving for the cameras had poked into my thoughts. I was too sensible to be drawn into pointless daydreams.

Then, I was almost twenty-four years old, and my parents had started hounding me about getting married. They would talk about endless suitable matches I had been dodging all along. I knew, though, that the time had come when I had to bury Dev for good and give my heart another try. My mom's uncle, who wasn't really her uncle but was something like the uncle of a cousin whose family was very close to my mother's growing up, had suggested a match for me. His name was Gurinder Walia, and he worked for PWC in New York City, where he also lived in his own apartment in Gramercy Park. He was looking to settle down with an educated Sikh girl from a good family.

"Really, Mom, his name is Gurinder, like the John of English names. Could he sound any more common?" I fussed.

"You are so ungrateful to Uncle. He especially spoke to the boy's parents about you, and now you must meet him as a courtesy."

"Hardly a boy, I'd say; he's twenty-nine." I rolled my eyes.

With her hand in the air to warn me of a slap for my obvious arrogance, I grudgingly agreed to meet this "boy." His picture was okay. How much charisma did I really expect an accountant at PWC to have? Apparently, my mom had sent a recent picture of me dressed in a lengha for a wedding we had attended, and Uncle said that Gurinder had liked me and wanted to meet me. The date was set; it was to be dinner at an Italian place in Midtown where he could meet me after work and I after school. I wore a casual but pretty spring dress in lavender. It was the only one I had that wasn't revealing, of course, but also didn't make me look like a nun. Mom had made me promise that this time I would put effort into my appearance. The last two guys I had met, I had showed up with jeans and my hair in a bun straight from class. Not that my appearance had led them to reject me. Rather, I had no interest in being married to someone who continued to talk about himself the whole night, and the other one had bad breath, a total turnoff. I did not expect anything better than those last two setups, but since I had made a promise, I had my long, silky hair down, and I wore a hint of blush and lipstick to brighten my pale face.

Gurinder Walia turned out to be "decent." He wasn't strikingly handsome, but his height at six foot two and his broad chest gave him a masculine stature. He looked very fashionable and seemed to take pride in his sense of dress: Ferragamo shoes polished under his slim trousers, his button-down shirt stiff at the collar, and what looked like an expensive watch around his broad wrist. He seemed to have tied his turban and beard with great precision, neat and proper. And the way he smiled with a little twinkle in his large eyes and how he could make me laugh with his witty sense of humor was unexpected given the fact that he was a numbers guy. He seemed so interested in learning about what I liked to do and what my dreams were. Gurinder, well, Inder, as he liked to be called, had a steady but intense gaze, and I seemed to be under its surveillance the whole night. After we had exchanged numbers and said goodnight, I thought about how it felt to finally go out with a guy and not think about Dev. Inder did seem a little taken with me, which secretly felt nice.

Inder and I continued to meet for a few more months, until both of our families pestered us to decide as to whether we wanted to marry or not. Six months later, after I had turned twenty-five, Inder and I were engaged, and the following year at twenty-six, I was married.

Ritu had been married a few years earlier to a Punjabi boy from New Jersey. After her divorce from Manny, she and her future husband had been introduced by Dad's cousin and seemed to make a good connection. Jazz had met a couple of girls when he finally started to earn a living but could not hold a relationship for too long without sabotaging it in some way, usually his temper when he was drunk.

Inder and I had hardly been married a year when our parents had started to ask for grandchildren.

"Mom, you have grandchildren! What's the rush?!"

"I know Ritu's two boys are there, but I have no hope from Jazz, so you need to have a child as well!"

"I'm not having this conversation, OK? Inder and I need more time for each other, and we want to travel, and I need to establish my career. I'm not ready to have a kid!"

"Stop rushing her!" Dad interjected.

Inder's parents were not as direct with me but did nudge Inder to start having a family since he was now in his thirties.

When I was twenty-nine, I became pregnant, not for very long, though. At three months, I woke up with blood staining my pajamas and sheets. I cried for a long time, and Inder never let go of me. He held me in his arms long and hard until I could cry no more. Our parents stopped pressuring us. They let it be. It was God's will, when our child would come.

That same week, as I mindlessly scrolled through Indian gossip magazines on my laptop, anything to distract myself, I saw Dev. He looked distraught. He was pictured leaving his chauffeur-driven car. The headline read, "Prince Bala Divorces."

Dev had been married to a rich and famous model from Mumbai. She had come from the Amba family, who had a textile business. Her picture right below the article was from one of her catwalk days and she was clad in something too little to be called a dress. Apparently, after only two years, the couple had ended what was already called a rocky marriage. Dev's marriage was dissolved without too much issue as a prenuptial had been in place. Why did Waheguru keep bringing him back to my attention? Well, perhaps, Dev being a global figure had something to do with it. But I couldn't help but think it was because I had to learn something from it. Perhaps Waheguru was reminding me of how far I had come. My grief, my heartbreak had not broken me. I survived, and with that strength, I was blessed again, with love from Inder. Inder may not have been the passion of my life like Dev, but he was my rock, and I loved him a great deal.

Dev's life and his destiny were no longer my concern. I had run away from his deception, from his memory. I had moved on, and I was sure he had too.

• • •

I closed my Instagram app and pulled myself up to wait by the doors that would open to the underground platform at Pennsylvania Station. I hurried up the steps to the main floor and up the escalators to Two Penn Plaza, where I was Head of Marketing in the business publishing division at McGraw Hill. I threw my coat on the back of my black chair, and Dana, my marketing assistant, brought my cup of green tea.

"Good morning, Dana. Thanks, you can leave it on my desk." My mind was foggy, and I wanted to be left alone to recenter myself.

"I left your mail next to it," she said a moment later, while tossing her ginger hair over her shoulder. "Oh, and Marty says that we have a new-author lunch on Wednesday, and he wants you to be there because it's someone from India."

"Really? Did he mention the name of the author or book?" I was suddenly awake and inquisitive.

"I think the book is called something like *The Empire*... Oh, it's called *The Indian Empire*, by...Bala? I think that's the last name?"

It was as if I had been hit by a thunderbolt. My heart had left its cushiony position atop my chest and dropped to the pit of my stomach. It couldn't be the same Bala. Or could it? The color draining from my cheeks did not go unnoticed.

"Are you feeling, OK?"

"Dana, bring me the file on this new author. I want to get some background information on him and his book before lunch." As she left the room, I collapsed onto my chair to compose myself. My relationship with Dev ended years ago, so if this author did happen to be him, what did it matter? I was a professional, so I was not going to let his presence affect me.

Whatever—I was overreacting as usual. I tried to encourage my mind to think about other things, but my damned ego was so strong it kept pulling me into my memories with Dev—how he looked, how he felt.

• • •

The dreaded Wednesday arrived, and I had by then secured the comforting knowledge that even though it was Dev's book, his coauthor, Rajan Mehta, a friend of his and the head of international relations of Bala Industries, would be coming in his place, so I was much more relaxed.

When it was time for lunch, I took a quick glance in the mirror in my office and dabbed on some gloss. The years had been kind to my face, which still had a youthful glow; my hair was still long and glossy, with my new chestnut highlights to cover a few pesky grays; and overall, I had maintained my figure, through countless hours of strength training and Soul Cycle. I brushed down the wrinkles in my pink blouse and straightened my light-gray skirt before throwing on my tailored cream trench coat.

The elevator doors opened onto the massive white marble lobby, cold and unemotional like the occupants of the Fortune 500 companies who were most of this building's inhabitants. I stepped out, and I felt my heels glue themselves to the stone tile.

"Ah, Mira," called Marty, the editor in chief, "let me introduce you to both authors of our first edition of *The Indian Empire*. This is Rajan Mehta, and this is Dev Bala, the CEO of Bala Industries himself."

Marty's words echoed in my ears as my gaze fixed on Dev. He looked as handsome as ever. Other than the few streaks of white in his hair and the stubble of salt-and-pepper on his face, he was the same man I fell for twenty years prior.

His eyes looked straight into mine without reservation, like he was looking down into a deep, dark pool and could see the hollows of my heart.

"Mira."

I immediately snapped out of my trance and moved forward to shake Mr. Mehta's hand. "Very nice to meet you." I beamed.

Dev extended his hand to me. I looked at him without graciousness and then down at the tile, trying to find a pattern in its white surface, avoiding giving my hand for longer than a split second.

• • •

Sitting opposite Dev at the Italian restaurant was excruciatingly painful. I could barely eat a bite.

"I think Mira will be ideal in helping you through the marketing process," Marty gushed. "She has years of experience with entrepreneur publications, and she can really do justice in terms of the cultural aspect of your work." Marty grinned at me, and I let out a meek smile.

"We will be happy to work with Ms.—"

"Mrs. Walia," Marty corrected.

"Yes, with Mrs. Walia," Dev repeated in a sullen tone. Dev's face looked downcast for most of the lunch. He said a few words but mostly just nodded.

I was anxious to leave and relieved when the meeting ended. Back in my office, I shut my door. It was just too much to take in, his presence, his eyes, his memories. I heard a knock, probably Dana.

"Come in," I responded with my eyes still shut.

"I'm sorry to disturb you, but I wanted to talk privately."

My eyes flew open to the sound of Dev's voice. I rushed to stand up, startled and breathless. My mouth opened to ask Dev why he was in my office, but no words came out.

Chapter 33

As the train pulled out of Penn Station, I was bewildered by what Dev had said only minutes earlier. Basically, he had asked me to reverse time. That was not possible. How could I give myself what I had always secretly desired?

When I got home, Inder was waiting on the couch with Zenith, both entranced by one of the *Frozen* movies.

"Hi, guys," I said as I took my shoes off at the front door and walked to the kitchen sink to wash my hands.

"Hooray, Mom's home!" screamed Inder, and Zenith followed with the same excitement, "Yay, Momma!"

I had barely finished drying my hands when Zenith jumped against my legs, urging me to pick her up.

"Long day?" asked Inder as he kissed my cheek.

"Yes, a long, unusual day."

"Oh, really?"

Caught by surprise as I had slipped too much information, I added, "I just meant, you know, the same old crazy at work." I laughed it off, trying to not draw any more attention to my meeting at work. I quickly changed the topic. "So, I picked up some marinated chicken and a side of vegetables from Whole Foods on my way home. Do you mind boiling some water for the pasta?"

"Sure, hon, I'm on it." Inder grinned. Inder wasn't like the typical Desi man who wouldn't enter the kitchen, but instead he was very helpful when it came to cooking. I really should not take him for granted, I thought, a hint of guilt creeping into my chest. After dinner and cleanup, Zenith insisted that tonight she wanted me to read her a story, not Daddy. She picked up *Goodnight Moon,* one of our favorites, and I read it to her while she laid her head on my lap.

"Goodnight Moon, Goodnight Room..." I read until Zenith yawned and rubbed her eyes. At the end of the story, she wrapped her arms around me and whispered, "I love you, Momma."

"I love you, my sweetheart." After I put her in her bed and dimmed the lights, I just looked at her asleep. I could never do that to my baby, I thought. I could never replace her happiness and well-being with my own selfish desires.

That night in bed, I lay tossing and turning, thinking about the conversation Dev and I had in my office. What would my answer be? Was this my chance, or was this a test from God?

Chapter 34

"Mira, Mira, are you real, or am I having another dream?"

His voice saying my name was too much to bear. I felt my body trembling. He came closer to where I was standing behind my desk and put his hand on my shoulder. His touch was just as electrifying as it was years earlier.

"I've spent years trying to understand why you left without a word." I remained frozen under the touch of his hand and the gaze of his eyes. He spoke more gently now. "Why did you leave me, Mira?"

I had secretly hoped, in a small, dark corner of my imagination, that this day would come, and now that it was here, I could not own up to it. I could not bring myself to accuse him of his infidelity, how he broke my heart, how I hated him for taking away my ability to love. I could not stir the anger I had harbored against him all these years. I was transported back to 1998, and love swelled like a balloon in my heart.

"Mira, I never forgot you. I've searched for years." His face wrinkled in anguish as he recounted how he tried to look for me after I left NYU. Years later, he found Katy through Narinder's friends list on Facebook. "Then I went through her friends list to find your picture. That was when I learned your new last name, and then I searched for Mira Walia on Google and found that you worked here."

"So, this whole book project was a setup to meet with me?" I said with a look of astonishment.

"Yes, in a way. Mehta had been asking me to coauthor a book with him for years, and I just saw this as an opportunity."

"Wow, I mean, if I didn't know you better, I would say you're a stalker." I paused. I didn't know him. "Well," I finally said, straightening taller, "what is it you need?"

"Come on, Mira, how could you live with yourself after how you just dumped me and left me for no reason?"

"Did you say no reason?" I said with half a laugh and half a snarl. "I left you because you cheated on me!" My voice was rising.

Running his hands through his hair, frustrated, he said, "Why would you think that? I never cheated on you!"

"I had proof!" I yelled. "I was sent photographs of you and a girl in India, kissing."

Dev looked like he had seen a ghost. He began to pace, and I knew he was thinking. Dev shut his eyes for a few seconds and blurted, "It was my mother. Recently I learned she set up my wedding with Tanya for a big business gain in textiles. And I learned other stuff about her crafty ways. She wouldn't have approved of you, so I guess she set us up to break up."

"You expect me to believe this story?" Yet Dev's solemn expression told me he was telling the truth.

"She was an old friend my mother insisted I meet for her parents' sake, and she just came on to me, against my will. I never met her again, nor was I interested in her. I missed only you and tried to send you emails, but there was always something wrong with the modem and the computer. Besides, I thought as I returned, we would be together and work something out with your parents. Little did I know that you would be gone, leaving me with no trace of you."

"I told my sister about you, and she encouraged me to tell our parents. I was so excited about seeing you and telling you that I was finally ready to stand up against my parents for you. And then you know the rest. I was so…heartbroken that I could not stand being there without you…" My voice trailed into tears that had not bled for twenty years.

"Oh, Mira!" Dev swooped my waist into his arms, pulled me close to his chest, and planted the deepest kiss on my lips. My body broke into a fire that I hadn't felt burning since we last embraced in college.

I was engulfed in the warmth of his mouth and felt myself sinking, only to hear a voice within me say, *Inder… Zenith…* I immediately pushed Dev's chest away with my hand. "We must stop! Dev. Don't forget, I'm married."

"Does that matter, Mira, after how both of us have been wronged by fate, and we kept blaming each other? I know you want this too. I could feel it in your kiss. You still love me; I know you do. You've never stopped loving me, like I have always loved you." We stared into each other's eyes in silence. I felt lost in a haze not knowing what to do, what to say. It was already too much to absorb.

"Meet with me tomorrow at five o'clock, after work. I'm staying at the Pierre. Think about us. Sleep on it tonight; don't say anything now. Meet me tomorrow, Mira. I will be waiting for you in the lobby." He took my hands into his. "My Mira, I love you, and only you. I'm so happy I found you. Please let us be together." From his blazer pocket, he took a little silk pouch and put it in my hand.

"I've been holding on to this for years. I bought it for you."

He opened the pouch, and inside was a small diamond pendant of our most sacred religious mantra, Ek Onkar, in the symbol form, meaning in its most literal meaning, One God. "I had it made for you because you were always so spiritual and had such strong faith, I thought you would appreciate it more than any other expensive ornament."

"Thank you, it's beautiful."

He smiled. "I'll see you tomorrow." And with those words, he walked out of my office. My body acted of its own accord, nodding its head and reassuring Dev with a smile. Thoughts of my husband and child were swept under the rug of denial in a far corner of my mind. Reality seemed far away and unimportant. My dream of being with Dev was coming true. Nothing else mattered.

"What are you thinking about?"

"Huh!" I gasped as Inder had interrupted my thoughts about my conversation with Dev. "I'm not thinking of anything."

"Oh, come on, I know you, Mira. I can hear you thinking, and it must be something serious this time. It feels heavy even from over here." Inder laughed. He took me into his arms. "Stop thinking, you'll hurt yourself, ha-ha." He loved to tease me.

"Stop, you're mean." I hit his arm as the smile crept into the creases of my cheeks. Inder always knew how to make me smile. A few minutes later, I fell asleep in the embrace that always kept me safe.

Chapter 35

In the morning, I felt the fog from the previous day had lifted, and I experienced a strange and sudden sense of clarity. I whispered the Chaupai Sahib prayers on the train, as I did every morning. These prayers protected me and shielded me from dangers that lurked in the world but also from the darkness hidden within myself.

As the workday began to wind down and five in the evening approached, I felt strong and assured in my decision. I was finally free.

I called Inder. "Hi, love, I'm going to be a little late tonight, something came up at work. Please put Zenith to bed for me. OK, OK, see you then."

The Uber drove up to the Pierre, and when I crossed the street toward the hotel, I saw Dev waiting anxiously outside.

"Oh, Mira, you're here. I'm so relieved to see you. I couldn't even wait in the lobby. I had to come outside to make sure you didn't leave."

"No, I wouldn't leave without speaking to you," I said with a smile.

As we walked into the lobby, Dev's eyes stayed on me. "You look so beautiful. I wanted to tell you yesterday, that you haven't aged at all."

"Neither have you," I said. "You look the same, except for the salt and pepper on your face," I remarked confidently with a smile.

"Let's sit here. It's quieter, and we can talk without being disturbed, unless you prefer to come up to my room. I have a big suite with a living room." Dev motioned me to lounge chairs in the side corner of the lobby a little away from the reception desk.

"No, I'm absolutely fine here."

"Are you still afraid of coming to hotels with me, Mira?" Dev smirked with a knowing twinkle in his eyes.

"That's funny." I smiled in return as I sat.

"Mira, you know I've been waiting for this day for twenty long years. Although I did marry under the pressure of my parents, I never loved her, and we were divorced two years later."

"I know," I interjected.

"Really? Have you heard of my news?" Dev was bewildered.

"You never told me who you were, Dev. I eventually stumbled across it online."

"Yes, I'm sorry about that Mira, but I had my reasons, one being I wanted you to care about me and not my money, like all the other girls I had previously dated. I was planning on telling you, of course, after we became close."

"But this is all ancient history, Dev. I don't know why we're talking about this when we've both moved on in our lives."

Dev looked offended and hurt by my words. "I haven't moved on, Mira. That is what I'm trying to tell you. It was always you. No matter how many other women I dated, it was always you."

His words stung me because I knew them to be true, but it was a tragic end to a beautiful romantic dream world that I did not live in. How did this successful man remain haunted by disillusions of an old first love?

I took his hands in mine. "Look, Dev, you were right when you said yesterday that I loved you. I did love you."

Dev's grip became tighter on mine. "Don't deny me your love, Mira, that I have wasted my years yearning for."

I continued with the calm strength I didn't know I had. "Dev, I didn't waste my years for a love that no longer existed. My heart loved again and created a beautiful flower, my daughter. My family, my husband, my daughter, these are all the people who I love and who are my today, and my tomorrow."

"Mira, I won't hear it. You didn't give us a chance."

"I did," I said, still holding onto his hand. "I did give us a chance, but I realized our lives and worlds are too different. If I left my husband and child, how would I reconcile their existing relationship with yours, and the fact that you don't live in this country, and that your family wouldn't approve of me still today?"

"I don't care about them. I don't need their approval anymore. I'm a grown man now," he responded.

"Yes, and I am a grown woman now. I am a mother now. I have loyalties and responsibilities toward my child and family. Abandoning them to pursue a selfish dream is not who I am, Dev, and I realize you don't know enough of who I have become to really understand me."

"You don't have to sacrifice your love for your family, Mira. Many people divorce and live well. I am happy to accept your daughter. I understand you cannot leave her. I can live here in New York and travel to India for work. We could make this work. I have the power to make this work!" Dev's voice was in a panic, as if I had already slipped out of his fingers.

I felt myself distancing myself from our discussion. "I am not eighteen anymore. I am not the naive girl you fell in love with. I know my family was a roadblock in the past, but I forgave them a long time ago. My family and I are made of the same fabric, everything we went through, we faced trauma together, and we have learned to live with it. They would be heartbroken too if I destroyed my beautiful little family. Dev, try to see that I have created a life for myself. I have created love and joy."

Dev looked unconvinced.

"This is not only about betraying my husband and giving up my child—this is more about me!"

I turned his shoulders so he would face me.

"I am proud of myself, Dev. It took me a very long time to overcome my grief after we broke up. And, yes, you're right, this beautiful necklace you gave me is the symbol of my spiritual strength that has always guided me in my life." I removed from my purse the necklace Dev had given me the day before and opened his palm, placed the necklace in it, and closed his strong but soft hand over it.

"Does this mean you are saying goodbye forever this time, Mira?" Dev's eyes seemed to look damp with brimming tears.

"I wish things between us could have been different. We have great chemistry between us, I know, but that's not enough to build a happy and successful relationship. I guess we were not meant to be."

"Don't say that. I've been waiting for you all these years because I believed that we were meant to be."

I let go of his hand.

"I know you love me. You are saying all this because you don't want to betray your family."

"No, you're wrong, Dev," I said with a smile. "I am saying this because I won't...I won't betray myself."

After a long pause where we both stared into each other's

eyes and those final words sealed my intentions, Dev, with pain in his eyes, finally swallowed the lump that was choking his throat. Holding my shoulders lightly, he planted a long kiss on my forehead before saying, "I will miss you."

Without a further word, he stood, turned around, and walked away. I watched his broad back diminish into the distance as he hurried to the elevator, rushing perhaps to not give himself the chance to return to where I stood.

"You will stay a beautiful memory, and nothing more," I murmured to myself as I lifted my purse and left the hotel.

Chapter 36

I sat on the late train from Penn Station to Great Neck, staring at the dark landscape flying past my window, until a young couple sitting across from me on the other side of the aisle caught my eye. Because of my meeting with Dev, I had taken the later train, which was much less crowded than the earlier one, and I had a clear view of this handsome young couple. They were taking selfies of each other kissing; they were doused in their love for each other. Their young faces looked fresh and tender with so much opportunity and future ahead of them. I smiled at their natural ability to be unaffected by the glances of others around them. They lived in their fantasy bubble. I thought about what their future may look like. Would they stay together, or would they have a heart-breaking split? Where would their lives take them? I was so curious to figure out their destinies, maybe because I had just figured out mine, for the time being. I felt like a big burden I had been carrying on my chest had been lifted. I was free of the memories of Dev. I knew now more than ever that I had made the right decision.

When I got home, I felt a new sense of gratitude and appreciation for my beautiful family. Inder had fallen asleep alongside Zenith on our bed with a storybook in hand. His strong, dark-haired arm held little Zenith firmly even in his sleep. She lay in her pajamas with her hair tousled over her forehead in complete peace. I quickly washed up and plopped into the bed with them. Smiling over their sleeping whimpers, I thought about how the years I had spent with Inder and raising Zenith were not in vain; they were, in fact, the best years of my life. And as I had wondered about the couple on the train, I was curious to know where the Guru would take me from here.

Acknowledgments

I am grateful to Kevin Atticks and the entire team at Apprentice House Press for making my dream of publishing this book and my promise to my deceased son, Kabir, come true. I thank God for giving me the strength to follow through and complete this novel, as it began as a self-therapy to help myself cope with loss. I am thankful to my developmental editor, Sienna Whalen, for her tremendous help in the editing process as well as her authentic feedback, which helped me pave my way to complete my never-ending story. Thank you to Claire Marino for all her help and patience with the final edits of my manuscript and cover design and to Corrine Moulds for marketing design. I'd also like to extend my appreciation to Deborah Jayne, who streamlined the entire process of getting my manuscript into the hands of publishers and introducing me to an excellent early editorial reviewer and copy editor, Kristin Thiel. I could not have promoted this novel to its potential without Jessie Glenn and the amazing team at MindBuck Media Book Publicity. A very big thank you to Hannah Richards, my social media manager at MindBuck, and her team for branding and marketing the book as well as running my Instagram and Twitter accounts. Thank you to Emily Keough and Bryn Kristi for building a great website and press kits, and for all their marketing efforts. And of course, a big thank you to Dr. Rochelle Almeida, my professor and friend from NYU, who always guided me and gave me encouragement and support. My parents, who I am eternally grateful for, I hope I've made them proud. And of course, I would like to thank my husband, Sonu, who was the first person I allowed to read my novel that I had been hiding for years. His encouragement and belief in my work gave me the confidence to complete one of the largest and most important projects of my life.

About the Author

Krishma Tuli Arora immigrated to the United States from India when she was five years old, and like her protagonist, Mira, she grew up on Long Island and then attended New York University. She is a poet, writer, and public speaker. For a few years, she was the author of "Free Spirit," a monthly column in her hometown magazine, *Brookville Living*. She has a master's degree in education, as well as a master's in marketing. She has also worked as a high school social studies teacher for eleven years. She lives in New York with her husband and four children. She began writing *From Ash to Ashes* seventeen years ago, after the death of her first child. This loss was the inspiration for her book, and she has dedicated it to his memory. In addition to *From Ash to Ashes*, she is also writing a nonfiction book, a collection of essays on womanhood and motherhood as seen through the eyes of a woman of color.

Apprentice House Press is the country's only campus-based, student-staffed book publishing company. Directed by professors and industry professionals, it is a nonprofit activity of the Communication Department at Loyola University Maryland.

Using state-of-the-art technology and an experiential learning model of education, Apprentice House publishes books in untraditional ways. This dual responsibility as publishers and educators creates an unprecedented collaborative environment among faculty and students, while teaching tomorrow's editors, designers, and marketers.

Eclectic and provocative, Apprentice House titles intend to entertain as well as spark dialogue on a variety of topics. Financial contributions to sustain the press's work are welcomed. Contributions are tax deductible to the fullest extent allowed by the IRS.

To learn more about Apprentice House books or to obtain submission guidelines, please visit www.apprenticehouse.com.

Apprentice House Press
Communication Department
Loyola University Maryland
4501 N. Charles Street
Baltimore, MD 21210
Ph: 410-617-5265
info@apprenticehouse.com•www.apprenticehouse.com

CPSIA information can be obtained
at www.ICGtesting.com
Printed in the USA
LVHW021214180523
747360LV00003B/39